"I am yours until dawn. There is no need for such haste.

"You need a few lessons in the art of seduction."

"I…" Julia's lips parted, and even in the lamplight he could see color suffuse her face. A shaft of desire, hot and fierce, pierced him at this maidenly response. Nicholas found himself wanting to push her up against the wall and begin the lesson now.

His fingers closed around her arm in a tight grip. "So, what exactly do you want, my dear?"

She stared up at him, the mask completely hiding her expression. "You."

"I think, then, we had best be certain." He yanked her to him, his mouth crashing down on hers in a merciless kiss. She froze and then began to struggle. He released her abruptly.

She stepped back, stumbling a little. "Please get in the carriage."

He stared at her, then his eyes dropped to the pistol pointed at him. "What the devil?"

"I am abducting you, my lord. Get in or I will be forced to shoot you!"

* * *

My Lady's Prisoner
Harlequin Historical #680—November 2003

**Harlequin Historicals is delighted
to introduce Mills & Boon author
ANN ELIZABETH CREE**

DON'T MISS THESE OTHER
TITLES AVAILABLE NOW:

MY LADY'S PRISONER

ANN ELIZABETH CREE

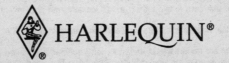

TORONTO • NEW YORK • LONDON
AMSTERDAM • PARIS • SYDNEY • HAMBURG
STOCKHOLM • ATHENS • TOKYO • MILAN • MADRID
PRAGUE • WARSAW • BUDAPEST • AUCKLAND

ISBN 0-373-29280-5

MY LADY'S PRISONER

First North American Publication 2003

Available from Harlequin Historicals and
ANN ELIZABETH CREE

My Lady's Prisoner #680

Prologue

London, 1817

She had never expected to see the ring again. And certainly not on the hand of Nicholas Chandler, Viscount Thayne, a man who, as far as she knew, had never crossed paths with Thomas.

So, at first, when Thérèse Blanchot had told her that she had spotted the ring, she was certain Thérèse must be mistaken. But she had gone to Thérèse's exclusive and very discreet gaming house to see for herself. And when she stood by the hazard table and watched Thayne throw the dice, her heart had taken a sickening dive. For on the fourth finger of his left hand was a ruby signet ring. A ring with an intricately carved gold band, the stone surrounded by two small diamonds. The ring was unmistakable. Her eyes had gone to his face: a lean masculine face, just bordering on handsome with a pair of cool dark eyes. His hard gaze went briefly to her masked face and she froze. But he returned to the dice, clearly uninterested.

She must obtain the ring. And discover what he knew. No matter what it took.

Chapter One

Julia, Lady Carrington, paused in the door of Thérèse Blanchot's richly appointed saloon, her legs suddenly shaky. There was no reason to be so apprehensive, she had merely to find Lord Thayne and, at the appropriate time, abduct him.

She glanced around the elegant room, its colours muted reds and golds. Already the saloon was crowded with patrons. Both men and women frequented Thérèse's saloon, where the suppers were superb, the guests carefully chosen and the stakes high. Admittance was by invitation only. Many of the women chose to come masked, although Julia had no trouble recognising the Duchess of Langston at the EO table— but perhaps that was because she took no trouble to hide her flaming red hair or disguise her husky laugh. Julia's own hair was a muted brown and completely unremarkable. Not that she was likely to be recognised at any rate; since her return to England she rarely graced London society.

She moved into the room and looked more closely around, hoping to spot Thayne. But there was no sign of his tall, broad-shouldered figure. Or of a man with tawny brown hair that glimmered with gold. Thérèse had sent word he would be here tonight. Perhaps he was in one of the private parlours. It would be too awful to contemplate if he was to change his mind. She hadn't come up with an alternative plan and she wasn't quite sure if she could work up the courage to do this again.

Thérèse materialised at her side. 'My dear, you have arrived. I was not certain you would come.' In her early thirties, she was still a beauty with high cheek-bones and violet eyes under a crown of thick black hair.

'Yes.' Julia took a deep breath. 'Is Lord Thayne here?'

'He is. In the gold saloon. However, he is not in the most jovial of moods.' Her brow creased with worry. 'My dear, I do not know what you have planned, but he is not a man you can cross. If you only would tell me, I could help.'

Julia shook her head. 'No. I do not want you implicated in any of it.' Thayne's hard gaze sprang to mind. She did not want his wrath to fall on Thérèse.

'That does not matter to me.' Thérèse hesitated. 'My dear, I wish I could convince you that it is most unlikely he knows anything about Thomas's death.'

'Perhaps not, but he has Thomas's ring. If anything, I want to at least know how it came to be in his possession.' She put a reassuring hand on Thérèse's arm. 'I will be careful.'

'I only want you to be safe.'

'I will be. Eduardo is waiting for me outside so I will be well protected.'

'Yes.' Thérèse still appeared unconvinced.

'Will you take me to him, then? I wish to play a game with him. Perhaps piquet.'

'And what then?'

'I will, I hope, have my ring,' Julia said lightly. She had no intention of telling Thérèse that she planned to abduct one of her most wealthy and powerful patrons. 'And one more thing—I think it would be best if you would pretend you do not know me.'

'If that is what you wish. What should I call you?'

Julia frowned. 'Jane, I think.'

Thérèse's brow shot up. 'Jane? Such an ordinary name.'

'I am less likely to forget it.' She had thought of taking something closer to her own name, Juliana, for instance, but she feared she would blurt out Julia instead. And certainly she did not want him to connect her with anything related to her real identity.

'Then come with me.' Thérèse led her through the saloon.

Several patrons greeted Thérèse as they passed but, to Julia's relief, no one gave her more than a cursory glance as they crossed the rich-hued oriental carpet, winding their way among the baize-covered tables. And then she caught sight of someone she knew all too well, her neighbour, Lord George Kingsley. He was hovering near the EO table. The Even-Odd wheel had just been set into motion as Julia and Thérèse passed by. Preoccupied with the spinning wheel, he did not even glance up. Thank goodness for that. If anyone were likely to recognise her under the mask it would be him. She quickly averted her gaze and prayed she could avoid him.

Thérèse stopped in front of the door of one of the

private parlours. She looked over at Julia. 'Are you certain this is what you wish, my dear?'

Julia took a deep breath to steady herself. 'Yes. I do not think I have a choice.'

Her knees started to shake. She was about to confront the man who perhaps held the only clue to her husband's murderer.

Nicholas polished off the remainder of his brandy in one smooth move and leaned back in his chair. 'Another game?' he asked his companion.

Henry Benton gave the pile of vouchers in front of Nicholas a meaningful stare. 'No, thank you. Not if I hope to keep my shirt. Believe I'll try my luck at Faro. Dammit, Thayne, I think your wits only sharpen the more you drink.'

Nicholas laughed, but his laugh was hardly amused. 'Then after another bottle or two I should break the bank.'

Benton frowned. 'Don't know why you're drinking like a fish. You'll have the devil of a head tomorrow. If you don't pass out before then.'

'Which is precisely what I plan to do.' Perhaps in drunken oblivion he'd be able to get through the rest of this anniversary without the images that had haunted him for the past two years.

Benton rose, the frown still on his face. 'Perhaps you'd do best to continue at home.'

'No,' Nicholas said curtly.

Benton opened his mouth as if to say more, but merely bowed and walked off.

Nicholas slouched back in his chair and reached for the bottle. His hand stayed when he realised someone had entered the small, dim room. He saw Thérèse and then his gaze flickered to the woman with her.

She was of average height and slender. The low-cut silk gown she wore revealed a glimpse of soft curved breasts. She was masked, not an unusual occurrence among ladies of the *ton* who did not wish to be recognised in such a risqué place. She looked vaguely familiar. He frowned and had a sudden recollection of her watching him last evening. Her still, watchful manner had seemed out of place in one of London's most exclusive and high-stake private hells. The thought had crossed his mind that it must be her first time in such an establishment. Apparently he had been mistaken. She looked quite confident as she followed Thérèse towards his table, her eyes behind the mask fixed on his face.

Thérèse stopped, the young woman a little behind her. She clasped her gloved hands in front of her in a way that suddenly reminded Nicholas of a schoolgirl. Thérèse's expression gave nothing away as she addressed him. 'Nicholas, may I present Jane? She wishes to play a game of cards with you.'

'Does she? I fear I am not in the mood.' He would prefer to polish off his bottle in solitude.

'She assures me she is a very skilled player. And she came here specifically to play with you. Surely you do not wish to disappoint her?'

His eyes flickered over the woman. He could think of no reason why she would wish to challenge him. She met his gaze boldly but he saw her fingers tighten around her reticule. So she was nervous. In spite of his desire to remain detached, he felt the faintest stirring of curiosity. 'How skilled is she?' he asked.

Thérèse shrugged and glanced quickly at her companion. 'I cannot say.'

He looked back at Thérèse. 'I don't waste my time on amateurs. Tell her I must decline.'

The young woman turned her masked gaze on him. 'I can hear and speak, my lord.' Her voice held more than a touch of annoyance. 'And I am hardly an amateur. I never lose.' Her voice was low and well bred.

His eyes narrowed. He wondered what the devil she wanted, but there was nothing he could think of. Her voice was completely unfamiliar. 'Don't you? Then sit down,' he said curtly.

She took the chair across from him. As she sat, he caught a whiff of soft rose. The scent evoked memories he'd prefer to forget. He should undoubtedly send her away after all.

A servant entered the room and spoke to Thérèse. She turned to Nicholas. 'I fear I cannot stay. A small crisis with the supper. But I shall be interested in the outcome. My dear,' she said to Jane, 'I wish you all luck.'

Jane nodded and then looked back at Nicholas. He saw her swallow, although the rest of her demeanour was calm.

'What is your game?' he asked.

'Piquet.'

'Very well. What odds?'

She looked straight at him. 'Anything you wish, my lord.'

'Anything?' he asked, his voice suggestive. He allowed his gaze to rest on her lips and then drift down to where her creamy breasts plunged into her bodice. Despite the amount of drink he'd consumed and his indifference, he felt the faint stir of desire.

Her gaze faltered a little. 'Anything.'

He smiled coldly. This was a new tack—usually women expressed their interest in a more direct fashion and never by challenging him to a card game. 'And if I lose?'

She hesitated and then spoke, her eyes on his face. 'Then, my lord, you will give me what I wish.'

His loins tightened unexpectedly, the thought of what she might want damnably erotic. His eyes went to her lips, soft and slightly parted, and the idea of crushing them beneath his was becoming more enticing by the moment.

What the devil was wrong with him? Apparently he had not consumed enough drink after all. The last thing he should want was a woman, particularly tonight. Except for an occasional one-night liaison, he'd been nearly celibate for the past two years. On the other hand, perhaps a night in a stranger's arms was exactly what he needed to make it through this anniversary. He leaned back in his chair and regarded her through half-closed eyes. 'Fair enough. If I lose then I will be at your mercy. However, I would prefer to call you something besides Jane.'

'What is wrong? You do not like Jane?' She sounded affronted.

'No. I'd expected something more exotic from such a woman of, er…mystery. I don't suppose that is your real name?'

'No, but I shouldn't mind if it were.' She lifted her chin.

He nearly laughed. 'I suppose your given name is something quite extraordinary that makes you long for a name such as Jane.' He hadn't expected to feel amused.

'No, it is also quite ordinary.'

'Mary? Elizabeth? Harriet?'

'No. Perhaps we should start the game, my lord.' Now she sounded cross as if she hadn't much time to dally with him. Certainly her voice held no trace of flirtatiousness. In spite of himself he was beginning to feel rather intrigued.

He picked up the cards. Her gaze was suddenly riveted on his hands. 'I assure you I've no intention of cheating,' he said. 'And if I did, watching my hands with such concentration would not reveal a thing. But if that worries you, you may deal the cards.'

She looked up and smiled, although her smile appeared forced. 'I am not worried about that at all, my lord. I was merely curious about your ring. It is quite unusual.'

'Yes,' he said curtly.

'Where did you get it?'

His brow snapped together. 'It was given to me.'

'Indeed. By someone close to you?'

'It is, my dear, none of your concern. I believe you expressed a desire to play a game with me.' He pushed the cards towards her.

'Yes.' She picked up the cards and he noticed her hand trembled a little. However, her movements as she first shuffled and then dealt the cards were quick and practised.

He made the first move and waited for her countermove. She merely stared at the cards in her hand as if mesmerised. He was beginning to wonder if she was a trifle mad.

'Your play. Although I suggest you do it some time within the next hour. I've no desire to stay here until

dawn. Unless you would rather forgo the game and
leave now.'

Her head jerked up. 'Leave?'

'Yes, leave. Together,' he added carelessly.

'I…' She caught her lower lip between her teeth.

'Well?' he asked. She still hesitated. What the devil
was she playing at? For a woman who wanted to seduce him, she was remarkably reticent. He suspected
he was dealing with a complete novice. 'Then I will
decide. I forfeit the game. Under our terms I am now
at your command.' He threw down his hand.

She stared at the cards and then looked back up at
him. 'Oh. Well, yes.'

'You seem surprised. Perhaps I misunderstood, but
I thought we agreed that if you won I would do what
you wish. I assume you had something in mind.'

'Yes.' She rose, stumbling against the chair a little.
'I would like you to come with me.' She sounded
rather prim.

He stood. 'Would you? Very well, I am at your
service, my dear Jane. Although I am curious as to
where we are going.'

Her lips parted in a nervous little smile. 'It will be
a…a surprise.'

His brow rose. 'Indeed.'

'Yes. So, if you will please come.'

He moved to her side and looked down at her. Her
demeanour was hardly that of a seductress—if anything her stiff manner reminded him of a governess.
He stepped closer to her.

She nearly jumped away. 'Shall we go, then?'

'Perhaps we should before you change your mind,'
he said drily. 'I must own at this point I am quite
curious as to what you want.'

'Oh.' She hurried from the room as if it was all she could do to keep from running.

He followed her into the passageway and took her arm. Her bones felt delicate under his hand. He pulled her around to face him. 'There's no need for such haste, my dear. Unless you are that eager to have your way with me.'

'No…that is, yes.'

'Are you? Most women who have expressed such a desire show more, er…enthusiasm for the task.' He released her arm.

'I fear I haven't much practice,' she said crossly.

He folded his arms and leaned against the wall. 'So, why exactly did you decide upon me to improve your skills?'

'I…' She stopped, her eyes fixed on the door of the parlour next to the one they had just vacated. She stiffened and then yanked her gaze away. 'I would rather discuss this outside.'

He glanced in the direction she had been looking. Lord George Kingsley and Carleton Wentworth had stepped out of the room. He looked back at her. 'I see. You wish to converse with me in private. Then let us depart. I am agog with curiosity.'

She threw one last glance at the two men and dashed across the hallway to the staircase. He caught up to her just before she started to descend. 'There is no need for such haste. I am yours until dawn.'

She gave him a startled look. 'Oh. Yes, of course.'

He nearly laughed then. He took her arm again and started down the stairs. He led her to the small front parlour where they waited for the footmen to fetch her cloak. She stood near the door, her posture stiff as if she were about to flee. He came to stand in front of

her and then lifted her chin with gentle fingers. 'You
need a few lessons in the art of seduction.'

'I...' Her lips parted and even in the lamplight he
could see colour suffuse her face. A shaft of desire,
hot and fierce, pierced him at this maidenly response.
He found himself wanting to push her up against the
wall and begin the lesson now. He dropped his hand
and backed away. He was beginning to think that she
was perhaps a most accomplished seductress after all.

They stepped into the foggy London night, the brisk
air cooling his cheeks. It also had the effect of clearing
his mind. He glanced down at his companion. She now
wore a long, rather unfashionable cloak which hid her
figure, but he could see the material was of good qual-
ity. What was she exactly? A demi-mondaine? But her
speech and carriage were those of a well-bred lady and
even in her nervousness she had not slipped into other,
less refined accents. 'Well?' he asked. 'Where to?'

'We will go to my carriage,' she said firmly.

They walked in silence along the fog-shrouded
street. But when they turned the corner of the square
on to a dark, nearly deserted side street his hackles
rose. Although he heard nothing he had the prickling
sensation of being watched.

His companion apparently noted nothing amiss. She
halted next to a carriage. 'We are here, my lord.' Her
voice was quite calm. Too calm.

His fingers closed around her arm in a tight grip.
'So, what exactly do you want, my dear?'

She stared up at him, the dark and the mask completely hiding her expression. 'You.'

'I think, then, we had best be certain.' He yanked
her to him, his mouth crashing down on hers in a

merciless kiss. She froze and then began to struggle. He released her abruptly.

She stepped back, stumbling a little. Her hand dipped into her reticule. 'Please get in the carriage.'

He stared at her, then his eyes dropped to the pistol pointed a few inches away from him. 'What the devil?'

'I am abducting you, my lord.'

'Are you?' He gave a short, surprised laugh. 'Are you that desperate? My dear, after that kiss such measures are hardly necessary. I would be more than happy to oblige you without the use of force.' His eyes roved over her figure.

'Get in, please, or I will be forced to shoot you.' Her voice was still polite, as if she had just requested he take her in to supper at a ball.

'Can you really use that thing?' he asked carelessly.

'Yes.' She motioned with the pistol. 'Will you just get in?'

'No please this time?' His mouth quirked. 'I will if you kiss me again.'

'I did not kiss you the first time!' she snapped. 'Get in.'

He raised a brow. 'I don't think so, my dear.'

He made a lunge for the pistol and she jumped back. He felt a blow to the back of his head, and the next thing he knew he was pitching forward.

Julia stared at the man sprawled at her feet, then looked up to see Eduardo.

Eduardo gave her an apologetic look. 'Thought I'd best step in before you decided to shoot the lad. Didn't want a scene. You'd best get the ring. What do you want me to do with him?'

'Put him in the carriage, if you please.'

He stared at her for a moment and then nodded. 'And then…what?'

'I…I want to take him back to Foxwood. I need to find out where he got the ring.'

'Very well.'

He glanced over at the coachman who had been watching with a disinterested look. 'Come on, lad, we'll put him in the coach for the Countess and bind him up good and tight. A pity, however, he isn't a less robust man.'

'Yes, 'tis a shame,' Julia said weakly. Her legs were beginning to shake. She watched while they managed to bundle Thayne in the carriage, worried Eduardo might have hit him too hard. But then he groaned and let out a string of curses and she almost wished Eduardo had hit him harder.

She stood by the carriage, her nerves on edge, praying no one had seen the assault. There was only one other coach on the other side of the street, but it was doubtful the coachman could have noticed anything. When they finished, she finally climbed in the carriage and took the seat opposite him. Guilt assailed her when she saw they had not only bound her prisoner, but had gagged him with his cravat as well. She leaned back against the uncomfortable cushions and closed her eyes. Whatever had she done now? She just prayed they would make it to Foxwood without incident.

Brunton watched the carriage turn a corner. They had been following it since it left the French woman's gaming hell. From all appearances, the carriage was about to leave town. He cursed, causing his horse to startle.

Smithers urged his horse next to Brunton's. 'Now what? They're leaving town.'

'Yes.' Brunton scowled. He'd not figured this into his plans. He'd anticipated either waylaying Thayne in a dark street and nabbing the ring or, if he had to, ambushing him while the Viscount rode his big grey through Hyde Park in the early-morning hours. When Thayne had entered Madame Blanchot's he'd been certain his opportunity was at hand. Until Thayne had left with the masked woman. He'd followed them down the street and around the corner. They had stopped in front of a carriage but, instead of climbing in, had seemed to be arguing. Brunton had been forced to dodge across the street when a large, burly man had suddenly appeared out of nowhere and had stopped to watch the two as well. Brunton hadn't actually seen Thayne enter the carriage, but when it had finally rumbled away Thayne and the woman were gone. The burly man now sat on the box next to the coachman. A glimpse of the masked woman in the window of the carriage confirmed she was inside. And, unless Thayne had vanished into the air, he was in the coach as well.

'Don't think the guv'nor will be pleased if he gets away,' Smithers said.

'No.' Never idle, Brunton's brain latched on to an alternative plan. A slow smile crossed his face. 'But he won't. We'll hold them up.'

Smithers grinned, showing several blackened teeth. 'Always wanted to be a highwayman.'

'Keep your wits about you. If we snuff out Thayne the guv'nor will have our heads.'

'Thayne won't argue with this.' Smithers patted the

pistol at his side. 'Dare say he'll be occupied with the wench.'

Brunton grinned. 'We'll hope she keeps 'im busy enough so he'll not notice us.'

Chapter Two

The carriage hit a bump and Julia winced. She glanced over at her prisoner. He had not made a sound since they had left London but she had no doubt he must be horribly uncomfortable. The fifteen miles from London to Foxwood had never felt so long. She leaned forward. 'I am sorry, but I assure you I mean you no harm. You will be more comfortable as soon as we reach Fox—I mean, our…our destination.'

The low sound issuing from beneath the gag was not encouraging. Even with his hands and feet bound, the set of his shoulders indicated he was furious. And his eyes. If they were weapons she would be dead. She suspected he would have no qualms in strangling her if he could. At least the bindings looked sturdy and Eduardo was skilled in tying knots. She hoped they were not cutting too deeply into his flesh.

She sat back against the cushions, wishing she could ride on the coach box as Eduardo was. Despite his incapacitated condition, Thayne's presence seemed to fill the confines of the carriage. It was like sitting with a caged tiger and the sensation was not comfortable. He was quiet, leaning against the cushions, long legs straight in front of him, but she could almost feel his contained power.

She tried to keep her eyes off of him as the coach rumbled through the foggy London streets. She wrapped her cloak more tightly around herself. At least she still wore her mask but it provided little barrier from his hard gaze. Or from the memory of his ruthless kiss. Even now her cheeks heated and her legs felt shaky just thinking about it.

Whatever had she done? She remembered Thérèse's words that he was not a man to cross. She knew little else about him except he had some sort of scandal attached to his name and that his grandfather, the Earl of Monteville, was one of the most powerful men in England. He was unlikely to take the abduction of his grandson and heir lightly. She would undoubtedly end up in Newgate or worse.

But what other choice did she have? She had considered offering to buy the ring or, if necessary, robbing him, but that would still not tell her where he obtained it or tell her if he had had anything to do with her husband's death. Asking him point-blank seemed ridiculous. He would hardly admit it if he had; so, the idea of abducting him and forcing him to give her an answer had seemed the only recourse.

Except she had not counted on his being so, well, unmanageable. She stole a glance at him and saw his eyes were now closed. Not that it made him appear any less unyielding. They hit a bump and he winced. She averted her eyes. Inflicting pain on her fellow man was not something she took pleasure in doing. She peeked out the window. They were finally leaving London. The carriage hit another bump. This time Thayne made a sound like a muffled groan.

'Are…are you all right?' she asked. A stupid question.

He shook his head and made another groaning noise. Concerned, she shifted on the seat and peered more closely at him. The light was dim but she thought he did look rather pale. A dreadful thought occurred to her. 'You are not going to be sick, are you?'

This time he nodded. She nearly groaned herself. Why hadn't she thought of such a thing? She could not possibly allow him to cast up his accounts wearing a gag. She must untie it.

The sway of the carriage told her they were now outside of London. 'Very well, I will untie your gag.' She moved to his seat and nearly fell on him as the carriage lurched. She was beginning to think the coachman was not a particularly skilful driver. He had been in her employment just a fortnight. She only hoped he was not tipsy.

She righted herself and forced her hands to reach up to the back of Thayne's head. His hair was thick and surprisingly soft under her hand. She managed to locate the knot, her fingers trembling. Her face was hot beneath her mask.

Unfortunately, the knot was tight and working it loose proved difficult. She finally pulled her gloves off, but the swaying carriage hardly helped. As much as she tried to avoid it, her body was forced into contact with his hard length. She finally managed to loosen the knot and she tugged. He made a noise like a muffled yelp and her hands fell away. Was he about to become ill? 'Please, try to hold on. I am almost done,' she said. She tugged more violently at the cloth and this time the sound was nearly a growl. Then she realised what was wrong. A strand of his hair had become entangled in the knot.

'Oh, drat!' she muttered. 'I will try not to pull too hard.'

She somehow managed to free the knot without further mishap. The gag fell away and the carriage slammed to a halt. She found herself smashed against Thayne's side. A shot rang out followed by shouting.

She managed to sit upright on the seat, her heart thudding uncomfortably. Her face had hit his shoulder and her mask was completely awry.

'What the devil is going on?' Thayne said.

Julia peered out the window and then her heart sank when she saw two masked men. Eduardo had already climbed down from the coach box and stood by the carriage, his hands up. She sank back on the seat. 'I think we have been set upon by highwaymen.'

Thayne stared at her. 'Good God! I don't suppose you could loosen these damnable bindings?'

'I will try.' She knelt in front of him and started to work on the knot at his feet. Thank goodness, Eduardo had not tied it too terribly tight as her fingers did not seem to want to co-operate. She had just started to slip the thin rope over his boots when her mask slipped completely off. She looked up for a moment and his eyes widened in surprise. She realised this was the first time he had seen her face. And then he glared at her, not at all grateful for her assistance.

The door was yanked open and a nasty-looking pistol was thrust in the opening of the coach. 'If you will be so good as to step out, madam.' The voice was exceedingly polite for a ruffian.

'I would rather not,' Julia said. 'Perhaps another evening.' She sat back down and managed a smile.

Where ever was her pistol? It was unlikely she could shoot the man, but if there was the slightest chance she intended to use it. Her hand finally contacted the cold metal and she thrust her hand with the pistol into the folds of her cloak.

The highwayman gestured with his pistol. 'Alas, I fear another evening is not convenient for me. And I should hate to find myself obliged to assist you in a more forcible manner.'

She dared not look at Thayne. She stepped down into the cold foggy night and was relieved to see Eduardo appeared unhurt. He held the horses while the coachman leaned against the carriage with his eyes closed.

'The gentleman as well.' The highwayman waved his pistol at her.

He had spotted Thayne. Her heart sank even further. Surely they would not harm a man in such a helpless condition. 'I fear he is rather unwell at the moment.'

'Not at all,' Thayne said coolly from inside. 'However, I will need some assistance. I am rather incapacitated.'

The highwayman peered into the coach and then reeled back. 'Egad! The man is trussed up like a chicken.'

'I am the lady's prisoner,' Thayne said. 'Perhaps you would be so good as to untie me.'

'Don't think I will. You look a trifle too brawny. So, he's your prisoner, milady?' He turned his masked gaze back on Julia. 'Why would a lovely lady such as yourself be needing such drastic measures to capture a man? Most men would come willing enough.' Beneath his mask, his mouth curved in a smile revealing a blackened tooth.

'I presume you have stopped my coach for some reason other than mere conversation,' Julia said pointedly. She had no idea whether she was afraid or annoyed. Why must they be robbed tonight of all nights? And why didn't the man just get on with it? She glanced over at Eduardo who still had a pistol trained on him. The coachman's eyes were now wide open and he looked as if he was about to swoon.

'Get your prisoner out.'

'I beg your pardon?' Julia said.

The highwayman jerked his head in the direction of the coach. 'Get him out.'

She blinked. 'How?'

'I'll come out on my own,' Thayne said. He suddenly appeared in the door of the coach, his feet no longer bound. Julia gaped at him, too shocked to speak as he awkwardly climbed out of the coach. His hands were still tied behind him. He met her eyes with a grim mocking look.

He glanced at their captor. 'Perhaps you would proceed with your robbery. We'd like to continue our journey.' His voice was bored.

The highwayman chuckled. 'Not so well trussed after all. Hand over your valuables, milady.'

'I do not have any. Unless you want a paste necklace.'

'Give it to me.' The amusement had left his face and he looked like the thief he was.

'Good God,' Thayne muttered.

'Best do as he asks, lass,' Eduardo called.

She fumbled with the clasp and reluctantly gave it to the ruffian.

The man turned to Thayne. 'Your ring, my lord.'

Julia's heart nearly stopped. 'No.'

The highwayman ignored her. 'Your ring.'

Thayne leaned against the coach. 'I am hardly capable of removing it myself.'

'Then you remove it, milady.' The highwayman gestured with his pistol.

Julia stepped closer to Thayne, her hand, still hidden in the folds of her cloak, gripped her pistol tightly. The highwayman's eyes fell to her side.

'What is in your hand?' he demanded.

'Nothing.'

'Show me your hand.'

She backed up against the coach. 'No.'

'You'd best do as I want, milady.' His tone had lost all affability. He pointed the pistol at her.

'Hell,' Thayne muttered. 'Give the damn thing to me.'

'But you don't have any hands,' Julia said in a low voice.

'Put it in my hand. Behind my back,' he said between gritted teeth.

The highwayman levelled the pistol. Beneath his mask, his mouth had tightened into a nasty line. 'I should hate to shoot you or your, er…gentleman. Show your hand, milady.'

Reluctantly, Julia brought her hand forward. In a sort of dream she heard the shot and at the same time Thayne slammed into her. She hit the hard road and gasped, the breath knocked from her. A heavy weight pinned her to the ground. After an eternity, she heard more shouting and the pounding of horses' hooves and finally silence.

'Are you all right?' Thayne's voice was near her ear.

'Yes,' she managed to say.

The weight rolled away from her and she heard a groan and then he cursed. She managed to rise to her hands and knees, dizziness overtaking her for a moment. When she sat back, her hand encountered something thick and sticky on her cloak. Puzzled, she realised it was blood, except she could feel no pain.

And then she saw Thayne. He was sitting up, less than a foot away from her, a dark stain spreading on his coat. She crawled over to him and was horrified to see the hole in his coat sleeve on the upper part of his arm. She briefly registered his hands were no longer bound. 'You've been shot,' she said stupidly. With a sick feeling she realised he had taken the ball meant for her.

He looked at her and his eyes held a sardonic gleam. 'It appears so.' Then promptly shut his eyes.

Before she could say more, Eduardo appeared. He knelt down at Thayne's other side. He glanced at the wound and looked over at Julia. 'We need a pad for his arm. You'll need to hold it to the wound while I bind it.'

Thayne's eyes snapped open. 'Keep her away from me.' His voice was nearly a snarl.

She supposed she couldn't blame him for being so bad-tempered, but he needn't sound as if she was about to poison him. 'I am only going to help you.'

'How? By knifing me?'

'No!' she snapped. Her face heated when she saw Eduardo's amused look.

She rose, her mind starting to shift into focus. 'I have my handkerchief, and there is his cravat in the carriage.' And the new ribbon she had purchased at Grafton House earlier today. It seemed centuries ago.

Between them, she and Eduardo managed to stop

the bleeding and then bind his wound. To her relief the shot had only grazed his arm, but she knew even then there could be complications.

Thayne had said little, his face growing paler; by the time they helped him into the coach, she feared he was about to swoon.

The coachman was revived with a shot of whisky. 'Never thought I'd live to say I was held up by a highwayman. I'll have a tale to tell!'

At least someone was delighted with the night's events. She climbed into the coach and reluctantly decided she'd best sit next to Thayne. If he fainted or started to fall off his seat, she'd at least try to prevent it. His eyes were closed, but he opened them as she sat down. He looked at her vaguely and then grimaced. 'Good God. Not you. Hell.'

He closed his eyes again and she strongly suspected hell was exactly where he wished her. And she could hardly fault him.

Chapter Three

His head felt like it had been kicked by a horse and his arm was on fire, reminders that last night had been more than restless dreams brought on by too much brandy and a conscience filled with remorse. No, he'd been shot by a highwayman. That was after he had been abducted by a woman with the face of an angel who was undoubtedly mad. He opened his eyes and looked up at a ceiling with a brown water stain directly over head. No, it was most certainly not a bad dream. He recalled the stain from last night when his captors had poured whisky into his wound. He struggled to sit up and then groaned as pain shot through his head. He closed his eyes. Fate had seen fit to finally punish him after all.

'My lord?'

He vaguely recognised the soft male voice from last night. He forced his eyes open and saw the stocky grey-haired man who had bound him up hovering over him. 'How are you feeling, laddie?'

'I've felt better.' He barely managed to form the words around his dry mouth.

'You need some water.' The man moved across the small room to a pitcher on a chest.

At least they weren't planning to kill him yet. He'd had some half-formed notion that was exactly what they intended as they forced some vile concoction down his throat last night. He'd drifted into unconsciousness with the brown-haired angel bent over him, something surprisingly like concern in her face. And that was the last he knew until now.

He watched the man pour the water and then bring the cup to the bed. Although his captor was undoubtedly on the shady side of fifty, his tall body was well muscled and he moved with the grace of a much younger man. He placed the cup on the table next to the bed. 'I'll help you sit.'

He supported Nicholas with one arm while holding the cup with the other. Nicholas took a few sips, the water soothing to his parched throat and then fell back against the pillows. He fixed his companion with a cool stare.

'Who the hell are you?' he managed to ask.

'Eduardo Mackenzie.'

'Eduardo's a damnable name for a Scotsman.'

'My mother was Italian.' He looked down at Nicholas, a slight grin tugging at his lips. 'Must be feeling better. You had a bit of a fever last night but in a few days you'll be on your feet.'

'I am delighted.' He stared hard at Mackenzie. 'However, I'd rather know precisely what I am doing here. Or more to the point, why the hell did you abduct me?'

'You will need to ask the Countess.'

Nicholas raised a brow in his most sardonic fashion.

'I presume the Countess is the madwoman I met last night? Perhaps you would be so kind as to fetch her.'

Mackenzie looked apologetic. 'She is out.'

'Doing what? Searching for another victim? Does she make a practice of luring men into her clutches and then finding novel means of torturing them?'

Mackenzie's lips twitched. 'Nay, you're the first.'

'Splendid,' Nicholas said bitterly. 'How was I fortunate enough to be chosen for the honour?'

'She'll tell you soon enough. Since you were still abed she went out to care for the animals.'

'Animals?' Had he heard correctly?

'This is a small farm.' Mackenzie took in Nicholas's expression. 'Some of the animals she prefers to tend to herself. And one of the mares is about to foal.'

'I see.' Nicholas closed his eyes briefly as tiredness overtook him. From the lingering taste in his mouth he suspected the potion last night contained laudanum.

'You'd best rest and then you'll be ready for a bite,' Mackenzie said. 'I'll be outside the door if you need anything.'

More likely to guard the door. Not that he was in any shape to attempt an escape. And even if he was, he certainly had no intention of leaving before he found out exactly what he was doing here. Nicholas watched Mackenzie cross the room and then he spoke, one more question coming to mind. 'Who is the Countess?'

Mackenzie paused at the door. 'I will let her tell you.'

He quit the room on quiet feet. Nicholas fell back against his pillows and swore, not only from the lack of answers but at his own helplessness. The Countess, or whatever she chose to call herself, had better have a good explanation for why he was lying under her roof with a gunshot wound in his arm—or she would rue the day she had ever laid eyes on him.

Julia closed the door to Betty's pen. The goat gave her a reproachful look, but Julia had no doubt Betty would find a way to escape again. It was nearly impossible to keep the goat contained anywhere. She preferred to follow Julia about like a dog and make everything her business.

Julia pulled the long wool cloak more tightly around her. The spring air was crisp and cool, but there were hints of warmer days to come. She paused by the barn and looked towards the old farmhouse. She had spent most of the day outside, dreading the moment Thayne would wake and ask for her. He'd slept the entire morning while she had attended to business in the study and then she had escaped after the noon meal to the barn. She had already spent more time than usual with the horses and then had played with the new kittens in the barn. From the position of the pale sun, it appeared to be late afternoon. She could not delay facing Lord Thayne any longer, not after he had saved her life.

This had completely confused her. Only an imbecile would fail to realise how angry he had been with her. She would hardly have blamed him if he had stood aside while the highwayman had shot her and then tried to make his escape. Instead, he had taken the bullet himself.

Perhaps Thérèse was right after all and he knew nothing about Thomas's death. For instance, it did not make sense that he would wear such an unusual ring that would be certain to attract notice. The cool intelligence she had seen in his eyes last night told her he was unlikely to do something that foolish.

He deserved to at least know why he had been hit over the head, bound and gagged and stuffed into a coach, and then shot by a highwayman. Every time she thought of last night she wanted to run. Thomas had always warned her that she was far too impulsive. 'You jump first and then think. You must make your plan, think of the possible outcomes, and then act, my sweet Julia.'

Not that he had always followed his own advice. And in the end, all the planning in the world had not saved him.

She reluctantly walked towards the house, the yellow cat, Wellington, trailing behind her. When she entered the house, Mrs Mobley, her housekeeper, appeared in the small hallway, dusting the flour off her hands on her white apron. She was tall with a magnificent figure and a mass of flaming red hair that was never quite concealed under her mobcap. 'Good thing you're back. His lordship is getting a trifle peevish, asking for you. Has the devil's own temper, I can see. Just brought him a tray and I thought he was likely to throw it at me. Said the gruel was only fit for babes, unless we now planned to starve him. Finally sent him some of the roast beef.'

'Splendid.' Julia's stomach was starting to knot up. So he was awake. She should be grateful he was finally conscious, but the thought of facing the man and his temper was hardly pleasing. 'How is his wound?'

'Wouldn't let me look at it. Or Eduardo. Said he wanted to wait for you.' She grinned. 'He's handsome enough, although he'll not tame easily. You'll have your hands full.'

'I have no intention of taming him. He will be leaving as soon as he is well enough.'

Mrs Mobley looked sceptical. Julia forced herself upstairs. Eduardo sat in a wooden chair outside of the door of the small bedchamber Thayne occupied. He rose when he saw her. 'Ah, 'tis you at last. The lad has been waiting impatiently for you.'

'He is not asleep?' Julia asked, praying that he was.

A smile touched his mouth. 'Not at all. He has just finished his meal. I think, however, you'd best tell him why you've brought him here. He's becoming a trifle impatient.' He opened the door and Julia entered the room.

She paused, her heart thudding. Thayne was in bed, propped against the pillows. His cool gaze found her and the dangerous light that leapt to his eyes nearly made her back out the door. 'So you decided not to run after all,' he said softly.

'I had some business to attend to.' Unfortunately, her voice was not as strong as she might have wished. 'I hope you are better.'

He ignored her inquiry. 'Come here,' he commanded.

'I....' She glanced behind her, relieved to see Eduardo had not completely closed the door. She moved across the room and looked at him with no little degree of apprehension and tried to remind herself that, after all, he was her prisoner. And wounded. Despite that, he hardly looked vulnerable. In fact, with the dark shadow of beard around his mouth and powerful shoulders visible beneath the thin linen of his borrowed night shirt, he appeared even more male and deadly than he had last night. Her heart thudding, she halted by the bed. She saw his face was still very pale. 'How is your arm?'

He stared at her. 'It hurts like the devil.'

'I really am very sorry,' she said, feeling wretched. 'I never thought we would be held up or that you would be hurt. And you saved my life as well.'

'In retrospect I've no idea why.' His hard gaze focused on her face. 'So, my dear Jane or is it my dear Countess? Or is that merely another one of your pretences?'

She tried not to flinch at his cold, sardonic tone. 'No. My husband was an Earl.'

His brow rose. 'Was?'

'He is dead,' she said quietly. 'I suppose you wish to know why you are here.'

'The thought had crossed my mind. We've no dealings together that I can recollect and I already told you I would have been willing to provide my services without such a rash measure on your part. I am still willing.' His eyes raked over her body in blatant insult. 'Of course, I would prefer to know your name first.'

Her sensible, high-necked gown suddenly seemed as transparent as glass. Heat crept up her cheek. 'That is not what I wanted at all! Certainly you are the last man on earth I would…' She stopped and collected herself. Losing her temper would hardly help. 'I am Lady Carrington.' She kept her eyes on his face, watching for his reaction.

'Lady Carrington?' His gaze sharpened for a moment. 'Have we met before?'

'No. But perhaps you once met my husband.'

'Not to my knowledge.' If he had met Thomas before there was nothing in his face that gave it away.

He regarded her from under lowered brows. 'What does this have to do with your abducting me?'

'I abducted you because of the ring.'

'The ring?' He looked blank.

'The ring you are wearing.'

He glanced down and then quickly back at her face. 'Ah, yes. My ring. The one you expressed an interest in last night.' His eyes narrowed. 'So, you wish me to believe you abducted me merely for my ring?'

'Yes, but there is more.'

'Is there?' He stared hard at her and gave a short laugh. 'I pray you will enlighten me. For you see, you are not the only person that has expressed an interest in this particular item in the past week.'

A chill ran down her spine. 'There has been someone else? Who?'

'I've no idea. The interested party sent an agent, but wished to remain anonymous.' He studied her face for a moment and then his brow drew together. 'What is this about?'

She took a deep breath. 'The ring belonged to my husband. When he was killed, nearly three years ago, it was removed from his finger.' She looked away. 'Most likely by his…his murderer.'

'How do you know it is the same ring?' he asked sharply.

'I purchased the ring in Spain. It is very old and I think it unlikely there would be another. Most certainly not in England. Our initials were carved on the inside of the band.'

'If they were there, they are no longer. How did you come to know I had the ring?' Then he smiled, but it did not reach his eyes. 'Ah, I remember. You were watching me play Hazard one evening. An amazing coincidence you happened to be there that very night. Or do you often visit Madame Blanchot's premises?'

The knowledge that he had recognised her was more than disconcerting. 'Thérèse told me you had the ring. I came that night to be certain.'

'And then a night later you decided to abduct me. Why?'

'Because I needed to know if you had anything to do with my husband's death. I did not think you would tell me if I merely asked you so I decided I would need to abduct you instead. And I wanted the ring.'

'I see.' Amusement briefly touched his mouth. 'Before we proceed further, I think you'd best look at the ring and be certain it is the same one. It would be a pity to discover you had gone to all this trouble for naught.' He pulled the ring from his finger, wincing slightly at the effort, and then held it out to her.

She took it, her hand trembling as she held the ring for the first time in nearly three years. The band still held the warmth of his hand. She ran her finger over the intricate carving on the band, remembering the surprise and pleasure on Thomas's face when she had presented it to him. And afterwards he had pulled her to him...

She forced the memory away and willed herself to look inside the band. Thayne was right, any initials there might have been were gone. When she touched the spot where they should have been, she felt a slight roughness. She moved to the window and looked more closely. The gold was scratched.

'Well?' Thayne said.

'I think they have been removed,' she said. She crossed to the bed. 'See, if you put your finger here.'

She bent over him and held out the ring. He glanced at her and then touched the spot.

'Possibly.' He fell back against the pillows. A lock of hair had fallen over his forehead and he suddenly appeared rather vulnerable. She had the most discomforting urge to smooth it away. She jerked up, flustered by the notion.

He looked tired again. 'Shall I leave you?' she asked. 'Perhaps you should rest. We can continue the conversation later.'

'No.' He fixed his hazel gaze on her and frowned. 'Precisely why do you think I had something to do with your husband's death?'

'You have his ring.'

'Then I must be either a fool or remarkably arrogant to flaunt it in public where anyone might recognise it.'

'I had thought of that,' she admitted. She forced herself to look directly at him. 'Did you have anything to do with his death?'

He met her eyes squarely. 'No.'

Was he telling the truth? Some instinct told her he was. Despite his arrogance, she sensed he would not kill a man unless he had no other choice. Not for a piece of jewellery, no matter how valuable. And if had to kill, he would not lie about it. She looked away, shaken at the certainty of her thoughts. Why should she trust a man she had just met and under such bizarre circumstances?

His sardonic voice broke into her thoughts. 'And so, where do we proceed from here? Have we established my innocence or not? Or am I to enjoy your hospitality until you make up your mind?'

She frowned at him. She may have decided to believe him but it did not mean she planned to tell him that. Not until he answered the rest of her questions. 'I still would like to know how you came to be in possession of my husband's ring.'

He eyed her. 'I would like my ring back first.'

The slight emphasis on the 'my' set her back up. 'It is not your ring.'

'No? Then why is it in my possession?'

'That is what I'm trying to discover!' She fought back her exasperation. 'Can you not tell me?'

He gave her a cool smile. 'Not until you return the ring.'

'I have no intention of returning it!' She clenched her hands together in pure frustration.

'Then you will need to come up with another plan. Perhaps you could coerce the information from me at gunpoint. Or threaten to starve me. I presume you have a cellar. Does it have rats? You could lock me up there until I—'

She glared at him and resisted the urge to throw something at him. 'I think you are quite mad! Do you think I would do such a thing when you are so unwell?'

'So you will wait until my arm is better and then lock me in the cellar?' he asked maddeningly.

'Possibly. I would hope you will change your mind by then.'

'It is unlikely. Not until I get my ring back.' His expression was grim. 'For you see, my dear Lady Carrington, that ring is much more to me than a mere piece of jewellery. I have no intention of letting it go.'

'Then I've no choice but to keep you here.' She fought to keep her voice calm, but inside she wanted to scream at him.

His smile was wicked. 'I look forward to it. And to

furthering our acquaintance.' His eyes locked with hers.

To her chagrin, her legs suddenly felt weak and her face heated. 'Good day, Lord Thayne. I trust you will change your mind soon.' She turned and forced herself to walk calmly across the room. She could not let him see how much he managed to fluster her. It would only give him all the advantage.

Nicholas fell back against the pillows, loath to admit even to himself that he was exhausted. Certainly he had no intention of letting his lovely gaoler suspect it had taken all his strength to finish their conversation, although it could hardly be called that. More of a verbal fencing. His mouth briefly lifted as he remembered the way her dark eyes flashed before she left.

Then he frowned. What the hell was going on? He knew of her husband, of course. One of Britain's most celebrated agents, Lord Carrington's name had been on every tongue after he had returned to England with his lovely wife, but even more so after his brutal murder. No one, to Nicholas's knowledge, had ever been arrested for the crime. He knew little of Lady Carrington, although that was hardly surprising. Since Mary's death, he had rarely ventured into society and so it was unlikely they would have crossed paths.

Had the ring indeed belonged to her husband? Certainly Lady Carrington had no doubt, not if she was desperate enough to abduct him for it. And how did the rest of it fit in? The man who had approached him had made him an offer that was staggering. He had found it peculiar but, because he had no intention of relinquishing the ring, had put it out of his mind.

And there was last night. The highwayman had requested Lady Carrington's necklace but had appeared oddly uninterested in any other valuables except for the ring. The fact the men had panicked and run off after shooting him had suggested they were amateurs.

So had that been the doing of the same person who had made him an offer for the ring? Or was the robbery a mere coincidence? If not, the implications, combined with Lady Carrington's revelation about her husband's murder, were not pleasant.

His frown deepened. He had no idea what to make of her, which had been his downfall. He had not been able to make up his mind whether she was an accomplished seductress or an innocent playing a game way over her head. So, due to a lethal combination of alcohol, lust and blasted curiosity, he had gone with her.

She had proved to be neither. She was a woman who would go to any lengths to solve her husband's murder. Except she needed to be more ruthless if she hoped to succeed. Instead of showing concern for his wounded state, for instance, she should have threatened to march him into the cellar straight away if he did nòt comply. A grin tugged at his mouth. At the very least she needed to curb her tendency to blush every time he teased her. He should perhaps drop a hint or two in her ear.

His grin faded. The last thing he wanted was to become embroiled in her affairs. He intended to retrieve his ring as soon as possible and escape. Even if it meant he held her at gunpoint.

The ring was all he had of Mary.

Chapter Four

Nicholas put his fork down on the plate. He grimaced as he surveyed the remainder of the meal sitting on the tray across his lap. The chicken was stringy and nearly tasteless, and the vegetables so overcooked they fell apart before they reached his mouth. If all the meals were this inedible, he would starve.

With his good arm he managed to shove the tray over onto the small table near the bed. After that he forced himself to sit on the edge of the bed. His head spun for a moment before his vision cleared. But when he stood and took a few steps, he broke into a sweat as a wave of nausea rolled over him. He was forced to sit back down.

He swore, cursing his weakness. Even if he did manage to escape his room he was hardly in any condition to make his way down to the stables and steal a horse to ride back to London. Not until he rid himself of this blasted lightheadedness.

The weakness passed and he forced himself to stand again. This time he waited before attempting a step. Nicholas had just made it to the table near the mantelpiece when he heard the key turn in the lock. Half-expecting Lady Carrington's Amazonian housekeeper, he was startled to see Lady Carrington instead. She carried a basin and a cloth was draped over her arm.

She stepped inside the doorway and then saw him. Her eyes widened as they fell on his half-bare legs and quickly focused on his face. 'Whatever are you doing out of bed?'

'Attempting an escape.'

She frowned. 'You are ridiculous. Please get back into bed.' She set the basin and cloth down on the table and fixed a disapproving look on him.

'I would rather not.' Despite the fact his stomach was beginning to feel heavy again.

'I think it would be in your best interest to do so.'

He raised a brow. 'Why? Do you plan to shoot me if I do not?'

'No, of course not!' she snapped. He was gratified to see that she looked as if she wanted to hit him. 'You are far from well and you must be rather…rather cold in only a nightshirt.' She kept her eyes fastened on his face, slight colour rising to her cheeks.

So that was the problem. 'On the contrary, I feel rather warm. I had considered removing it since I normally do not wear such things to bed.'

Her reaction was all he had hoped for. She blanched as if she expected him to pull the garment off now. 'I…I…' She swallowed. 'Perhaps you are a bit feverish.'

'Perhaps.' Although he was loath to admit it, his head was starting to spin. He reached out for the table to support himself.

Lady Carrington was at his side in an instant. 'I am going to help you to bed.' She took his good arm in a gentle grasp. 'Come.'

Blast. He hardly wanted her leading him to bed as if he were an elderly invalid. 'No.'

'I fear you will swoon if you do not lie down.' She gave his arm a little tug. 'And if you do not do as I ask I may have no choice but to shoot you after all.'

'Very unsporting of you,' he managed to say and then was forced to close his eyes for a moment as sudden dizziness overtook him. When he opened them, he found her looking up at him, her face full of concern.

'You are most definitely going to bed,' she said.

Except for his sister, no woman in the past two years had ever looked at him in such a way, or touched him with such gentle hands. The sensation was more than disconcerting.

He pulled his arm out of her grasp. 'I will put myself to bed,' he said coolly. He turned away from her and managed to make it back to the bed without stumbling. He sat down on the edge. To his chagrin, his head swam and he was forced to lay back on the pillows. Lady Carrington had followed him and now stood next to the bed. He looked up and scowled. 'Now what do you want?'

She levelled a frown at him. 'I need to look at your wound.'

'Why? To pour salt into it, perhaps?'

'Do not be so absurd! I wish to make certain it is not infected. Eduardo will be in with a new dressing in a moment. If you will sit up a little more, I can remove your bandage.'

'I've no intention of having you faint all over me at the sight of blood. I'll wait for your bodyguard.'

'I have seen worse injuries. Much worse.' She was beginning to look exasperated. 'I am going to remove your bandage. And it will hurt much more if you do not cooperate,' she added severely.

'Are you threatening me?'

'No. Merely telling you that if you attempt to pull away you may hurt your arm.'

The last thing he wanted was to have her touch him again with her soft, gentle hands. Or see his bare arm. 'What is your given name?' he asked, hoping to distract her.

'Julia.' She sat down on the bed next to him.

'Julia,' he murmured. 'Much more suitable than Jane.'

From the slight colour that stained her cheeks, he knew he had flustered her again. Good. He intended to fluster her enough so she would leave him alone.

'I need to see to your arm, please.' She did not look at his face. A few strands of fine brown hair had come loose from the knot at the back of her head and he resisted the sudden urge to tuck the hair behind her ear. He forced his gaze to her lips, which proved to be a mistake for a surge of desire shot through him.

He nearly groaned. Lust was the last thing he wanted to feel for her. He had undoubtedly been without a woman for too long. Perhaps it was time he gave up his celibacy and accept Marguerite Anslow's not too subtle offer after all.

'Is something wrong?' she asked. Her brow was creased in a tiny frown. Apparently she had no idea of the effect she had on him.

If she did she would probably run like the devil, which might work to his advantage. He stared down at her pale oval face with its thin, delicate nose and rosebud lips and resisted the urge to pull her into his arms. Instead his gaze lingered on her mouth. 'I might consider telling you what you want to know if you will kiss me,' he said softly.

She stared at him as if he had gone mad. 'I…I beg your pardon?'

He smiled wickedly. 'I am making you a bargain. If you kiss me, I will consider telling you where I got the ring. With a little more enticement I might decide to let you keep it.'

She leapt up and backed away from the bed. 'I think you are delirious!'

'Not at all.' He turned his head a little on the pillows and then allowed his gaze to run insolently down her softly curved body. Even in the candlelight he could see the colour on her pale ivory cheeks. 'I believe you offered me that and more last night.'

'I…I did not!'

'No?'

She jumped when the door opened and gave a little gasp. Mackenzie entered. He glanced at Julia's dismayed face and then looked at Nicholas. A hint of a smile touched his mouth but he only said, 'I was a bit delayed. How does his wound look?'

'I…I have not yet had a chance to look at it.' Her voice was a trifle breathless. 'In fact, I believe it would be best if you saw to Lord Thayne yourself.'

'I see.' Eduardo gave her a curious glance before moving to the side of the bed where, as Lady Carrington had before, he sat down next to Nicholas. Before Nicholas could protest he had started to unwrap the bandage.

'I thought she was planning to leave,' Nicholas said. He gritted his teeth against the sudden pain that shot through him when Mackenzie's hand brushed his tender flesh.

'How is his arm?' Lady Carrington asked, ignoring Nicholas. She had come to stand next to the bed again.

Mackenzie straightened and stood up. 'A bit red. We'll clean it with a spot of brandy and then wrap it again.' He glanced at Nicholas. 'Afraid you'll need to accept our hospitality a bit longer. Can't have you leaving with that arm.'

Nicholas scowled at him. 'I had no idea leaving was a possibility. Lady Carrington does not seem inclined to release me.'

'So you haven't reached an agreement yet?' Mackenzie asked.

'No.' Nicholas looked past Mackenzie to Lady Carrington. 'We are still negotiating. I have laid out my terms. I am certain when she has the time to consider them she will see they are quite reasonable.'

Her mouth fell open and then she glared at him. 'Reasonable? You may count yourself fortunate if I let you go before the next century! Good evening, my lord.' To his immense satisfaction, she backed out of the room and slammed the door.

Mackenzie regarded him with an interested expression. 'You might try a less heavy-handed approach, laddie. Unless you're wanting to stay on for a while.' He moved to the table and picked up the basin.

'No.' Nicholas watched Mackenzie approach him and braced himself for another assault on his arm. He fully intended to be back in London before another night had passed. Unless he had completely misread Lady Carrington, a few more improper offers should have her eager to return his ring and rid herself of him in no time.

Julia entered her bedchamber and then sank down on her bed. She got up again almost right away and stalked to her window, her fists clenched. She forced herself to take a deep breath before she did something childish such as heave a vase across the room.

Whatever was wrong with her? He wasn't the first man who had offered her a *carte blanche*. Thomas had posed as a charming gamester. He rubbed shoulders with some of the most practised rogues in Europe and more than one of this circle had assumed Julia would be amenable to an illicit affair. She had learned to shrug off most advances with a polite smile and had become expert at dodging the more persistent admirers.

So why could she not shrug off Thayne as well? He was proving to be exactly the sort of man she despised; a man who was not beneath attempting to force a woman into his bed. She should treat him with icy contempt instead of losing her temper and slamming doors. Certainly she should not be blushing like a schoolgirl every time he looked at her with an insolent gaze.

Except she had the most stupid feeling he really did not want her in his bed at all and was merely trying to aggravate her. In fact, she suspected he did not even like her very much. Worse, there had been a moment or two when she had looked at him and actually felt the same mixture of exasperation and sympathy she had felt for Thomas when he had been ill. More disconcerting, she had felt the same desire to take care of him.

She wanted to groan. However had she got herself into this fix? She had Thomas's ring—perhaps she should just release Thayne and try to discover whatever information she could on her own. If someone

had approached him about the ring, then there was a
chance the person might approach her.

Unfortunately, she suspected it would not be all that
easy. However else Thayne might confuse her, of one
thing she was certain: he was not going to give up the
ring without a fight.

The next morning Julia decided she would let Eduardo and Barbara Mobley nurse Thayne. She tried to
justify her cowardly behaviour by reminding herself
that she did have to attend to other matters and could
not spend all of her time worrying about her ungracious patient. Not that she was allowed to forget his
presence. Barbara seemed to think she needed frequent
reports on his arm, which was less red, his manners,
which were surly, and his demands, which included a
shirt and breeches instead of the nightshirt.

She finally escaped to the stables; when she returned
to the house, she went directly to the tiny room that
served as her study. She sat down at the old desk. The
first thing that met her eye was the most recent letter
from Francis Abbot of Abbot and Sons, Solicitors. Mr
Abbot had written to advise her, not for the first time,
that she would be wise to sell Foxwood. On sunny
days with blue skies showing outside the study window, and roses and larkspur in bloom, it was possible
to be optimistic about keeping Foxwood. But on cold
rainy days such as today, with leaks in the roof and
the dilapidated garden, she was tempted to give in and
sell the farm after all.

Foxwood had been Thomas's dream; a peaceful
country farm to raise his horses. But he had been killed
before the first foal was born.

She had not wanted to give up his dream. She had

leased out the land to her neighbour, Lord George Kingsley, and sold several of the horses. There was little of the money Thomas had left her and none of the amount his uncle had left with the farm. She refused to give Thomas's remaining relations the satisfaction of admitting defeat and selling the farm. Or her own relations. Where would she go? To live as a companion to Cousin Harriet? She could hardly take Eduardo and Barbara with her.

'Daydreaming again?'

Julia's head jerked up. She stared at the man who stood in the doorway. And then wanted to groan. A visitor was the last thing she wanted and this particular one was even less welcome. She stood. 'Oh, George. I…I hardly expected you. I thought you had left for Maldon.'

He sauntered into the room and raised a brow. He was of medium height with dark brown hair and a thin, arrogant face. As usual, he was exquisitely dressed, with an elaborately tied cravat and shirt points to his chin. 'Disappointed, my love? No, I had meant to leave London and travel to Maldon today, but, alas, my dear father had other plans. There seems to be a matter or two at Amberton that cannot go without my attention. I would have thought Seton could capably attend to the problem but, alas, my parent decided otherwise with the gentle hint that if I declined, I would find myself without funds. I fear some of my creditors are becoming a bit, er…persistent.'

Which meant he had probably racked up another mound of gambling debts. But why, of all times, must he pay one of his infrequent visits to Amberton? He much preferred Maldon where he kept a small cottage and docked his yacht. 'I see.'

'He also commissioned me to inquire after your well-being.'

'I am well, of course. Would you care for refreshment?' She prayed he would say no.

'Perhaps a glass of claret. However, I will forgo anything of an edible nature. I do not wish to risk breaking a tooth.'

Mrs Mobley suddenly appeared as if on cue. She regarded George with a suspicious eye and stalked out after Julia made her request. George watched Mrs Mobley leave. 'I expect to find myself cursed,' he remarked as he settled himself in one of the wing chairs. 'I have no idea why you surround yourself with such grim servants. Actually, I have no idea why you persist in living in such a grim place.'

'I do not find it particularly grim.' She cast a nervous glance towards the door. She hoped Mrs. Mobley had remembered to lock Thayne in his bedchamber. The thought of him appearing while George was here was enough to give her palpitations.

'Well, perhaps one becomes used to it although that is a rather troubling thought. So, I take it you are not planning to take up my offer and sell?'

'No.' She nearly jumped at the sound of footsteps, but it was only Barbara returning with the claret and a plate of cakes. She watched George take the glass and hoped he would quickly finish it.

He did not. He took a leisurely sip and sat back. 'So, my dear, what have you been about since I last saw you?'

'Nothing very interesting.' Was he looking at her oddly? She gave him a quick smile. 'How is London?'

'Tedious in the extreme. The usual *on-dits*, although the latest gossip is most interesting.'

'Indeed,' she said flatly, hoping to discourage him from elaborating.

'Yes. Indeed.' He took another sip. 'Viscount Thayne has disappeared without a trace.'

'V…Viscount Thayne?'

'The Earl of Monteville's grandson. He was to meet with Monteville yesterday morning and never showed up. He also failed to appear for a dinner at Norwood House last night without a word. The rumours have already begun. Everything from foul play to an elopement. He was last seen at Thérèse Blanchot's establishment the night before.'

'R…really.' Oh, Lord. Was there any chance she had been recognised? But she could tell nothing from George's bland gaze. 'Perhaps he merely decided to go away.'

'Perhaps. But his carriage was found in a nearby street and the coachman reported he never returned to it. And there is the mysterious female with whom he was said to have left Thérèse's.'

Julia managed a laugh. 'A mysterious female as well? How odd. It is beginning to sound rather like a Minerva Press novel. Perhaps he decided to elope and hired a hack.'

George raised a brow. 'My dear, one does not miss appointments with Monteville in order to elope in a hack. Unless one has run mad.'

'I suppose not. At least from what I have heard about Lord Monteville.' The reputation of the cool powerful Earl was well known. The thought of what he would do if he discovered she had abducted his grandson made her feel rather ill.

'No. Which is why that scenario is most unlikely. I

am surprised you have not met the formidable Lord Monteville. He is a friend of my father's.'

Monteville and Phillip were friends? The situation was becoming worse by the moment. 'I did not know that.'

'He is not a man one would want to cross. If Thayne's disappearance was not voluntary, one could almost feel sorry for the perpetrators.'

'Oh,' Julia said faintly.

George suddenly polished off his drink and set the glass on the table. 'As much as I am loath to do so, I suppose I must deal with the local peasantry.' He rose in a leisurely movement and looked down at her. 'My lovely Julia, you look most unwell.'

'Do I?' She stood. 'I am rather tired, that is all.'

He took her hand and bowed elaborately over it. 'I am not surprised. You must come and dine with me soon. As dull as Amberton can be, at least I have a decent cook. And by the way, my dear Aunt Sophia has asked me to tell you that you are always welcome to stay with her in London.' He released her hand and picked up his hat and gloves and strode to the door. He opened it. Betty stood outside. She fixed him with her dark unblinking stare. George paused and turned to look back at Julia, a look of disgust on his countenance. 'My dear, I really advise you to sell the place. If it ever gets about you have livestock running about the house, you will be considered a complete quiz.'

He left the room. Betty wandered into the study and spotted the cakes whereupon she reached up and neatly helped herself. Julia sat back down in her chair, her thoughts in turmoil. Had George recognised her as the unknown female? But surely he would have said something or asked more probing questions if he had.

More disconcerting was the knowledge that Lord Monteville and Phillip were friends. What if Phillip decided to make one of his visits to Amberton? George always stopped at Foxwood and she would be forced to ask him to dine, an invitation he never turned down despite Barbara's cooking. And if something went wrong and Thayne managed to escape from his room…she shuddered at the thought. How could she ever explain how he came to be here? Perhaps she could drug Thayne and lock him in his room, but that seemed utterly barbaric.

Aside from that, it was hardly fair to Thayne's family to let them think he was dead or hurt. She had best release him as quickly as possible. But would he leave without the ring? Even if she told him he was free to go?

She fingered the chain around her neck. She had finally decided this was the safest place for it. It was unlikely he would look for it there. At least she hoped not; the thought was enough to make her blanch. Particularly after last night.

Now, instead of persuading him to stay, she must persuade him to go.

Without the ring.

Nicholas swung his legs over the side of the bed and rose. He was still a little shaky and his head tended to spin for a few seconds after he changed positions, but his arm was better. Not that he had any intention of letting Lady Carrington know that. Better if she thought he was still incapacitated. His mouth curled. She had not been by to see him today, but instead, had sent either Eduardo or Mrs Mobley to tend to him. However, he planned to deal with his captor himself. Tomorrow, if possible. He forced himself to move to the window. His room faced the back of the house and looked down on the stable yard. In the fading light he could see the outline of the stable.

Earlier today he had positioned himself in the chair in front of the window. He had been interested to see that Lady Carrington had spent considerable time in the stables. Mrs Mobley had been willing enough to tell him Lady Carrington generally made a daily visit to the stables to attend to the horses. So, he merely needed to make his way to the stables at the same time she was there. Slipping past her two guardians might pose a problem, but he had noted that today his door was frequently left unguarded. The lock was so old he doubted it would take much effort to break it. Once in the stables, he had no doubt he could persuade her, although she may not like his methods, to give him the ring and a horse. And a pair of boots as he'd not managed to locate his own. Then he was leaving.

There was a sound behind him. He turned, expecting to see Eduardo who'd been the last person outside his door. Instead, Julia stood there. His body tensed in anticipation almost as if he had been looking forward to her visit. He forced the feeling down.

'So, you've deigned to visit me after all,' he drawled.

'Yes. I had something I wanted to discuss with you.' She looked at him, biting her lip a little as if she were nervous and did not know quite what to say. 'How are you feeling?' she finally asked.

'Better.'

She frowned. 'Why are you up? Shouldn't you be in bed?'

'No. What do you wish to discuss? Have you come

to accept my offer after all?' He had no idea what to do if she said yes.

'No! I most certainly have not.' A touch of colour washed over her cheeks but she held his gaze. 'In fact, I have put it quite out of my mind.'

'Indeed.' He gave her a disbelieving smile. 'What is it you want?'

'Must you be so rude?'

'Am I? I was not aware there was a protocol for when addressing one's abductor.' He had no idea why he was sparring with her except he wanted to keep her at a distance.

She looked completely discomfited. 'Won't you at least sit?'

'After you.' He gestured towards the wooden chair near his bed.

She hesitantly advanced into the room and perched on the edge of the chair like a schoolgirl. He climbed back into the bed, grateful to be sitting and determined not to let her know. He stared at her. 'What is it?'

'I have decided to release you.'

That was the last thing he had expected. 'Why?'

'Well, I...I cannot keep you here forever.'

'But I thought that was the plan if I did not tell you what you wanted to know. I was quite resigned to spending my life locked up in a small bedchamber with a leaking roof, subsisting on poorly cooked meat and overcooked vegetables with my only visitors two surly servants. And your delightful self, of course.'

'That was hardly my intention!' she snapped, and then seemed to collect herself. 'You may leave to-morrow.'

'So, why the sudden change of heart? I don't suppose George Kingsley's visit had anything to do with it?'

Her eyes widened in surprise. 'What do you know of that?'

'Your delightful Mrs Mobley told me. I am rumoured to be the victim of foul play, I believe.'

She coloured, looking extremely mortified. 'She had no business telling you that!'

'Why not? It is my life after all.'

'Yes, but she should not have been listening!'

'Apparently she fears for your virtue at Kingsley's hands.' At least that was the excuse the housekeeper had given for eavesdropping on Julia's visitor.

'That is ridiculous! George…that is…Lord George would never…' She shut her lips tightly. 'This is an inane conversation! And yes, if you must know, I did change my mind after his visit! I cannot have your family worrying about you and thinking you are dead! So you may go.'

'So you have decided to return the ring to me.'

'No, I haven't decided that at all!' Her hand went to a chain she wore around her neck.

'Then I am not leaving.' He settled back against the pillows and looked at her.

'But you cannot stay here!'

'Why not? What do you plan to do about it? Throw me into the rain and leave me to my own devices? I am hardly well enough to walk back to London. Then you would have my death on your conscience, although, of course, that may not matter to you. I suppose you could abduct me again and take me to my townhouse. But in that case, I might decide to press charges against you.'

'But then you would have to admit you were abducted by a woman. I cannot imagine you would like that getting about!'

He smiled sardonically. 'It matters little to me what tale gets about.' He allowed his gaze to wander over her face in a way that brought colour to her cheeks. 'Some men might actually be envious.'

'I cannot imagine why!' she snapped.

'Can you not? You are a lovely woman.'

Her colour increased and she glared at him. 'That has nothing to do with a thing! Why must men always make some idiotic remark about a woman's appearance that has no relevance to a conversation at all!'

'Referring to you as a lovely woman is hardly an idiotic remark.'

'That is not—' She stopped and shut her mouth tightly as if attempting to hang on to her temper. 'Perhaps we could stick to the point of the conversation.'

'We could, although we seemed to have reached an impasse. You wish me to leave your house and I do not plan to go without the ring. Although you could have Eduardo toss me into the rain.'

'You are ridiculous! I would hardly do such a thing!' She looked extremely flustered. 'I should think you would want to leave!'

He gave her a lazy smile, which had the desired effect of making her look even more disconcerted. 'Why? I've nothing more pressing to do. I will own, being abducted by you has been the most entertaining thing that has happened to me in a long while.' Which was, he realised with some surprise, the truth. His days mostly seemed to stretch out in a predictable pattern of appointments and activities designed to fill the time.

She stared at him, a peculiar look crossing her face.

'I cannot imagine why anyone would find being forced into a carriage at gunpoint entertaining.'

'You've left out being bound and gagged, jostled over rough roads, and finally being shot by a highwayman. Then there is the nearly inedible food and the—'

'I think you are quite mad! Why can you not go? I will be more than happy to have Eduardo drive you to London.'

'But then you won't know where I got the ring. I thought you wanted that information.'

'Yes, but...' She bit her lip. 'Why must you make this so difficult?'

To his consternation, she looked as if she were about to cry. After living with a younger sister, he recognised the signs all too well.

'Don't,' he said roughly.

'Do...don't what?' She avoided his eyes and sniffed. She looked vulnerable and tired and he had the damnable impulse to pull her into his arms and comfort her.

'Cry.'

'I am not crying. I never engage in such...such missish behaviour!' She abruptly rose to her feet, stumbling against the chair a little. 'I will leave you for now. I...I hope you will consider my...my offer.' She turned and dashed from the room, leaving Nicholas to stare after her.

He fell back against the pillows. 'Hell!' he muttered. Now he'd managed to make the indomitable Lady Carrington cry. Hardly the effect he had wanted. Not that he was sure what he had wanted from her.

If he had an ounce of sense he'd take his leave from this house as quickly as possible. He had no desire to involve himself with the lovely Lady Carrington. No more than she wanted anything from him—her evident desire to rid herself of him as quickly as possible told him that. She was willing to let him go without the information she sought.

But, of course, she still had the ring. And he could not leave without it.

Chapter Five

At least he hadn't propositioned her again. That was the first thought Julia had on awakening the next morning. The next was that it was raining and the roof was undoubtedly leaking.

And then she heard a curse followed by an indignant bleat. Her eyes shot open and she sprang out of bed, hardly noticing the hard cold floor. Oh, heavens! Whatever was Betty doing inside? And why must she choose to enter Thayne's room?

Betty stood at the foot of his bed, staring at him. He had sat up, the cover falling from his chest. His eyes went to Julia's face. 'There is a goat in my room,' he said.

'Yes.' Embarrassed, she stepped inside. 'It is Betty.'

'Indeed.' He continued to stare at her with an unreadable expression.

'She…she sometimes comes in the house.' Actually, it was on a nearly daily basis, but Thayne didn't need to know that.

'Perhaps you could tell her I'd prefer that she'd find another room. Waking up nose to nose with a goat isn't particularly appealing.'

'No.' Her face crimson, Julia crossed over to Betty who had a cloth in her mouth. She saw it was one of the clean bandages. 'Just give me that,' she hissed, grabbing the other end.

Betty stared at her with unblinking dark eyes. Julia tugged and the cloth tore. 'Drat!'

'Perhaps you should use what's left of it as a rope,' Thayne suggested. His voice held a slight hint of amusement.

Julia quickly tied the cloth around Betty's neck, not daring to look at him. She tugged on the makeshift lead and Betty reluctantly followed her, her hooves clicking on the wood floor. Julia returned to her bed-chamber and shoved her bare feet into a pair of slippers before leading Betty down the narrow steps and to the kitchen. Because of the rain, the door had swollen and would not shut properly which was how Betty had made her way in. Julia supposed it was her fault for raising the orphaned goat in the house in the first place.

She pushed the reluctant Betty out of the door. The goat gave her a reproachful look as if she considered Julia the epitome of cruelty for shoving her into the rain. Julia looked at her sternly. 'You can go into your shed! And please, if you must come in, stay away from Lord Thayne.' He probably thought her mad enough already without a goat roaming about the house.

She watched Betty amble into the garden and then attempted to shut the door. It closed, but barely, and she had to use all her strength to push it tight enough so she could fasten the latch. By the time she was done, she was breathless. And then she noticed the leak in the roof. She stifled a groan and went to fetch a large pot. It seemed as soon as they repaired one leak, another heavy rain would come and bring another.

'Do you frequently have livestock running about the house?'

She whirled around, her hand going to her throat. 'Wh…what are you doing here?'

Thayne was leaning against the doorway. 'I came to see if you needed help evicting Betty. And I was hungry.'

'Hungry?' She stared at him, her heart pounding. He was dressed in a shirt and breeches that had belonged to Thomas. They were a trifle loose on him, but failed to hide his lean, muscular build. His injured arm was in a sling. The faint outline of his beard made him look a little rough and not at all like an elegant lord. She was suddenly aware she was clad only in her nightrail, her feet bare except for her slippers, her hair in a thick braid past her shoulders. No matter that it was a voluminous gown with a high neck and she wore a shawl. She pulled the ends of the shawl tighter and crossed her arms.

'Last night's stew was not exactly edible,' he said. 'What meat was that anyway? For a moment I feared I was eating pieces of boot.'

'Mrs Mobley does her best. And please do not say anything to her! You'll hurt her feelings.'

'I wouldn't dream of it.' He fixed his penetrating stare on her. 'Where is she, by the way, as well as your other faithful retainer?'

'Still sleeping, I imagine.' At his look, she added defensively, 'It is not yet dawn.'

'Leaving the mistress of the house to contend with escaped goats and leaking roofs. And prisoners.'

'They both work very hard.' She gave him a cold

look. 'If you want something to eat, I suggest you sit down and keep your unwelcome observations to yourself.'

His brow shot up, but none the less he sauntered into the room and sat down in one of the wooden chairs at the heavy old table. He swayed a little and she frowned. 'What are you doing out of bed? You still look far from well.'

'I am well enough,' he said curtly.

'I doubt that.' Arguing was undoubtedly fruitless. 'What do you want to eat? There is bread and cheese and ham.'

'Bread and cheese will do. I am not certain I trust the ham.'

She moved to the pantry, aware his eyes were on her as she pulled out the bread and found a carving knife. She prepared the food, put it on a plate and set it in front of him. 'Would you like something to drink?'

His cool gaze settled on her face and then drifted down to the high neckline of her gown. 'You have surprising talents.'

Colour rose to her cheeks. 'Hardly. And unless you wish your meal taken away from you, I suggest you make no further remarks in that vein. And I pray you will not say a thing about the fact I am not suitably dressed!'

Amusement leapt to his eyes. 'And risk having my food snatched away? I assure you I would not be so ungentlemanly.'

She backed away, unnerved by the unexpected laughter in his face. 'Anything else, my lord?'

'No. Come and sit with me.'

'I...'

'I have something to say to you.'

Her heart began to pound again. She swallowed and forced herself to look at him. There was no reason to think he was going to make her another improper offer. 'What is it?'

'I apologise for making you cry last night,' he said abruptly.

Her mouth fell open and then she flushed. 'You really did not.'

'Then why did you dash from the room like that?'

'I…I was merely rather tired.'

'And had a sudden urge for your bed, I take it?'

'Well, no.' She felt rather foolish under his penetrating gaze. Of all the men to abduct, why did it have to be someone who seemed to see through her? 'Would you like something to drink? I can make coffee or there is ale.' She jumped up.

Nicholas caught her hand and a tremor ran through her at his touch. 'There is no need to run away. I am not planning to eat you. So, do you accept my apology for upsetting you?'

He was too close. She looked into his eyes which no longer seemed so cool and impersonal and, for a moment, no one seemed to exist except him. His own gaze darkened and he dropped her hand. She stepped back. 'Yes, of course.' Except she hardly knew what he was talking about.

She brought him the ale and forced herself to sit down. She had no idea what to say. Sitting with him in the dark kitchen with the rain pattering on the roof created an intimacy she found unnerving. She stole a glance at him. A lock of hair hung over his forehead, making him look rather boyish. He seemed to have lost some of his defensiveness and for a moment she suddenly caught a glimpse of a younger, more vulnerable man. A man she could quite like.

Disconcerted by her thought, she quickly turned away. She could not possibly allow herself to like him. She might be tempted to forget they were at daggers' drawn.

'What do you do here?'

She started. 'I beg your pardon?'

He was looking at her. 'On this farm. Do you actually farm?'

'No. I have leased out most of the acres to Geor…Lord George. I keep some in pasture for the horses and some is still rather wild although Geo…that is, someone has suggested that I should farm that as well, as it is very good land.' After last night she did not want to bring George's name too prominently into the conversation.

'But you obviously do not wish to.'

'No, I like it the way it is. Part of an old ruined cottage sits there which looks rather romantic, and there are berries and a family of foxes. And a lovely view of the countryside.' If she leased it, she would never feel quite as comfortable about going there when she wanted to think.

'Why are you here? I would imagine such an isolated farm would be rather lonely for you.'

She looked away. 'Foxwood was where my husband wished to live. He much preferred it over his family estate in Hampshire. He used to come here when he was a boy to visit his uncle; when his uncle died, he left the farm to Thomas. And when Thomas died, he left the farm to me.'

'I see. What about your family?'

She looked back at him, surprised. 'My father died

when I was six and my mother when I was thirteen. I
have no brothers or sisters. Eduardo and Barbara—that
is, Mrs Mobley—are my family.'

He frowned. 'There are your husband's relations
and your stepfather and your cousin. Do they not care
about your welfare?'

She was even more shocked he should know that
much about her. 'Thomas and I eloped. My stepfather
had wanted me to marry someone else; when I married
Thomas, he disowned me. And Thomas's family disowned him when he married me. So, no, to answer
your question, they do not care about my welfare.'

'There is no one you can apply to?'

'For what?' She gave a little laugh.

'After a night or two in this place it becomes quite
apparent it is in dire need of repair. I've no idea what
you are leasing your land for, but it is obviously not
enough to keep the roof over your head. Did your
husband not leave you enough to at least keep the farm
up?'

She stared at him, more than a little angry. 'I cannot
see that it is your business, my lord. It is hardly polite
for a guest to make such rude comments anyway.'

His brow rose a fraction. 'I have now been elevated
from the status of hostage to that of guest?'

She ignored that. 'You are free to leave, you know.'

He leaned back in his chair. 'As soon as I get the
ring.'

'It is not yours! Can you not understand that?'

'Not at all. I had it in my possession for the last
two years. I consider it mine. And so far you have
given me no solid evidence it belongs to you.'

She stared at him, frustrated. 'It belonged to
Thomas! I gave it to him!'

'How do I know it is the same ring? Perhaps there are two such rings. You admitted yourself you could not read the inscription.'

'It should be quite obvious the inscription was scratched away! Why must you be so stubborn?'

'You are equally stubborn, my dear. And for all I know the inscription had someone else's name.'

'Could you at least tell me where you got the ring?'

'I could, but not until you return the ring. Or until you kiss me. Of course, I still might not leave until I have my ring.' The slow smile that crossed his face nearly made her legs turn to water.

Something she had no desire to let him see. She gave him a cool smile in return. 'I can see you still plan to be unreasonable. Very well, my lord, you may stay and enjoy my hospitality in your leaky bedchamber with inedible meals as long as you wish!' She rose with as much dignity as possible in a nightrail and shawl.

He leaned back even further and regarded her with infuriating calm. 'Thank you. I fully intend to do so.'

'Good. Well, I have too much to do today to entertain you. You may do as you wish. If you need anything, Mrs Mobley will be delighted to assist you.'

'I somehow doubt that.'

She gave him one more scathing look and then stalked to the door. Without looking back at him, she left the room, quite aware that his eyes were fixed on her back.

After dressing, she went downstairs to her study. Barbara had left a tray on her desk with toast, butter and coffee. The rain had stopped and, to her surprise, the clouds actually showed signs of dispersing. She sat down at her desk and stared out at the back garden, which seemed to be nothing but a mess of tangled weeds and forlorn-looking plants. Betty was nibbling on a tall weed. At least one member of the household had time to garden.

She poured herself a cup of coffee and sighed. The condition of the garden was the least of her worries. Whatever was she to do about Thayne? Instead of gratefully accepting her offer and leaving, he seemed determined to stay unless she gave him the ring.

But how could she do that? She touched it gently. She had found it in a shop in Madrid. The ring had been curious and old, and she had been instantly drawn to it. The proprietor's unlikely tale of love and magic had only added to its mystery, and after a bit of haggling she had purchased it. Thomas had been as intrigued as she had, and until the day he died had worn it.

So how could she possibly give it to Thayne? And however was she to persuade him to tell her from where he got the ring? She could hardly hold him at gunpoint again. Besides, it was doubtful if even that would convince him. He'd probably just look at her in his sardonic way and tell her to shoot him, which, of course, she wouldn't do…as he undoubtedly knew quite well.

Or she could kiss him.

She quickly dismissed that thought. After this morning she was convinced more than ever he merely intended to tease her. It would quite serve him right if she did tell him she wanted to accept his offer. But if he called her bluff…her face heated at the mere thought.

She rose and stood in front of the window. And

what of his family? She could hardly justify letting them think he was gravely injured or even dead. Why had she not considered that when she abducted him? But then, she was not thinking about anything but her own desperate need to find Thomas's killer. Thayne had been nothing to her but a means to an end. Certainly not a man with a family that might worry about him.

But there was a way she could solve at least one of her problems of conscience.

A half-hour later she found Eduardo in the barn. He listened to her request with an impassive face. 'So the lad still refuses to leave?' He set the pitchfork against the wall and looked at her.

'He will not leave without the ring.'

'And I take it you will not return it to him.'

She scowled. 'No. Not unless he tells me what he knows. And even then I am not certain I will do so.'

His lips twitched. 'Then you may have him on your hands for a very long time.' He sobered. 'Very well, but are you certain he's wanting his family to know his whereabouts? I do not suppose you told him your intentions?'

'No.' That he would be displeased would be a vast understatement. 'But I cannot think of any reason why they should not know. I remember how worried and desperate I would feel the few times Thomas disappeared for days without word. I cannot inflict that sort of worry on someone else.'

'I doubt you can,' he said quietly. He hesitated. 'Are you certain you'll be all right with Thayne for a few hours?'

'Of course I shall be. Barbara will be here. At any

rate, I do not think he is well enough to do much harm.'

'I wouldn't be too sure of that,' Eduardo said. 'I'll take Isabella and return as quickly as possible. At least the rain has let up so the road should be passable.'

She watched him go and prayed she had done the right thing.

A few hours later she finally sat back on her haunches and surveyed the small garden plot near the kitchen door with more than a little satisfaction. Most of the weeds had been pulled and it now appeared quite ready for the vegetables she planted each year. Usually, she set young Joe Partridge from the village to clearing the plot, but her anger and frustration with Thayne had made a physical task most attractive. No matter she had managed to tear a glove and her old gown was hopelessly dirty from the muddy soil. At least she had accomplished something.

She rose and dashed a stray lock of hair from her forehead with a muddy hand, undoubtedly leaving a streak in its place. The cat, Wellington, who had been sleeping on an old wooden bench, rose and stretched, then jumped down. Betty ambled over to the pile of weeds and then paused, looking at something behind Julia's shoulder. Her tail twitched and she bleated.

Julia glanced around but saw nothing near the garden fence. Then she heard a sound as if someone was walking rapidly away. Puzzled, she walked across to the gate and peered over but saw no one. Had someone been there? Surely Barbara would have said something. Or could it have been Thayne? But why would he watch her in such a manner and then steal off?

A drop of rain hit her on the nose and she shivered.

She had best go in anyway. The clouds were beginning to look rather ominous. She quickly made her way to the kitchen door, Wellington and Betty trailing after her. She managed to keep Betty out, but Wellington slipped past her.

Barbara was at the long wooden table rolling out a pastry. She glanced up and her brow creased in a disapproving frown. 'Out in the dirt again, I see. You had best change before you sit on any of the furniture. Or before Lord Thayne sees you. He'll think we're unrespectable if he sees the mistress of the house does her own gardening.'

Julia strongly doubted there was much else she could do to lower herself in his eyes. 'Were you outside a moment ago?'

'Now why would I want to be outside in a rainstorm?' Barbara patted the pastry into a dish. 'I don't like the rain any more than the cat.'

'Where is Lord Thayne? Did he go out?'

'He's in the drawing room. I don't suppose he went out either. Not unless he likes to ramble around in his stockings. Eduardo hid his boots.'

'Did he?' She would have to find them straight away in the unlikely event Thayne decided to leave. She wouldn't want him to be deterred by a lack of boots.

Barbara was regarding her with a little frown. 'Was there someone outside?'

'I thought perhaps there was, but I must have been mistaken.' She glanced down at her gown and made a face. 'You are right, I must change.'

But first she would see if Thayne was in the drawing room. Had he decided to leave, boots or no boots, without saying a thing? But that hardly made sense.

She left the kitchen, Wellington at her heels, and walked quickly to the drawing room.

Nicholas had just dozed off when something heavy and wet landed on his chest. His eyes flew open and he struggled to sit up. The weight fell off him with an indignant meow and pain shot through his injured arm when he hit it against the cushion. He managed to sit back and, after the usual wave of dizziness passed, he saw with no little astonishment a yellow cat sitting on the floor in front of him. He looked up and was even more astounded to find Lady Carrington regarding him with a dismayed expression from the doorway. 'Do you always send animals in to wake up your house-guests?' He asked. He looked at her more closely. She wore a faded pink gown that was streaked with dirt. Her fine brown hair hung about her shoulders and there was a dab of mud on her cheek. She looked nothing like the impeccably dressed women he knew in London.

He found her absolutely charming.

The thought displeased him enough that he scowled. 'What the devil have you been doing? Ploughing the fields yourself?'

She sniffed and stared at him with an indignant look. 'I have been gardening. Some people do not have the luxury of lying around on other people's sofas!'

The corners of his mouth lifted. 'I beg your pardon.' He started to rise, but the sudden movement made his head spin. He sat back down.

She dashed forward. 'What is wrong? Are you feeling ill again?'

'It's nothing,' he grated out. 'I am still a trifle dizzy whenever I first sit up or stand.'

'And your arm. Does it still hurt?' She sat down next to him, her leg under the faded cotton gown brushing his. He flinched. 'Perhaps I should look at it.'

'There's nothing wrong.'

'You are very pale. Why ever were you down here anyway? You should have been resting.'

His mouth curved in a faintly sardonic smile. 'And you were planning to send me off today.'

'I will own I was wrong. You are certainly not well enough to go anywhere. And I think now you'd best go directly to bed and allow me to check your arm,' she said sternly.

Nicholas looked into her lovely brown eyes with their flecks of green and gold. Why the devil must she look at him with such concern? Of course, she was probably worried she would have his death on her hands if he died. His gaze fell to her cheek. 'You have mud on your face,' he said.

'Oh.' Slight colour rose to her face. 'I had best fetch Barbara and we can help you to bed.'

'Later.'

She sighed. 'Then I will look at your arm here.'

'There is no need to look at my arm.'

'I fear an infection may have set in.'

'And how would you know if you saw one?'

'I do have some familiarity with wounds, including those made by a gun.'

'Indeed.'

She looked both exasperated and concerned. 'I promise I won't hurt you if that is what worries you,' she said more gently.

'And if you don't, my lord, we'll be forced to take matters into our own hands,' Mrs Mobley said from the doorway.

'Good God.' The last thing he wanted was to have two females pouncing on him. Under other circumstances the idea might have its appeal, but Mrs Mobley had the look of a governess about to box his ears. For that matter, Julia hardly looked much more amenable.

He settled back on the sofa and the cat jumped up beside him. 'Very well, look at my arm.'

Clearly affronted, Julia sniffed. 'There is no need to be so rude.'

'You should have thought of that before you abducted me.'

'I can hardly help it now!' she snapped. 'I am going to remove your shirt.'

'No!'

'How can we look at your arm, then?' Julia sounded completely exasperated. 'You must take it off.'

'No need for maidenly modesty,' Mrs Mobley said. 'I dare say we've all seen a bare manly chest or two in our time.' Which was not a particularly noteworthy sight, if her disparaging tone was any indication.

If he refused to cooperate, he feared they'd forcibly rip the shirt off his back. He fixed Julia with his most cold gaze. 'Very well. Remove it. I would be grateful, however, if the rest of the audience, including the cat, would depart. Where the devil is Mackenzie, by the way?'

He was surprised to see Julia flush. 'I sent him to London on an errand.' She turned to Mrs Mobley. 'Perhaps you could fetch some clean bandages and water.'

'Behave yourself, my lord,' Mrs Mobley said.

'Good God,' Nicholas muttered. He was hardly in any condition to think of seduction.

But he wasn't so sure after Julia sat down on the sofa next to him and untied the sling from around his neck. Then her gentle fingers fumbled with the buttons of his loose linen shirt. She studiously avoided looking at him and kept her eyes on her task, presenting him with a delicious view of the back of her neck. She slowly eased the shirt from his shoulder and down his arm. The movement was so sensuous he almost forgot the pain. Except now his groin was beginning to tighten most uncomfortably. He shut his eyes for a moment, trying to regain control.

'What happened?' Julia's concerned voice forced his eyes open. She was looking at a long thin scar on his chest.

'I was wounded. In a duel.'

Her face registered shock. 'I am sorry.'

'Don't be. I deserved it.'

'No one deserves such a wound,' she said quietly.

'I must disagree. Perhaps you will get on with the task.'

'If I hurry too much I might hurt you.' She began to unwrap the bandage from his arm. He closed his eyes, willing himself to ignore her soft sweet scent and the fact the gentle touch of her hands was arousing him to a painful degree. Otherwise, he'd be tempted to pull her down on the sofa with him.

'It looks rather inflamed.'

He opened his eyes. 'What does?'

'Your wound.'

'My wound?' he asked stupidly.

'The wound in your arm. You are not feverish, are

you?' She looked worried and placed a cool hand on his forehead. 'Your head is a bit warm.'

'Is it?' His eyes strayed to her mouth. Perhaps he was feverish. 'You are very lovely.'

She jerked back as if she'd been slapped. 'I beg your pardon?'

'You are a lovely woman.'

She frowned. 'I hope you are not about to tease me again with another ridiculous offer. I really do not have time for such things.'

'Don't you?'

'As soon as Barbara returns we will clean your wound and bandage your arm.' Her voice was cool and composed and she shifted away from him on the sofa.

So she planned to ignore him, did she? He suddenly had the most devilish urge to tease her. He allowed his gaze to wander over her face. 'I suspect you are very kissable as well,' he said softly. 'I do not suppose you would consider kissing me? I've no doubt it would help my arm considerably.'

'Really!' Her eyes flashed with a mixture of annoyance and anger and he had no doubt she could cheerfully box his ears. And then a peculiar expression crossed her face. 'Very well.'

'Very well what?'

'Very well, I will kiss you.' She sat back, a little smile on her face as if she knew he would turn her down.

'Why?' He fully intended to call her bluff, but he wanted to see how far she was willing to go.

She opened her eyes wider in feigned innocence. 'To help your arm, and for the information you promised me, of course.'

He smiled, a little wickedly. 'Then come closer, my lovely lady. You cannot kiss me properly from that distance.'

A trace of panic fled across her face and he fully expected her to leap up and run. Instead, she scooted next to him. And then she leaned over and brushed her lips over his. Desire, hot and swift, shot through him at her sweet cool taste, but before he could react she had pulled away.

His only consolation was that she was breathing as hard as he was. 'I believe you have something to tell me, my lord.' Her eyes did not meet his.

He scowled, angry with her for taking up his challenge, but even more angry with himself for wanting her. 'That was hardly the sort of kiss I had in mind.'

This time she did look at him. Her eyes were icy. 'Are you trying to back out of your bargain, my lord? I believe you have told me on at least two separate occasions that if I complied with your terms you would tell me how you came to have my husband's ring. You did not specify how I was to kiss you.'

He stared at her and then laughed shortly. She had managed to best him at every turn. 'You are right, I did not. So, my dear Lady Carrington, I will tell you what you wish to know, which I fear is not very much.'

'Well, well. This is most certainly an interesting scene,' a voice said from the doorway.

Julia gasped. 'Oh, no,' she said faintly. She rose, her face turning pale.

He looked over and nearly groaned. Lord George Kingsley stood in the doorway, surveying the room with a sardonic air. His gaze wandered over to Nicholas. 'It appears you've not been murdered after all, Thayne,' he remarked.

'Obviously not,' Nicholas drawled.

'So, that leaves us with the second theory, although who would have guessed the reclusive Lady Carrington would capture the interest of the elusive Lord Thayne?'

Nicholas forced himself to stand. 'I fear your second theory is in error as well.'

'Indeed.' He ran his eye down Nicholas's bare chest in a suggestive fashion.

'George,' Julia said. 'You are mistaken. Lord Thayne was wounded. By…by a highwayman. He made his way here and we took him in. I was just looking at his wound. I fear it is slightly inflamed.'

'I see.' He swung his sardonic gaze to Julia. 'How fortunate he was wounded so near to Foxwood. And that you were here to bind his wounds in such a tender manner.' He managed to sound as if he didn't believe a word she had said.

Nicholas quelled the desire to mow him down. 'I trust you have a purpose in coming here other than insulting Lady Carrington.'

'Was I insulting her? I had merely intended to make a statement of fact.'

'Then keep your facts to yourself.'

Kingsley turned to Julia, who stood rooted to the spot. 'My dear, it appears you have a new protector.'

She unfroze and glared at him. 'He is not my protector!'

'I did not mean it in the usual sense, more of the chivalrous knightly sense in which he will stand up for your honour. Much as the good Mrs Mobley does, whom I see has just entered the room.'

Mrs Mobley eyed Kingsley coldly. 'Good day, Lord George. Here to cause a bit of mischief, I see.' She carried a basin of water and some clean linens.

'Not at all. I was on my way to Maldon and wished to bid Julia adieu. I will own, I was a trifle surprised to find Lord Thayne secluded at Foxwood. I am certain his family will be delighted to know he is not dead. When you deign to tell them, that is.'

'I trust you do not plan to take that task upon yourself,' Nicholas said coolly.

'I wouldn't think of it. My lips are sealed. I am certain you have reasons for your secrecy.' His gaze wandered back to Julia who still looked as if she wanted to vanish. 'I have the sense I am somewhat *de trop*. I will take my leave, but you know, my dear, if you need anything you have only to send for me.'

Julia's smile was strained. 'Thank you, George.'

He moved towards the door and then paused and looked back at Nicholas. 'I would not wait too long, however, before announcing your whereabouts. Your grandfather has asked my father for help in locating you. I do not know if you are aware, Thayne, but the former Lord Carrington was my father's godson. So, Julia, you see, is practically one of our family.'

Nicholas waited until Kingsley had left before swinging around to stare at Julia. 'Why did you not tell me Lord Stanton was your godfather?' he demanded.

'I had no idea it mattered. Besides, he was Thomas's godfather, not mine.'

'Indeed.' He stared at her. 'Were you aware that my grandfather and Stanton were old friends?'

A light flush stained her cheeks. 'George did mention something when he called yesterday. I do not see why it is a concern.'

'It is.' He bit back a curse. 'There's not a chance in hell we'll be able to keep the fact I've been under your roof for three days from my grandfather. Not that there was much hope of keeping this from leaking out now that Kingsley has been here.'

'You should have thought of that before you decided to come downstairs.'

'How the devil was I to know that Kingsley runs tame here?'

Her colour mounted. 'He does not run tame here!'

'No?'

'No.' She looked at him, clearly dismayed. 'Was it really so important to keep the fact you are here from your grandfather?'

'Yes. He has the most uncanny ability to ferret out the truth whether one wants him to or not. I only hope he doesn't discover precisely how I came to be here.'

She paled so much that for a moment he thought she might faint. He bit back another curse, this time at himself. He had no business taking out his frustration on her. 'I beg your pardon,' he said stiffly. 'I did not mean to ride roughshod over you.'

'You undoubtedly have every right to do so,' she said in a small voice. 'If you will pardon me, my lord, I believe I will allow Barbara to tend to your arm.' She walked quickly from the room without looking at him.

This time he did swear. When he turned, he found both Mrs Mobley and the cat staring at him. He raised his brow. 'Well?'

'You'd best sit down, my lord,' Mrs Mobley said mildly.

He did. Mrs Mobley sat down next to him and began to gently clean his arm. He winced and then frowned. 'I assure you my intention was not to overset her.'

Mrs Mobley looked up. 'Perhaps, my lord, you should decide exactly what your intentions are.'

Julia rose from her chair by the fire. As much as she longed to stay in the cosy quietness of her drawing room, she could not put off her mission any longer. The clock showed the hour to be nearly a quarter past eight; if she waited much longer Thayne might be asleep.

She had decided she must give him the ring. And then he would have no reason to stay at Foxwood any longer.

Her hand went to the chain at her neck. The ring felt familiar and strange at once. She had worn it against her skin for the past day, but it had not made Thomas's presence more real. Perhaps because it had been on another man's hand. Somehow the ring had become entwined in her mind with Thayne.

She could not keep him here any longer. Not after this afternoon. Every time she thought of the kiss, she wanted to sink. How could she have done such a thing? It was just that he had been so arrogantly certain she would back down and the thought of actually disconcerting him had been too tempting. And by the time she realised he intended to call her bluff, a mad impulse had propelled her to neatly block him into a corner. She had not, however, counted on finding the brief taste of his lips beneath hers so intriguing. Or having the most insane desire to prolong the kiss a few moments longer.

Thank goodness, she had not. If George had seen them in an embrace… Her face flamed at the mere thought. It was bad enough that he had discovered Thayne on her sofa with his shirt off and her sitting next to him. She could imagine how the scene must have appeared to George, who delighted in viewing any situation in the worse possible light. From the cynical look in his eye, she doubted very much that he believed her halting explanation about the highwayman.

At least Barbara had appeared with the water and clean bandages which surely must lend some credence to her tale. Despite his assurances his lips were sealed, she very much feared he would let something slip for George was a notorious gossip.

But even without the complications George's visit had brought about, she could not keep Thayne under her roof any longer. He was far too attractive and far too dangerous and she did not need a man like that in her life.

She knocked lightly on his door. For a moment she hoped he might be asleep, but his cool voice bade her to enter. She opened the door and stepped inside. He was in bed, his head propped up against several pillows. 'I was not certain whether you would pay your usual evening call tonight,' he said when he saw her.

She prayed he would not bring up this afternoon's débâcle. 'I need to speak with you.' Her stomach was beginning to clench again. She forced herself to walk across the room.

He stilled. 'What is it?'

'I…' She took a deep breath. 'I…I have decided to return the ring to you.'

He studied her face for a long moment. 'Why?'

'I can see you will not go until you have it. And I cannot keep you here. Not after this afternoon.'

'So, Kingsley's appearance distressed you enough that you are willing to give me the ring? Or,' he said softly, 'was it the other?'

'It doesn't really matter.' She looked away. 'It was very wrong of me to abduct you but I was desperate, you see. I was certain you would do what I wished, but you would not. And to make matters worse you were wounded. I fear I have done you a great wrong, I cannot blame you for being very angry.'

Her hand tightened around the ring she held in her hand. 'And it is only a ring. I had thought that having it again would bring something of Thomas back, but it has not. It has been away from him for so long that it no longer carries his…his impression. Perhaps it carries yours now.' She looked at him, having no idea if he understood or not. He was watching her very quietly, but she saw no censure in his face. 'But I want more than I want anything, even more than I want the ring, to find out who killed him.'

'If you recall, I still have my part of the bargain to fulfil. I fear, however, it is not much to go on.' He looked away towards the window. The curtains had not yet been drawn and raindrops drizzled down the panes. He watched for a moment before half-turning towards her. 'It was given to me by a lady shortly before she died.'

She stood very still, her eyes on his face. 'I…I did not know. I am so sorry.'

'Are you? I doubt if you would be if you knew the whole of it.' His mouth twisted in a bitter smile. 'She was married, but not to me.'

His words shocked her, but the stark pain in his eyes put a stop to any fleeting judgment.

He glanced back towards the window. 'She found the ring in a jeweller's shop in Sheffield. That is all I know.'

The disappointment she felt warred with compassion for him. The words he did not say spoke more than if he had told her all. He had loved this lady deeply and she had died. No wonder he was reluctant to give up the ring. It was, perhaps, all he had of her.

And they had not married. 'I am sorry,' she said again. At least she and Thomas had lived together and, although briefly, they had been united in every way. She lifted the chain over her head. She undid the clasp and removed the ring. 'Here, my lord.' She held it out in her palm.

He stared at it and then at her. 'I've not given you much to go on. And you do not need to give me the ring.'

She shrugged. 'But it is more than I had. I will proceed to Sheffield and see if there is anything I can discover. I have a sketch of the ring. Perhaps someone in the jeweller's will recognise it.' She tried to sound more optimistic than she felt. Despite the ring's uniqueness, the likeliness of anyone remembering the ring seemed impossible after such a lapse of time.

He still looked at her face, making no move to touch the ring. She took his hand and laid it in his palm and then closed his fingers over it. 'It belongs to you, I believe.' She removed her hand.

As if waking from a trance, he jerked back. For the first time since she had met him, his expression held uncertainty as if he did not know what to say.

'I had thought Eduardo would be back today. But

he seems to be delayed. He should be back tomorrow, however, and he could take you to London, if you wish. I dare say your family will be pleased to see you.' She was babbling, but the peculiar look on his face was making her nervous. For once he was neither attempting to intimidate or tease her.

'Just like that?' he asked.

'I beg your pardon?'

'You are returning me without further ado?'

She was puzzled. 'What do you mean? I would expect you would be anxious to leave. And you have what you wanted.'

'Do I?' His gaze flickered over her face. 'And do you have what you wanted?'

'Yes.' She hesitated. 'No. I want to find out who killed my husband.'

'I wish you all luck, then,' he said softly.

'I will need it.' She hesitated another moment. 'I will leave you then, my lord. And you can look forward to soon spending your nights in your own bed with no danger of the roof leaking.'

'Yes.' A bleak look crossed his features and then he closed his eyes. She watched his face for a moment, then left the room, quietly shutting the door behind her.

A few hours later, Julia started awake, her heart pounding. Had she heard footsteps or was it merely a product of an overactive imagination? Or had Eduardo finally returned? She sat up, hands around her knees. The rain still beat against the window so perhaps it was only the storm.

The floorboards creaked again. She had no doubt this time they were footsteps. She threw back the quilt and climbed out of bed. She made her way to the door and opened it. The hall was dark. 'Eduardo?' she called softly. This time she heard a familiar clop-clop. She nearly sank with relief. It was only Betty, who appeared to have made her way to one of the bed-chambers at the end of the hall.

No doubt she should put Betty out but the rain was pounding hard on the roof and she was cold and tired and wanted her bed. She could only hope Betty would stay out of Thayne's room. She started to turn when she heard a sound behind her. Julia had no time to react before the dark shape was upon her. A strong, rough hand was clasped over her mouth and an arm yanked her against a hard, smelly body. She struggled and managed to kick her assailant's leg until he subdued her. 'Don't scream or I will hurt you. I want the ring.' His voice was low and menacing and then he took his hand from her mouth.

'I…I don't have it.'

'Get it.'

'I…' She could hardly tell him Thayne had the ring.

There was the clatter of hooves and a loud indignant bleat. 'What the…?' Her assailant's hands fell away and then he shoved her so hard she fell. Julia's head hit the wall and pain shot through her skull as she tumbled to the ground.

The last thing she heard before darkness descended was another angry bleat.

Chapter Six

Something cold and wet shoved her in the face. She moved her head a little, but the pain that shot through her caused her to moan. She heard a familiar bleat. 'Betty?' she whispered.

'Move.' The rough male voice was certainly not Betty. 'Julia, can you hear me?'

Why was Thayne hovering over her? Surely he had not bleated. And why was she lying on the floor? She forced her eyes open. His face swam into focus and she vaguely realised he was kneeling beside her. His face was joined by a hairy one. 'So, Betty is here,' she murmured.

'Yes.' He scowled and shoved the goat away. 'Damn it. Are you all right?'

'There is no need to swear at me.'

'I was not swearing at you. Can you sit up at all?' His face was grim.

'Yes, I…I think so.' She struggled to sit despite the pain in her head. His arm came around her shoulders and she was forced to lean into his chest for a moment. She could hear his heart, strong and steady, beneath the fine linen of his shirt.

'Good girl,' he said softly. He held her for a moment, his warmth enveloping her. 'I am going to carry you to your bed.' Before she could protest, he had scooped her up in his arms.

'You cannot do this. Your arm.'

'My arm will be fine.' He carried her the few steps to her bed and laid her gently down. She winced as her head contacted the pillow.

He drew the cover up over her and sat down next to her on the bed.

'Julia,' he said gently.

She opened her eyes. He was close enough so she could see the shadow of his beard around his firm mouth. His eyes were dark with concern. And he was calling her by her Christian name. Perhaps she was having some sort of odd dream.

'Damn it, Julia, do you know what I am saying?'

She most certainly was not dreaming. 'You are swearing again, my lord.'

He made an exasperated sound. 'Yes, and I am likely to swear more if you do not give me an answer. Why the devil were you out in the hallway? I hear your goat making enough noise to wake the dead and when I go out to investigate, I find you nearly unconscious. You have a bump on your head. Did you fall?'

'No.' She forced her mind to focus. 'I heard footsteps—I thought that perhaps Eduardo had returned and I left my room. Then I heard Betty.' She faltered, suddenly remembering what had happened next.

'What else?'

'Someone…someone attacked me,' she whispered.

He stared at her. 'Are you certain?'

'Yes. He…he grabbed me from behind. He wanted the ring. And then Betty came. Perhaps she scared him for he shoved me away and I fell. I must have hit my head then.' She had no idea how to read the expression on his face. 'I know it sounds most improbable.'

'It does not,' he said grimly. 'Do you have any idea who did this?'

'No.' She shuddered. 'There was nothing familiar about him.'

He rose. 'Where is Mrs Mobley's room? I will send her to you.'

She sat up, not liking the harshness in his voice. 'Her room is at the very end of the hall. But where are you going?'

'Outside.'

'No! Please, I cannot have you hurt again!'

He glanced down at her, his expression odd. 'I won't be, my dear.'

He strode to the door. 'But you are not even dressed properly!' she exclaimed. He couldn't possibly go out in just a thin shirt and breeches! Her gaze went to his feet. 'And you've no shoes!'

He paused at the door and the corners of his mouth lifted in a brief smile. 'Don't worry. I found my boots.'

Nicholas straightened up from his slouched position against the wall when the door to Julia's bedchamber opened. Doctor Bothwell, carrying his bag, stepped out followed by Mrs Mobley. 'How is Lady Carrington?' Nicholas asked.

Doctor Bothwell regarded him with a slight frown. He was a tall, serious man and although his manner had been all that was polite, Nicholas sensed he did not approve of his presence at Foxwood and found the tale of his being shot by highwaymen and making his way to Foxwood somewhat suspicious. But if so, he had kept his thoughts to himself. 'She has a bad bump on her head, but since there are no other symptoms it does not appear to be a serious injury. However, she must remain quiet and in bed for a day or two. Nor must she be unduly upset.' He fixed Nicholas with a stern eye.

'She will not be,' Nicholas said coolly.

'I trust not. It could only be detrimental to her health.' Bothwell paused for a moment. 'She asked me to look at your arm before I left.'

'My arm?'

'She was concerned since you carried her to her bedchamber last night. So, if you will allow me to look at your arm, my lord.'

'My arm is fine.'

Doctor Bothwell allowed a slight smile to touch his lips. 'It will upset her if you do not.'

'The devil. Very well, do it, if you must.'

He submitted to the exam with ill grace. Despite last night, the slight inflammation from yesterday had gone and Dr Bothwell pronounced him able to travel when he wished. The dizziness he still felt upon rising was not uncommon after an injury and as long as he was not losing consciousness should eventually pass. Mrs Mobley entered his bedchamber just as the physician finished the exam. She waited until Dr Bothwell had left before speaking. 'So you will be leaving us soon, I expect.'

Nicholas awkwardly fastened the last button of his shirt before turning. 'No.'

A smile actually touched her lips. 'I thought not, my lord. You may see her now. She is awake.'

Julia was sitting in bed, eyes shut, her head propped

against several pillows. Wellington lay at her feet. For a moment he thought she was sleeping, but when he stepped into the room she opened her eyes. He walked to the bed and stood, looking down at her. 'How are you feeling?' he asked. Her face was pale and her hair fell around her shoulders in a light brown cloud. She looked fragile and very young, and he wanted to run the man through who had hurt her last night.

'Doctor Bothwell assures me I will live. And you? How is your arm?'

'My arm is fine. And, like you, I will live as well.'

'I am glad.' She fixed him with her clear gaze. 'Thank you for coming to my rescue and for going out into the rain.'

He shrugged. 'You do not need to thank me. I fear, however, I was too late to catch your assailant.'

'It was brave of you to try.'

'Hardly,' he said curtly, embarrassed by her gratitude.

'But it was.' She smiled a little and then she glanced away for a moment. 'Eduardo should return today. I expect you will wish to return to London as quickly as possible.'

'No.'

Surprise crossed her face. 'No?'

'No. I am not leaving this place until I am certain you are safe, and there are no repeats of last night.'

She looked stunned. 'Surely the man will not return. And as soon as Eduardo is here, I will be fine.'

'Have you thought this through? Someone knows I am here and suspects you retrieved the ring from me. This person was desperate enough to enter your house in the middle of the night and attack you. And have you forgotten the highwaymen?'

Her eyes searched his face. 'Do you think that is connected?'

'I believe so, yes.'

'Oh, dear.' If possible, she had grown paler. 'I had rather thought he was very interested in the ring but I had hoped it was nothing to signify.'

Hell. He was doing exactly what Bothwell had warned him against, oversetting her. He frowned. 'Do not trouble yourself. I won't let anything happen to you,' he said roughly.

She looked down at the bedcover. 'You are very kind, but you are not responsible for me. This is none of your concern.'

'You are wrong. From the moment you forced me into your carriage it has very much become my concern.'

She looked up. Anger flashed in her eyes. 'Well, I am releasing you from any obligation. At any rate, you now have the ring, so I doubt if I will be bothered again.'

'You don't know that, my dear.'

She glared at him. 'I am not "your dear".'

'No?' Why the devil was he goading her? And in her condition. She looked as if she wanted to throw something at him. He'd best leave before she did and he had the combined wrath of Bothwell and Mrs Mobley falling on his head.

He started when Mrs Mobley stepped into the room. Fully expecting her to take him to task over upsetting Julia, he was surprised to see she looked almost flustered. 'You'd best go downstairs, my lord. Eduardo has returned with company.' She paused. 'Your grandfather.'

'Oh, no,' Julia said softly.

He felt as if someone had punched him in the gut. 'My grandfather is here?'

Mrs Mobley nodded. 'That is what he tells me. So, if he's Lord Monteville, then he is.'

Nicholas paused on the threshold of the drawing room. The faint hope he'd entertained that the house-keeper was mistaken was dashed by the tall, lean and very familiar figure who stood near the window looking out over the drive. Betty was visible, nibbling on some tall grass.

Monteville turned when Nicholas entered. In his seventh decade, he was still a formidable figure with a cool commanding presence. Not quite knowing what to expect, Nicholas paused. 'Sir, I hardly thought to see you here.'

The earl's brow rose a fraction. 'No? You did not think I would come as soon as I discovered you had been wounded? I hope you do not think I am completely unfeeling when it comes to your welfare.' He did not give Nicholas a chance to reply. 'How is Lady Carrington? Mrs Mobley said she was hurt last night.'

'She is better,' Nicholas said.

'What happened?'

'She was attacked by an intruder.'

The brow rose higher. 'I think perhaps you had best tell me what is going on.' Monteville moved away from the window towards Nicholas. His expression gentled for a moment. 'Sit down, you do not look completely recovered.'

Nicholas took the sofa where he had so boorishly fallen asleep yesterday. As if on cue, the yellow cat appeared from behind the sofa and leapt up next to him. He tried to shove it away, but the animal merely looked at him and settled down, paws tucked under its chest and began to purr. Since he had no intention of fighting with the cat, Nicholas gave up. 'I am well enough. It is Lady Carrington who concerns me.'

'Of course. So, do you know why she was assaulted?'

'The man wanted a ring.'

'A ring?' Monteville looked at him, his expression curiously alert. 'What sort of ring?'

'A very old ring. With a ruby in the centre.'

'Perhaps the same ring you are wearing.'

Nicholas looked at him with more than a little surprise. 'Yes.'

'You do not seem to be particularly forthcoming on the matter. So I will guess that the ring you wear is the same ring that once belonged to her husband.'

This time Nicholas nearly reeled. 'How the devil did you know that? Sir,' he added belatedly.

'Phillip was with me yesterday when Mr Mackenzie arrived with Lady Carrington's note.'

'She sent a note? What the devil possessed her to do such a thing?' He'd have thought revealing his whereabouts would be the last thing she would want to do. She apparently knew nothing of his grandfather, because if she had, she would have known a note would bring him here straight away.

'I would imagine from the kindly impulse to relieve your family's mind. She wished to inform your family that you were not dead, but recuperating at Foxwood from a wound inflicted by a highwayman. I will own I am decidedly curious as to why you quit London, leaving your carriage and servants without word. You are usually not so forgetful.'

'I am not at liberty to satisfy your curiosity, sir.' He

was hardly about to tell his grandfather he'd been abducted.

'I see.' Monteville leaned back, regarding him with the piercing stare that had compelled more than one man to confess. Nicholas, although not exactly immune, had lived with it long enough to hold out against it, at least for a while. 'Curiously enough, Mr Mackenzie and Phillip knew each other quite well.'

'How?' The Marquis of Stanton was highly placed in the Home Office. He seemed an unlikely person for Mackenzie to know. He was also one of his grandfather's oldest and most respected friends.

'Lord Carrington and Mackenzie had both worked for Stanton. They were English agents.'

Nicholas started. 'Mackenzie was a spy, too?'

'Yes. When Lord and Lady Carrington returned to England, Mackenzie came with them. As well as Mrs Mobley.'

'Don't tell me she was a spy as well.'

A slight smile touched Monteville's lips. 'On occasion. Thérèse Blanchot was involved also. Carrington posed as a gambler. Information was often passed in the gaming saloon Madame Blanchot kept in Brussels.'

Which would explain why Thérèse had informed Julia of the ring. She had apparently known Carrington well. How the devil had he managed to land in such a hotbed of intrigue? 'Good God,' he muttered. 'But how did you know about the ring?'

'Carrington was killed in what appeared to be a robbery. Among the items stolen from his person was a ring.'

The tale was very familiar. 'Go on.'

'The ring, perhaps, the thief wanted. And the one you wear on your finger.'

'Yes.'

'Perhaps the ring explains how you and Lady Carrington came to cross paths?'

He had no doubt his grandfather would have the story from him one way or the other. Or manage to find out. 'She abducted me from Thérèse Blanchot's establishment at gunpoint,' he said coolly. 'She wanted the ring back.'

At least he had the rare satisfaction of watching his grandfather appear truly startled. 'Precisely why did she find it necessary to abduct you rather than merely rob you of the ring?'

'She wanted me to tell her where I obtained the ring.'

'I take it, then, you were a trifle reluctant to provide this information.'

'Yes, and a trifle foxed,' Nicholas said baldly.

'So where did the highwayman come in? Or did Lady Carrington shoot you?'

'Hardly. Although I think she might have liked to. We were robbed on the journey here.'

Monteville frowned. 'What did they take?'

'Not much. Although they were more than a little interested in the ring. I believe they were amateurs. They fled without much persuasion.'

'But not without shooting you.'

'No.' He had no intention of elaborating exactly how that came about.

Monteville regarded him for a moment. 'And in the end did you tell Lady Carrington where you obtained the ring?'

'Yesterday. After she returned the ring to me. She

had taken it from me and would not give it back unless I told her what she wanted to know.'

His grandfather merely looked at him. Nicholas scowled. 'I had no idea if it was even the same ring. The inscription had been scratched off.' Which made him sound the worst scoundrel who routinely doubted the word of ladies and failed to provide grieving widows with whatever help he could render. He could not tell his grandfather the ring had been given to him by Mary.

'So I assume you were planning to return to London once you had the ring.'

'I was. Lady Carrington has made it quite clear she can hardly wait to be rid of me.'

'And now?'

Nicholas frowned. 'That was before last night. I've no intention of leaving her here even under Mackenzie's protection.'

'You will not need to. Phillip will arrive tomorrow. Once we realised you had been under her roof we decided it would be best if she returns to London with Phillip. She will stay with Lady Simons.'

She would be safe at the house of Phillip's sister. Which meant he could be absolved of his responsibility towards Julia and could get back to his life. He thrust aside the disquieting feeling that the thought was not as appealing as it should be.

Chapter Seven

Julia looked up as Barbara entered her bedchamber. The housekeeper crossed the room and observed the barely touched supper tray across Julia's lap. 'You need to eat more than that.'

'I was really not hungry.' Although the chicken was actually tender tonight, her stomach had knotted up the moment she picked up her fork. 'Although it was very good,' she added.

'You'd best do better than this if you wish to keep up your strength.' Barbara picked up the tray. 'I suppose the cat will be grateful at any rate. By the way, Lord Monteville wishes to see you, if you are well enough.'

'Oh, dear.' Her stomach began to knot again.

'I doubt he plans to eat you. He has been most civil.'

'Then he probably has no idea I abducted his grandson.'

'I wouldn't be so sure of that.' She regarded Julia with a small smile. 'And he plans to stay for the night.'

'Oh, no,' she said faintly. 'Why would he wish to do that?' She doubted if Foxwood had two decent spare bedchambers whose ceilings did not leak. Why had he not taken Thayne back to London? Surely he couldn't want to spend the night in such a dilapidated house?

'Well, at least we won't be worrying about someone creeping about in the middle of the night.' Barbara headed towards the door with the tray. She paused and glanced back at Julia. 'Should I send them up?'

'Now?'

'Yes, now.'

'I…'

But Barbara had already quit the room. Julia straightened up against the pillows, her heart thudding. When she heard footsteps and the unmistakable timbre of masculine voices, it took all her willpower to keep from diving under the bedclothes.

The door opened and Thayne came into the room, followed by a tall, distinguished man with silver-flecked hair.

Thayne came to stand by her bed. She blinked. Not only had he shaved, he was wearing brown breeches and a pair of well-polished boots and over his shirt and cravat was a perfectly fitted blue coat.

'You are dressed,' she blurted out and then could have sunk through the floor at her idiotic and most improper remark.

His brow rose slightly. 'My grandfather brought a change of clothing for me.'

'Of course.' Her face heated. She felt uncomfortable under his scrutiny and his clean, civilised appearance made her feel even more at a disadvantage.

'How are you feeling?' he asked softly.

'Better.' She looked away, finding his intense expression unnerving.

Lord Monteville moved to stand beside his grandson. No one could doubt they were related. They had the same lean countenance, the same hawk-like nose, and the same cool intelligence in their eye. She felt more than a little intimidated.

'Perhaps you will introduce us?' Monteville said.

Thayne started and yanked his eyes away from Julia. 'Of course. Lady Carrington, may I present my grandfather, Lord Monteville. Lady Carrington.'

She found herself looking up into a pair of eyes that reminded her forcibly of Thayne's. 'I am pleased to meet you, Lord Monteville,' she said, feeling more than a little awkward. 'I must apologise for receiving you here instead of in the drawing room. I fear I am not allowed to go downstairs.'

'I would not have expected you to under the circumstances.' He smiled gently. 'I have looked forward to making your acquaintance. And to thanking you for looking after my grandson after he was wounded.'

She saw nothing in his expression to tell her he knew the true state of affairs. Feeling the worst hypocrite, she managed to say, 'You are very kind, but there is nothing to thank me for.'

'I must disagree with you on that point,' Monteville said firmly. 'I was sorry to hear of your assault. I fear neither you nor my grandson has fared very well in the past few days.'

'No. But my injury was a mere trifle compared to Lord Thayne's,' she said, trying to be fair. 'He was wounded when he—' She stopped, mortified at what she was about to say.

Monteville raised a brow. 'When he…?'

'Tried to…to…' She cast a helpless glance at Thayne.

A smile touched his mouth. 'There is no need to worry. He knows everything.'

Her eyes flew to Monteville's face. 'Everything?'

'Under the circumstances, I cannot blame you for abducting my grandson,' Monteville said. 'He told me the whole of it.'

'Oh, dear.' She briefly closed her eyes and then looked back at him. 'I am sorry.'

'My dear, there is no need to be.' For some odd reason, he looked almost amused. 'So pray continue, my grandson was wounded when? He has not yet told me exactly how it came about.'

'There is no need to say more,' Thayne said coolly.

She did not dare look at him.. 'The highwayman was about to shoot me. Lord Thayne shoved me aside and took the ball instead. I had a pistol, that I would not give to Lord Thayne, which was why the highwayman wished to shoot me. So, you see the fact he was wounded was entirely my fault.'

'Hardly,' Thayne snapped.

'So he was shot in order to save your life.' Monteville looked at his grandson. 'I must commend you,' he said softly.

To her surprise, a hint of colour appeared on Thayne's cheekbones. 'Any man would have done the same,' he said stiffly. The familiar scowl had returned to his face. 'Perhaps we could move on to the next matter of business.' He moved away from the bed and went to stand near the window. 'Lord Stanton will be arriving tomorrow.'

'Oh, heavens.' Her stomach jolted. 'Does Phillip know about this?'

'Not the entire story,' Monteville said. 'Only that Nicholas is here with you. Phillip was with me when

Mr Mackenzie delivered your message. He, of course, was concerned about your welfare. And my grandson's.'

'Oh, dear.' What an unfortunate coincidence. But why ever had she thought she could keep this from Phillip? She had no doubt George would say something sooner or later. 'Must Phillip know everything?'

'Most of it, I think,' Monteville said. 'In light of the assault on you, I do not think the matter can be dismissed. Phillip needs to be told.' He looked down at her. 'You must rest now. Try not to worry too much. We will see you are safe.'

She nodded, but it was hardly her safety that concerned her. It was all she could do, after they had quit the room, to not indulge in helpless tears. She lay back against the pillows and stared with unseeing eyes at the wall. She felt nearly as helpless as she had when Thomas had been killed. She had been told to rest and had gone to stay with Sophia while Phillip and George and the others had looked into his death. There had been nothing—no leads, no sign that his death had been anything other than a robbery.

But if it had been only a robbery, why would someone care whether the ring had shown up again or not? Was someone so worried the ring could be traced back to them? Or was it something more?

She was beginning to feel tired so she closed her eyes, her mind in a muddle. One thing she did know, however—she was not going to trust it all to someone else this time.

Stanton arrived mid-morning on the following day. Monteville had wasted no time in relating the events of the past few days. Stanton had listened impassively, although the revelation of Nicholas's abduction had startled him. He had asked to see the ring and Nicholas had removed it from his finger and handed it to him.

Stanton ran his finger over the ring. 'It appears to be the same ring.' He looked up at Nicholas. 'Julia—that is, Lady Carrington examined it herself?'

'Yes,' Nicholas said. 'In fact, she had it in her possession for a good day before she returned it to me.'

'I am surprised she did so,' Stanton remarked.

Nicholas had the grace to colour slightly. 'I forced her to.'

'I see.' Slight amusement crossed Stanton's face. 'And where did you get the ring?'

'It was given to me.' The words were not so difficult to say this time. 'But I know little else except it was purchased from a jeweller in Sheffield nearly two years ago.'

Stanton looked at him curiously. 'It is a very unique ring. Have I seen it on your hand before?'

'Perhaps. I have not worn it very often until recently.' Several weeks ago to be precise. On the second anniversary of Mary's death.

'A few days ago he was approached by a man who wished purchase the ring,' Monteville said.

Stanton looked sharply at Nicholas. 'Who?'

'A Mr Grayson, I believe.'

'Would you recognise him again if you saw him?'

'Most likely, yes.'

Stanton regarded him for a moment. 'It may have some bearing on the matter.' He moved to the mantelpiece. 'Thomas's murder was, as far as we could determine, a robbery. Ironically enough, he was killed after leaving Thérèse Blanchot's. He was involved in a matter of some importance with the Home Office, but no connection was ever established between that matter and the murder. However, there were several things that were puzzling if it were only a robbery. He carried several items of value but only the ring was taken.'

'So he was robbed for the ring?' Monteville asked.

'It appeared he was. It is very old and very valuable. I will own, I had not expected to see it again. I would have thought it would have been sold privately, if at all.'

'None the less, someone very much wants it,' Nicholas said. 'Enough to assault Lady Carrington in her own home and possibly enough to hold up a coach.' He frowned. 'Although it makes no sense for Carrington's killer to decide he wants the ring back now. Why would he have disposed of it in the first place if he did not want it to turn up again?'

Monteville spoke. 'It is possible he sold the ring and that person in turn sold it to the shop in Sheffield. Or the killer never expected the ring to be recognised, particularly by Lady Carrington herself. It is possible that there is something about the ring that might identify the murderer.'

'Possibly.' Stanton looked grave. 'Julia may very well be correct as well. Tracing the ring to Sheffield might provide a lead to his killer.' He glanced at Nicholas. 'I would have preferred she came directly to me, however, rather than taking the drastic and foolish step of abducting you.'

A brief smile touched Nicholas's mouth. 'It has been a most interesting experience. What is it you want from me? The ring, I assume. I own I would like it back.' As would Lady Carrington, he added silently. He didn't want to touch that yet.

Stanton read his mind. 'I've no doubt Julia does as well. No, if you would agree I would like you to keep the ring. There is a chance that whoever approached you might approach you again.'

'I see. A bait of sorts.'

'Yes, but there is a certain element of danger involved if this does indeed have anything to do with Thomas's murder. Once a man has killed he will have no qualms about killing again.'

Nicholas shrugged. 'I can take care of myself well enough.' He thought of Julia lying unconscious on the floor and then about her husband, dead by another's hand. If someone had killed Mary he would have gone to any lengths to discover her murderer. Including abduction. He made up his mind. 'Very well, I will do it.'

'Thank you.' Stanton looked at him, some strong emotion in his face. 'Thomas was my godson, you know.' He looked away for a moment before returning his attention to Nicholas. 'I would like Julia to stay out of this as much as possible. Which is the other reason I am grateful you are willing to help us. I fear she may try to take matters into her own hands. If she knows you are involved as well, she will be more inclined to let us handle the affair.'

Nicholas nearly choked. 'Indeed.' She would most likely kick up a dust when she found out. Or abduct him again.

Julia looked up as Phillip entered the tiny sitting room off her bedchamber. She had managed to convince Barbara she was well enough to be out of bed and spent the morning in a chair near the window. She rose and smiled, despite the quaking in her legs. 'Phillip, it is good to see you.'

'And you.' He moved across the room. In his early fifties, he was still a handsome man with receding dark hair and a pair of calm grey eyes. He took her hand. 'Although I wish you had come to me straight away instead of taking matters into your own hands.'

Relief flooded her. At least he was not planning to ring a peal over her. She sat back down. 'I had no idea everything would become so complicated. But do you not see what it means, Phillip? Thomas's death had to be more than a mere robbery. Otherwise why would someone want the ring so much?'

'Which is why I am taking you back to London with me.'

She stared at him, dismayed. 'Taking me to London? But why?'

'For several reasons. The foremost is to protect you from danger.'

'But surely I am in no danger. The intruder wanted the ring and I no longer have it.'

'We do not know if that is all he wanted. We do not want to take the risk that you might be harmed. You will stay with Sophia.'

'I should love to see Sophia, but I do not wish to go to London. At least not now.'

'You have no choice, I fear. I would never forgive myself if something should happen to you. Neither would Sophia. You are forgetting one more thing as well. Nicholas has been under your roof for several days. We will hope nothing of it leaks out but if it should, I would prefer to deal with the matter with you in London.'

'But I had Barbara here with me. And Eduardo,' she said, appalled.

'My dear, in the eyes of society they are servants. That is not the same thing as having a relative or a companion.'

'But there is nothing to gossip about. And no one knew he was here.' No, that was not true. 'Except for Dr Bothwell, who is very discreet, and…and George.' Who was not.

Phillip started. 'George knew Nicholas was here?' His brow snapped together. 'Then you most certainly have no choice. We will only hope he'll have the sense to hold his tongue.' He looked at her face and frowned. 'You still do not look well. I fear this whole affair has been too much for you. You must let Sophia look after you and try to think about something else. Perhaps balls and routs, for a change, instead of Foxwood.'

'I don't wish to be distracted. I want to find out who killed Thomas.'

'As I do. And like you, I hope to God that when we discover who is behind these attacks, we will find his killer. But killers are ruthless men, my dear. And dangerous, which is why I do not want you involved.'

'But, Phillip, surely there is something I can do.'

'Just take care of yourself.' He touched her cheek. 'And do not worry too much.' He started to move away and then paused. 'By the way, Nicholas has consented to help us.'

She started. 'Nicholas?'

'Yes.' He smiled a little at her expression. 'He was approached by a man who wished to buy the ring. He will put it about he is now interested in selling it. With any luck, he will be approached again.'

'He cannot do that! I do not want him involved in this at all!'

Phillip looked at her steadily. 'Once you made the decision to abduct him, you embroiled him in this affair. You have no choice in the matter. Nor does he.'

Which was precisely what made his involvement so intolerable. He had no choice. Once again, she had not only managed to muddle her own affairs but his as well.

Nicholas hesitated for a moment before tapping lightly on the door of Julia's sitting room. He waited for her soft reply before stepping into the room.

She sat in a wing chair near the window. The yellow cat sat on the quilt covering her lap. She wore another one of her high-necked gowns and a shawl was draped around her shoulders. Her eyes widened when she saw him. 'Lord Thayne? Oh! I…I did not expect you.'

A smile touched his lips. 'Disappointed?'

'Oh, no. It was just I expected Barbara as she said she would—' She broke off and then frowned. 'I am glad you are here. There is something I must discuss with you.' From her governess-like tone, he gathered she planned to argue with him. Phillip had certainly wasted no time.

She removed the cat from her lap and set him on the floor. He gave her a reproachful stare and then sat down and began to wash. Julia stood.

'There is no need for you to get up,' Nicholas said.

'I would prefer to.'

He moved across the room and came to stand in front of her. Her face was still rather pale. 'Sit down. I've no doubt you can upbraid me just as well from the chair.' His lips twitched. 'Otherwise I will be forced to help you.'

She gasped and fixed him with an indignant stare. 'Well, really!'

His brow shot up. 'Only fitting after all the times you threatened me.'

'I was merely trying to help you.'

'And I am merely trying to help you. Your face is nearly white.' He took a step towards her.

She plopped back down. 'There is another chair, my lord,' she informed him pointedly.

'Indeed.' Instead of taking it, he leaned against the window pane. 'What do you wish to say to me? Or should I guess? Phillip has informed you that I am to help him with his investigation and you want to tell me that you would rather I declined. Shall I tell you my response to that? I have every intention of helping Phillip.'

She looked at him, clearly agitated. 'I have no idea why. I would think you would be glad to wash your hands of the entire affair. I suppose Phillip told you that once I abducted you, you had no choice but to be involved. You did not ask to be so shabbily treated and so it is hardly fair that you should be asked to do this.' Her clear gaze met his. 'I cannot have you possibly put yourself in any more danger because of me.'

Taken aback, he stared at her. He had been prepared to meet any number of arguments but not this one. 'I doubt I will be in any danger.'

'But you might be,' she insisted. 'Someone broke into this house because of the ring. What if this person attacks you as well?'

'I will be careful.'

'But that is the point! I do not want you to worry

about being careful! You should return to your life as if this never happened!'

A wry smile lifted his mouth. 'I doubt I can do that. There is still my sore arm. And the ring.' He sobered. 'Phillip's argument was wrong, however. I was involved in this affair from the moment I decided to wear the ring in public although I did not realise it at the time. As long as I have the ring, I have no choice in the matter.'

'Then I wish I had not returned it to you!' she burst out. 'I should have kept it and waited to see if anyone approached me.'

'Someone did,' he said grimly. 'The results were not pleasant. Next time you might not have Betty around to fend off any assailants.' Her face was still worried and unhappy and he wanted to pull her into his arms and comfort her. A move that would border on insanity. The last thing he needed was to feel her soft curves against him. His body heated even thinking about it.

He ran a hand through his hair and frowned. 'I came to tell you that my grandfather and I plan to leave within the hour.'

'You are leaving?' She sounded stunned as if she had not expected it to actually happen.

'Yes. Is that not what you had hoped for?'

'No, that is, yes…' She stopped. 'I did not think you would leave so soon. But, of course, you must want to. I have no doubt you look forward to seeing London again.'

Hardly. If anything, the prospect seemed more flat than usual. In some damnably odd way, he would miss this place. With almost a sense of shock, he realised that, for the first time in two years, Mary's ghost had not been his constant companion. The sensation was foreign and he did not know if he welcomed it or not.

'I only wish I could persuade you to give up this idea that you have some sort of obligation to concern yourself with my affairs.' She had risen again and come to stand in front of him.

'It is my affair as well, now.' He looked down at her. Her face was raised to his and her brow was puckered with worry. Why the devil must she look at him like that? As if she truly cared about him. The idea made him feel vulnerable. He shoved the idea away and told himself that was quite impossible. 'I'll be fine,' he said roughly.

'I hope so.' She took a deep breath and gave him a shaky smile. 'Goodbye, then.' She held out her hand.

He took it. Her hand was soft and warm and delicate. He looked into her hazel eyes and suddenly felt lost. 'Goodbye,' he said. He released her hand. 'Perhaps we will meet in London.'

'Perhaps,' she said. 'I wish you a safe journey.'

'Yes. With no highwaymen.'

She gave him a tremulous smile. Without thinking, he bent and kissed her hard on the lips. He straightened. 'Goodbye, Julia.' He turned before he was tempted to do more, almost stepping on the yellow cat who was suddenly in front of him, and left.

Chapter Eight

Julia smoothed down the fine muslin of her pale green ball gown, her stomach churning. Why ever was she so nervous? She was just attending a ball, not an execution. It was only that she had not been to such an affair since Thomas's death. The last ball she had attended had been with him on the night he was killed.

She turned to the dressing table in the bedchamber Sophia had given her and picked up her fan. Best to not think of such things now—it would only make this even more difficult. She wished she had not let Sophia talk her into attending but Sophia had insisted.

'My dear, now that I finally have you in London, I am not about to let you hide away. And since your poor head is much better there is no reason why you cannot attend Lucy Bathurst's ball.'

Arguing with Sophia was impossible. She had taken such delight in having her mantua-maker fit Julia with a new gown that Julia feared further protests would only disappoint her. Sophia had always been kind and had taken Julia under her wing shortly after her marriage to Thomas. Julia had come to love her as the sister she had always longed for.

'Julia?' Sophia appeared in the doorway of the pleasant bedchamber. 'Are you ready?' She moved into the room with her light, graceful tread. She paused and looked at Julia. 'Oh, Julia, you look lovely. I knew the green would suit you.'

'And you look beautiful,' Julia said warmly. With her soft blonde hair, grey-blue eyes, and slender figure, no one would ever guess Sophia was nearly one and thirty. And that she had been a widow since the age of eighteen after a brief marriage to a man twenty years her senior.

'Thank you.' She smiled at Julia. 'Are you still nervous? There's no need to be. I promise to stay by your side at all times. Except when you are dancing, of course.'

Julia laughed. 'No, really, Sophia, I shall be fine. I suppose it is because I haven't attended a ball for so long that I feel a little apprehensive. I doubt that I remember how to chit-chat properly.'

'You can just smile.'

'Which can look rather empty-headed if overdone.'

'But harmless.' Sophia shot her a quick glance and said carefully, 'Nicholas will be there.'

Julia nearly dropped her fan. 'Will he?' She had not seen him in the six days she had been in London. Not that there was any reason he would want to call on her. Why would anyone wish to pay a social visit to the person who had abducted one? But the few affairs she had attended had seemed rather flat, for some reason; the one time she had caught a glimpse of a tall male figure with light brown hair her heart had beat a trifle too fast until she saw the man's face and realised she did not know him at all.

'His arm must be better, then,' she said, hoping to

sound nonchalant. She had avoided bringing up his
name although it would be perfectly reasonable for her
to inquire whether he had been approached about the
ring. Or to ask after his arm.

It was just she did not want Sophia thinking that
she had any interest in him, which of course, she did
not. Just as he had no interest in her, despite the brief,
intimate kiss he had planted on her lips before he
left…or his words that he might see her in London.
He probably wanted to put her out of his mind, which
was quite understandable, just as she wanted to put
him and his scowls out of hers. Except, at the most
unexpected moments, she would suddenly think of the
slight smile that would tug at his mouth when he was
amused and the vulnerability she had more than once
glimpsed in his face, which was why she needed to
avoid him. She could not afford to be thinking of anything but Thomas.

She realised Sophia was speaking. 'I beg your pardon. I was thinking about something else.'

Sophia arched a delicate brow. 'I can see that. I was
merely saying that Nicholas's arm is nearly healed.'
She hesitated for a moment. 'I hope you will not worry
about meeting him. I could see that it might feel rather
awkward but once you have this first meeting, the rest
will be easier. I have no doubt he will behave in a
gentlemanly manner.'

Julia gave her a wry smile. 'And I promise to behave in a ladylike manner. I will not do anything such
as force him from the ballroom at gunpoint.'

Sophia laughed, obviously relieved Julia was determined there would be no awkwardness. 'I hardly
thought you planned that, although it would create a
most interesting diversion.' She picked up Julia's silk

mantle from the bed. 'Shall we go, then? George should be here soon.' She made a small face. 'I do hope he will not be too difficult. I know he is my nephew but I sometimes find him so terribly trying. I had thought that when Arthur was sent to Italy George might step into his shoes, but if anything he is worse. Sometimes I feel such sympathy for it cannot be easy having such a paragon for an older brother. And other times I want to strangle him!'

Julia laughed and took the shawl from Sophia. 'I understand very well. I have had the exact same feeling. Then I remind myself that George can be kind. And Thomas said much the same thing as you. Living in Arthur's shadow would be difficult.' Actually he had said it would be enough to drive any man to vice, but it hardly seemed the thing one should say to Arthur's doting aunt.

'Well, we shall hope he behaves himself,' Sophia said. 'And do not worry about a thing. It is only a ball and, for the most part, they are dreadfully predictable.'

Two hours later, Julia stood at one side of the crowded ballroom. She wriggled her toes in her satin slippers and sighed. Her feet were beginning to ache, reminding her that although she was capable of walking for miles in the country in half boots, she was not at all used to executing dance steps in thin slippers.

Sophia seemed to know everyone and so Julia had not lacked a partner until now. Nor had Sophia. She was at this moment performing a country dance with a slightly balding gentleman who, from the look on his face, was quite taken with his lovely partner. A twinge of longing mixed with sadness shot through Julia. Thomas had looked at her in much that way the first time they had danced together. She had just returned to her stepfather's house from school and he had been a guest at the neighbouring estate. They had met at a local assembly. He had asked her for a dance and from the moment she laid eyes on the tall, dashing young man with laughter lurking in his eyes, she had been lost. And to her great amazement, her feelings had been reciprocated.

'Enjoying yourself, my dear neighbour?'

She started and turned to find George at her side. Tonight he was dressed in a bright blue coat over an embroidered waistcoat of an amazing yellow. His stiff collar was so high she wondered how he managed to turn his head.

'Very much,' she said politely. 'And you?' She had seen very little of him. He had asked her for one dance and then disappeared into the card room.

'The affair is a trifle dull.' His attention had drifted away from her and then his gaze sharpened. He leisurely brought his quizzing glass to his eye. 'However, I believe it has just become more interesting. Your most recent houseguest has arrived.'

'I beg your pardon?'

'The enigmatic Lord Thayne. He is over against the wall.'

Her heart jumped. She avoided the direction George indicated. 'Indeed.' She had been on pins and needles for the first hour or so, half-expecting to see Thayne, but when there was no sign of him, she began to relax. Although, for some odd reason, she had almost felt disappointed.

'Yes, indeed. Shall I present him to you as a possible partner?'

She turned her most furious expression on him. 'I

pray you will not! In fact, if you should even try to do so I will never speak to you again!'

George toyed with his quizzing glass. 'I take it that he was not the most agreeable of guests. Although I never would have guessed that from the day I found you bent tenderly over his wounded arm.'

'If you do not be quiet,' she said through gritted teeth, 'I vow I will endeavour, at the next opportune moment, to do damage to some item of your clothing.'

He held up his hands in mock defence and shuddered. 'I had no idea you felt so strongly. My lips are sealed. I will say no more.'

'Thank you.' Not that she trusted the speculative gleam in his eye one bit.

'My dear, I believe I will adjourn to the card room. Before I inadvertently say something to put you further in a temper.' He made her a bow and sauntered off.

She watched him go. Instead of heading towards the card room, he was heading in the opposite direction. Towards the side of the room where he said Thayne stood. She forced herself to look in that direction. Thayne was indeed there, standing near the wall, a familiar, half-bored expression on his face as he surveyed the room. Her heart began to thud and her hands felt clammy.

George stopped next to Thayne and said something. Her stomach lurched. George could not possibly be suggesting to Thayne that he dance with her! But when Thayne glanced in her direction she feared that was exactly what he was doing. Mortified, she jerked her gaze away and prayed he had not noticed her. She forced herself to look again and saw Thayne had moved away from the wall. He was not heading in her direction, however, but had stopped to talk to a woman she recognized as Lady Bathurst.

She nearly sank with relief. Thank goodness, she had been mistaken. She would rather die than stand up with Thayne. Particularly if George was in some way involved.

The musicians were tuning their instruments. Another dance was about to start. Perhaps she should find Sophia before she jumped to any more silly conclusions and made a cake of herself. She turned to walk towards the card room, but found her way blocked by a group of chattering young ladies. She started to step to one side when she heard someone say her name.

She turned around. Lady Bathurst stood behind her, a curious, almost excited expression on her pleasant, plump face.

With her was Lord Thayne.

Julia froze, her mind a complete blank. Lady Bathurst was speaking. 'My dear Lady Carrington, I have a gentleman here who is very desirous of making your acquaintance. And soliciting your hand for the next dance!' She beamed at Julia.

'In…indeed,' Julia said faintly. She finally stole a glance at him and tried not to notice how devastatingly attractive he was in his elegant evening clothes. His eyes met hers with a slightly mocking expression. A stab of annoyance shot through her. If he did not wish to see her, then why did he ask for an introduction?

'Yes, indeed,' Lady Bathurst said. She looked excessively pleased. 'Lady Carrington, may I present Lord Thayne?'

'How do you do, Lord Thayne?' she said as coolly as she could. She held out her hand.

He took it. His fingers, warm and strong, seemed to

burn through her glove. He bowed over her hand. But instead of releasing it, he gazed into her face. A smile touched his mouth. 'I have looked forward to making your acquaintance, Lady Carrington. And to standing up with you, of course.'

She pulled her hand out of his. 'Indeed.'

His brow rose in that irritatingly familiar way. 'I can see you are nearly speechless at the offer,' he murmured.

She was about to say 'indeed' again and then shut her mouth. Lady Bathurst glanced from Julia to Thayne with a puzzled expression, her smile fading. The musicians played the opening notes of the next dance. Her expression changed to relief. 'The waltz is starting. I do hope you enjoy yourselves.' She gave them a brief smile and bustled off.

Thayne glanced down at Julia. 'I believe we are obligated for this dance, my dear.' He held out his arm.

She ignored his arm. 'I really do not wish to dance. And I am not ''your dear''.'

'No?' He dropped his arm. His lips twitched in a most maddening way which made her wonder why she had ever entertained the slightest desire to see him again. 'I was informed you most particularly wished to dance with me. It is quite ungenerous of you to refuse me now that I have gone to the trouble of procuring a proper introduction.'

She gave a little gasp and stared at him in outrage. 'Who ever told you that?'

'Kingsley.' His voice was bland.

She closed her eyes for a brief moment and then opened them. 'I will strangle him.'

'Later.' He reached down and took her hand. 'For

now, we are going to dance. Otherwise, Lady Bathurst
will think we have already quarrelled, which will not
do.'

He led her to the edge of the floor. Before she could
protest, he had placed one hand lightly at her waist
and taken her other hand in his. The Spanish ring
gleamed on his fourth finger. He began to move in
time to the music and she promptly tripped on his foot.

Her face heated and she stared at the lace of his
snowy white shirt. 'I beg your pardon. I have not
waltzed for over three years.'

'I fear you have surpassed my record then. It has
been two and one-half years since I last waltzed.'

She glanced swiftly up at him and stumbled a little.
His hand tightened on her waist as he steadied her. 'It
has been nearly two years since I have danced with
anyone other than a relation,' he said conversationally.

She nearly stumbled again at that. 'Then you should
have asked someone with more recent experience.'
Her gaze had returned to his shirt front. 'I really did
not ask George to say anything to you.'

'I know.'

'Then why are you dancing with me?'

'Must you address my chest? It is disconcerting to
be conversing with the top of your head.'

'I will probably step on you again if I look up.'

He laughed. 'After other things I have survived at
your hand, I've no doubt I could survive that.'

The genuine amusement in his voice startled her.
She did look up and saw his eyes were alight with
laughter. It transformed his face, erasing the hardness
from his countenance, and suddenly she realised how
powerfully charming he could be. She swallowed, try-

ing to regain her equilibrium. 'I...I suppose so. How is your arm?'

'It is much better.' The corner of his mouth lifted. 'We are making progress. You have not yet tripped again.'

She stared at him. Was it possible he was flirting with her? The thought was so unexpected and so unnerving she nearly froze. She cast about for something to say. Nothing at all came to mind.

'I asked you to dance because I wanted to inquire about Foxwood. I assume Mrs Mobley is well, as are Betty and the cat,' he said.

'The cat?' He was unnerving her more by the second. 'Oh, Wellington. He is fine. So are Barbara and Betty. I think Wellington misses you, however. He sits in front of your...that is, the bedchamber you occupied and meows.'

This time he actually grinned. 'Probably hoping for another victim to pounce upon.'

She found herself returning his smile. 'Perhaps.'

His expression changed, the smile fading from his face. He stared at her, his eyes darkening with an awareness of her that made her catch her breath. Her hand trembled in his and for a moment she had no idea where she was. There was only him and he suddenly seemed completely familiar as if she had just come home.

The music stopped. He dropped his hand from her waist and then she was back in the ballroom in the midst of a crowd of strangers. She blinked, feeling as if she had just awakened from a dream. She glanced at Thayne and saw his expression was almost as dazed as hers. He cleared his throat and then frowned. 'I should return you to Sophia.' His voice was abrupt.

'Yes.' She took the arm he proffered, trying to make the least contact with him as possible. She felt shaky and odd as if something had just changed her forever.

Sophia stood near the edge of the ballroom with a man and a young woman she did not recognise. She felt Thayne stiffen. Puzzled, she glanced up at him. He met her eyes, a wry look on his face. 'My cousin and his wife. I've no doubt they wish to meet you, particularly now. By the way, I should warn you they know I stayed at Foxwood. After I had managed to escaped, wounded, from a robber.'

Before she could reply, they had joined the group. Sophia looked at Julia with a peculiar little smile but merely greeted Nicholas before introducing Julia to the others.

Adam Henslowe was a pleasant-looking man of perhaps five and twenty. His wife, Lady Jessica, looked to be several years his junior. She was extremely pretty with thick dark hair curled about her face and a pair of expressive eyes.

Mr Henslowe took Julia's hand, his eyes going over her with frank interest. 'We are delighted to meet the lady who rescued my cousin.'

She felt heat rise to her cheeks. 'I really did nothing.'

'No?' Mr Henslowe glanced at Nicholas with a raised brow and turned back to Julia with a grin. He dropped her hand. 'That was not my understanding. His arm has nicely healed due to your care.'

'I doubt he was the most agreeable of patients. Men are nearly impossible when they are laid up,' Lady Jessica added. 'Although perhaps he was not so bad if you actually agreed to waltz with him tonight.' She cast a laughing look at Julia.

'He wasn't really very horrible at all, considering the circumstances.' She had no idea why she felt obligated to stand up for him. Except it had been her fault he had been wounded. And he had come to her rescue. Twice, in fact.

'Wasn't he?' Lady Jessica looked at her and then at Nicholas. She suddenly smiled. 'I see I will have several interesting things to write Sarah tomorrow.'

Nicholas looked less than pleased. 'I doubt she will find any of them all that interesting,' he said drily.

'Oh, but she will. Do you not think, Adam?' Lady Jessica's eyes sparkled.

'In the interest of keeping the peace, I believe I will keep my speculations to myself.' Adam grinned and then gently took his wife's arm. 'Come, my love. I think a dance is in order. Before we manage to embarrass Lady Carrington or antagonise my cousin.'

Lady Jessica smiled at Julia. 'I am certain we will meet again soon. Perhaps I might call on you and Sophia?'

'That would be delightful.' Sophia glanced over at Julia. 'Would it not?'

'I would like that very much,' Julia said. She felt rather awkward particularly when Nicholas turned to look at her. She couldn't imagine that he would welcome any sort of acquaintance between herself and his family.

She avoided looking at him as Mr Henslowe and Lady Jessica said their goodbyes. Sophia turned to him. 'And I hope you will call as well, Nicholas. You are always welcome, you know. I am certain Julia would agree.' She gave Julia a meaningful look.

'That would be very nice.' She forced herself to meet his eyes.

He stared at her for a moment and then a slow smile touched his mouth. A smile that made her hot and cold at once. 'I look forward to it.' He bowed. 'Good evening, Sophia, Lady Carrington.' He sauntered off.

Sophia turned to Julia. 'Well! I can see I need not have worried about any awkwardness. Not only did he ask for an introduction, he actually waltzed with you. He rarely stands up with anyone and I cannot recall the last time he waltzed!'

'It was two and a half years ago,' Julia said automatically. 'The only reason he did so was because George told him I wished to dance with him. I dare say he only wanted to aggravate me.'

'George? I've no doubt of it, but for once his mischief worked out remarkably well, wouldn't you say?'

'I meant Lord Thayne.' Julia suddenly felt too tired to explain.

Sophia merely laughed. 'I doubt that is the whole of it. Well, you certainly have created a stir.'

Which was the last thing she wanted to do. If she had an ounce of sense, she would avoid him at all costs. The horrible truth was she found him dangerously attractive. She had hoped it might be due to their forced intimacy at Foxwood, but she was wrong. He was just as lethal in a London ballroom. Perhaps even more so, if tonight was any indication.

And she had not even thought of asking him about the ring.

Much later that evening, George strolled into White's. He was hailed by Carleton Wentworth, a foppish young man with an indolent air. 'My dear fellow, you have just come from the Bathurst affair, have you not? Bunty, here, has as well and has proposed a bet on which I've no doubt you'll want to lay odds.'

George ambled over to their table. 'Will I? And what has that to do with the Bathurst ball, Bunty?'

Bunty, who was more properly known as the Honourable William Buntford, raised a languid hand. 'Saw Thayne waltzing with your neighbour. Never waltzes with anyone.'

George started. 'Indeed. You are correct, Thayne never waltzes with anyone. Nor does Lady Carrington for that matter. So?'

'Actually smiled at her. Thayne never smiles,' Bunty explained.

'I will own that is a rare event.'

'Precisely, and so, my dear fellow, what are the odds he plans to make her his mistress? And that she will accept?' Wentworth asked.

'I begin to see.' George thought for a moment and then a slow smile curved his mouth. 'I will go further. What are the odds they will wed?'

'Marriage? Thayne?' Wentworth raised an incredulous brow. 'Do you perhaps desire to see the inside of debtor's prison? I doubt your sire will increase your allowance enough to cover such a wager.'

George smiled gently. 'My sire will go to any length to protect the family name from scandal. One of his offspring in prison would not further the cause. There would be the unfortunate effect of tainting my sainted brother as well. But that is a moot point. I doubt I will lose.'

Chapter Nine

Phillip called the next day, driving all thoughts of Nicholas from her mind. He was shown into the drawing room where Julia and Sophia were studying the most recent *La Belle Assemblée*.

He refused Sophia's offer of tea and took the wing chair near the sofa. He did not waste time on the preliminaries. He turned to Julia. 'I returned from Sheffield last night. I am sorry to tell you that I could discover nothing useful there.'

Sick disappointment washed over her. 'Nothing at all? The jeweller did not remember it?'

'No. His son has taken over the business in the last year and the father's memory is impaired. There was no record of any such transaction nor could either one recall such a ring.' His face held a disappointment that reflected her own. 'I am sorry, my dear. I know you had hoped there might be some clue to the identity of the person who took the ring. I do not wish to be harsh, but we may have to accept the fact that we may never know who killed Thomas.'

'I cannot.' She looked away, refusing to allow the tears to fall. She swallowed and glanced back at Phillip. 'There is still Lord Thayne. Perhaps someone will approach him about the ring.'

'Possibly. But that does not mean the person wants anything more than to purchase a valuable and unusual piece of jewellery. I am afraid that Thomas's death may be exactly what it seemed—a common robbery.'

A common robbery that resulted in her husband's murder. 'But why would it be so important for a mere thief to break into my house and demand I hand over the ring? I cannot believe that has nothing to do with his death!'

'You were perhaps mistaken. You did sustain a blow to the head.' Phillip's expression was not unkind.

'No. I know what I heard.' Distressed, she rose. 'I know I have asked you before, but please could you not tell me what Thomas was involved in before he died? I know it worried him very much.'

Phillip stood as well. 'You, of all people, should know I am not at liberty to tell you that information. And I will repeat what I have told you before: his work for the government and his death are not related.'

She looked at him, the frustration and hopelessness she had felt three years ago bubbling to the surface. 'Perhaps I should go to Sheffield. I could make inquiries. There must be something.'

'That is not necessary,' Phillip said coolly. 'And possibly dangerous. Furthermore, I cannot see what you could discover that I could not.'

'But there might be something!' She willed him to understand. 'Last time I waited and waited. You cannot know how frustrating it was! At least you were doing something! But I could only wait!'

'I know.' His mouth tightened. She had undoubtedly insulted him. 'I will still make inquiries, but I cannot allow you to put yourself in danger, if there is any. I promised Thomas we would watch out for you if he could not. And I plan to.'

His face had that uncompromising look that she had come to know well over the years. He had no intention of allowing her to do a thing. And now that she was in Sophia's home, it would be next to impossible to oppose him.

Sophia rose and put her hand on Julia's arm. 'I am sorry as well,' she said softly. 'But, oh, Julia! If anything happened to you we could not forgive ourselves. And I know Phillip is doing everything he can.'

'Of course.' Julia managed a smile, but she could not quite quell the twinge of resentment. Which was mean-spirited of her, because they were two people in the world who would never hurt her.

But her mind refused to let the matter go. That night after the dinner party she attended with Sophia and Phillip, and after the abigail had helped her dress for bed, she sat down at the small desk facing the window. The muslin curtains were parted and the pale light of the full moon bathed the room. She leaned her hand on her chin and thought.

Thomas had escorted her home after the ball and then gone to Thérèse's, which was not his usual habit for he almost never left her after such affairs. She had sensed he was meeting someone there although he did not say in so many words. And he was troubled again—she could tell by the way his ready smile did not quite reach his eyes. She had tried several times over that past week to discover what was behind the shadow in his eyes but he always managed to distract her.

Now she wished she had not been so easily bought off by his kisses and teasing. But hindsight was never useful. She rose and went to stand by the window. Thérèse had been questioned by Phillip and his men. But Julia had never asked her about Thomas's last night. Somehow, with the horror of his death and the mourning and condolences and then the horrible sensation of moving in a fog, she had never really questioned Thérèse herself—how Thomas had spent his time there had not seemed relevant in the aftermath of his death and had been too painful to discuss.

But time had healed some of the pain and made it manageable. So perhaps it was time she called on Thérèse and found out exactly whom Thomas had been going to meet.

She called on Thérèse the next day. Despite knowing Thérèse was the proprietor of a gaming saloon, Sophia had been pleased to have Julia visit an old friend and had offered the use of her carriage.

Thérèse greeted her in her office, a small room on the third floor. She rose from behind her desk. 'My dear Julia! I could not believe my ears when André said you were here.' She moved towards Julia and embraced her. She stepped back. 'You look well. I had heard you were in London.'

'Yes.' Julia smiled at Thérèse. She wore a sensible dark blue dress and her hair was pulled severely back from her face and caught at the nape of her neck. Her prim appearance only emphasised her exotic beauty.

'And Lord Thayne has returned also.'

Julia's pulse jumped at the mention of his name. 'I believe so.'

'I would hope you know so, particularly as you waltzed with him the night before last.'

Julia started. 'You know that?'

Thérèse arched a delicate brow. 'I am certain all of London know. Come, sit down and I will ring for refreshment. And you will tell me about Nicholas. I have been agog with curiosity since you left with him that night. Or should I say forced him to leave with you?' Her eyes twinkled at the expression on Julia's face. 'Do not worry, I doubt if anyone else noticed a thing. But what exactly did you do with him for five days?'

Her tale failed to shock Thérèse. If anything, except for the highway robbery and the intruder, she was highly amused. 'My dear, you would be the envy of half the women in London. Except they would have taken full advantage of having the elusive Lord Thayne helpless under their roof.'

'He was hardly helpless.'

'No?' Thérèse laughed. 'Perhaps difficult, then?'

'Yes,' Julia said shortly. 'It is not Lord Thayne I am here to discuss. It is Thomas.' She took a deep breath. 'That last night, the night he died. I think he was here to meet someone. Can you remember anything at all about that night?'

Thérèse frowned. 'I told Phillip what I knew, as did my servants. Have you asked him?'

'He will not tell me much about his inquiries. But I know Thomas was worried. Perhaps about something he was investigating. And Phillip will not tell what that was.'

'No. He would not.' Thérèse stood and moved to her desk. She took a ring of keys from a hook above the desk, removed one and then used it to open a drawer in her desk. She pulled out a small stack of papers. 'After Phillip left, I wrote down my observations as well as those of my household. I thought perhaps Phillip would come again or send someone else with more questions and so I thought to write down everything we saw that night. But he did not and then I heard it was decided Thomas's death was a robbery and nothing more. But I kept the papers.' She came to Julia's side. 'You may take them if you would like.'

'Yes, if you please. I will return them to you when I am finished.' She took the papers and for some odd reason found her hand was shaking. She glanced at them and then swiftly up at Thérèse. 'Do you agree with Phillip?'

'I do not know,' Thérèse said cautiously. 'I have wondered. And now with what you have told me about the ring…' She shrugged lightly.

'So you are not convinced it was.' Julia looked down at the precise, elegant writing. As in everything, Thérèse had been meticulous. The first page listed the patrons who had attended that night. The others were narrative accounts by each of her servants. She glanced down at the list of names and frowned. 'George was here that night? But I thought he had left for Maldon.'

'He was here for a very short while. He left early, I believe.'

She looked up, puzzled. 'He never said anything. Did he speak to Thomas?'

'That I do not know.'

Julia returned her attention back to the papers and then felt a surge of excitement. 'And Robert Haslett? He was one of Thomas's good friends. He worked under Phillip as well.' Her hope died down. 'But he has left England.'

'He returned six months ago. He is, in fact, a frequent patron.'

'I would like to speak to him. He was still working for Phillip then. Perhaps he knows something.'

A frown creased Thérèse's brow. 'My dear, are you certain this is wise? I will help you in any way, but I worry that you will only be disappointed. And hurt once again.'

Julia stood and clasped the papers to her chest. 'I cannot be hurt any more than I was. I need to find out why Thomas was so worried. Perhaps it means nothing and then I will accept that. But I cannot stand back this time.'

Thérèse's face still held worry. 'But you must be careful. You have already been injured once because of the ring. There is someone, perhaps, who does not want the past disturbed. I do not think Thomas would have wanted you in danger, even for his sake.'

'I am doing this for my sake,' Julia said quietly. Thérèse was right, as was Phillip, Thomas would prefer she remain innocent and out of harm even if it meant his killer was never brought to justice.

'I see.' Thérèse looked at her for a moment. 'So you want to speak to Robert Haslett. He will be here tonight. Can you come?'

'Yes.' A twinge of guilt shot through her. She and Sophia were to attend another coming-out ball. She loathed lying to Sophia, but knew that it was one thing for her to visit Thérèse during the day and another at night. Sophia would wonder why and there was always the possibility Phillip would find out. And this time, she wanted to do things her own way.

Julia arrived at Thérèse's house shortly after nine that evening. She finally decided on a lie that held a grain of truth—an elderly friend of hers and Thomas's had asked her to dine. Haslett was at least an old friend. If Sophia found it odd the invitation had been made so late, she said nothing, merely that, of course, Julia must go. And that it might be less tiring for Julia than a ball. Her kindness nearly made Julia confess everything, particularly when she offered to send Julia in her carriage.

Julia had assured her Mrs Sanders would send a carriage. Instead, Thérèse's plain, elegant carriage had arrived at half past eight to fetch her.

Despite the fact she had no intention of abducting anyone tonight, Julia's stomach still knotted as she was admitted to the house by André, Thérèse's butler. He took her card and glanced at it. 'Madame Blanchot awaits you in the saloon, my lady,' he said.

She nodded. 'Thank you.' She made her way across the small entrance hall and up the staircase. The main saloon was on the first floor. She paused in the doorway, her hand going to her mask to assure herself it was still in place. Then she stepped inside.

The room was already crowded. Most of the patrons tonight were men; if she hoped to find Robert Haslett on her own, it would take an age. She looked around and finally spotted Thérèse near the Faro table.

She moved across the room, aware she was the object of more than one curious glance. Thérèse looked up just as she reached the table. She left it and came to Julia's side. 'He is here,' she said quietly. 'I have told him that you very much desire to speak with him and he has agreed to meet you. He is in one of the small parlours. Shall I have Hayes take you to him now?'

'If you please.'

Thérèse nodded to a burly man in livery who stood near the Faro table. He came to her side and she spoke to him in a low voice and then turned to Julia. 'I wish you luck, *ma chérie.*'

'Yes.' She followed Hayes across the saloon and the small hallway. He paused in front of one of the rooms and Julia realised it was the same room where she had met Nicholas. The coincidence was not very reassuring.

'He is seated at the table in the corner,' Hayes said.

'Thank you.' Julia stepped inside, her heart pounding. Two men sat at the table near the fireplace. She saw a solitary man seated at the table in the corner.

She started across the room. And then gasped when someone caught her arm.

'Planning another abduction, Lady Carrington?'

She whirled around and stared up into Nicholas's sardonic face. 'Wh…what are you doing here?'

His brow shot up. 'More to the point, what are you doing here? Or did you decide you desire more entertainment than your dinner with an elderly lady provided?' Any of the warmth she had seen at the ball two nights ago had vanished.

Her mouth fell open. She gave him an angry stare, and then remembered it was probably wasted on him in her masked state. 'That is none of your concern. Will you please let go of me? I have an appointment with someone.'

He dropped her arm. 'With Haslett?'

'Yes. And if you will move out of my way, I will endeavour to keep it.'

'An assignation? My dear, I had no idea you had it in you, although I might have guessed,' he drawled.

His face had darkened and he suddenly looked as dangerous as he had the night she abducted him.

A shiver of fear coursed through her. What if he had no intention of letting her move past him? She could not allow Haslett to leave. 'Please, you must let me go. It is not an assignation. He was a friend of my husband's and it is very important I talk to him.'

He stared at her for a moment, his eyes searching her face, and she had the sense he could see beneath her mask. 'Very well,' he said abruptly.

'Julia.'

They both turned. Robert Haslett had risen and come to stand next to them. 'I trust there is not a problem, Lord Thayne.' His voice was polite but cool.

'I merely wished to determine that Lady Carrington was safe,' Nicholas said, equally coolly.

'I assure you she will be.'

'She had better be.' The slight menace in Nicholas's voice was not reassuring.

'I have known Robert for a very long time,' Julia said, attempting to break the tension.

The only result was to have Nicholas's brows snapped together. 'Indeed,' he said, ice in his voice. 'If you need anything, I am at your service.' He stalked off.

Robert looked at her, a quizzical expression in his blue eyes. But he merely said, 'Come and sit down.'

She followed him to the table and took one of the chairs. He seated himself across from her. 'It is good to see you, Julia. Or at least most of you.'

She smiled at him. 'And it is good to see you as well.' Except for his thinning hair, he had not changed much since she last saw him, a few months after Thomas's funeral. He had left for Austria shortly after that. He was not quite handsome but his thin intelligent face was very attractive. 'I hope you are well?' she asked.

A shadow crossed his face. 'For the most part.' He paused, and then said, 'I lost my wife a year ago.'

She touched his hand. 'I am so sorry.' She had not known he was married, but then she had lost contact with so many people after Thomas's death.

'So am I.' He looked away for a moment and then back at her. 'I did not mean to bring that up the very first thing.' His smile was wry. 'The anniversary of our marriage was today.'

'Then today must be very difficult for you.' She hesitated. 'Perhaps this is not a good time for me to talk to you.'

'No. It is actually better than being alone with my thoughts,' he said. 'What can I do for you? I assume that the matter must be rather grave if you chose to meet me here.'

'It is.' She leaned forward. 'It is about Thomas. I know you were here that last night—the night he was killed. Do you know if he came to meet someone here?'

He frowned a little. 'If he did, I did not notice. We played a few hands together. He spoke with a number of people, but I cannot recall that anyone in particular caught my attention.'

That was disappointing. 'There is something else, then. He seemed troubled, but he would not tell me why. I knew he was involved in some matter for the government and I wondered if that was what worried him. Do you have any idea what he was doing?'

His frown increased. 'Why the questions now, Julia?'

'Because some things have happened and I have begun to wonder if there was more to his death than a mere robbery.'

'Have you?' he said slowly. 'I will own I had wondered myself, but the investigation came to naught.'

'Do you know what he was involved with?'

'I suppose there is no reason I cannot tell you,' he said slowly. 'He suspected that someone in the Home Office was selling secrets to the French. No one was ever charged and, once Thomas died, the investigation was dropped.'

'Lady Carrington is ready to leave, my lord,' Haynes said in a low voice.

'Thank you.' Nicholas turned from the EO Table.

'But you've yet to place your wager,' the young Lord Lawton exclaimed.

'Later,' Nicholas said over his shoulder. He made his way through the saloon and went down the staircase to the front entry. André finished admitting a trio of young bucks and then saw him. He came to Nicholas's side. 'She is in the waiting room, my lord.'

Nicholas nodded and went to the small room off the hall.

Still masked, she sat on a wing chair, her hands clasped around her reticule. She looked up at his footsteps. Her body stiffened. She slowly stood. 'Why are you here?'

'I am escorting you back to Sophia's house.'

'Thérèse has provided a carriage for me.'

'I am taking you instead.' He levelled a frown at her. 'Don't argue. I'll go to the devil before I allow you to leave this place without me. I intend to see you get home without incident.'

'I have no idea what sort of incident you refer to,' she said icily.

He stepped towards her. 'No? Then you are either more naïve or more foolish than I thought.'

'I am neither, my lord.'

'Indeed? Then what sort of a game do you play? I doubt if either Sophia or Phillip know you are here.'

'I am not playing a game.'

It was all he could do to rein in the anger that had boiled in him since he saw her with Haslett. He refused to acknowledge he could possibly be jealous. 'Is this how you abuse Sophia's hospitality? By leading her to believe you are safely dining in the home of an old friend while you are all the while amusing yourself in a gaming hell?'

'I am not amusing myself! Nor is this a gaming hell!' she snapped. And suddenly seemed to fold. 'I would not dream of deceiving Sophia if I did not have to.' Her mouth trembled beneath her mask. 'Please, I do not wish to argue with you. I will go with you, if you insist.'

His anger vanished along with her capitulation. 'What sort of trouble are you in?'

'I am not in trouble.'

'Then what is wrong?'

'Nothing. Everything. I just want to leave this place.'

He picked up her mantle from the chair. She did not protest when he draped it about her shoulders. 'Come. My carriage should be waiting by now.'

They did not speak as they entered the carriage and took their places across from each other. He waited until the footman had closed the door and the carriage had started through the dark London streets before he spoke. 'You can remove your mask.'

Her hands went to the strings at the back of her head. She fumbled with them for a moment and then the mask fell away. He could barely see her face in the shadows of the carriage.

'What happened tonight?' he asked quietly.

'Robert Haslett told me that my husband suspected someone in the Home Office was passing information to the French,' she said dully. 'Before he was killed, he was attempting to discover this person or persons' identity.'

'And did he?'

'No. The investigation stopped with his death. His superiors concluded there was no evidence for his suspicions. Or at least no evidence was found.' She drew in a breath. 'I think he was killed because he did find something.'

'You did not know of this until tonight?'

'I knew he was still working for Phillip and that something was worrying him. But Phillip would not tell me what it was. He assured me it had no bearing on his death.'

Just as Stanton had assured him and his grandfather. 'Will you tell Phillip what you have discovered tonight?'

'I do not know. He returned yesterday from Sheffield. He found nothing. He still thinks, or wants me to think, Thomas's death was a robbery.' Her voice was tired.

'Perhaps to protect you.'

'I do not want to be protected. Not if it means hiding the truth.'

He frowned, not liking her implication. 'Do you really think he would do that?'

'I do not know what to think.'

The carriage had turned into Berkeley Square. The whole affair made him uneasy, but he did not like the turn things were taking. He especially didn't like the fact she was making her own enquiries. He leaned towards her. 'Don't do anything more.'

The carriage stopped. 'I cannot let this rest.' Under the street lamp he could see the stubborn look on her face.

'It may be dangerous. Let me help you.'

'I cannot have you involved any further.'

He laughed. 'My dear, whether you wish it or not, and for that matter, whether I wish it or not, I am involved beyond return in this matter. I am not about to back out now and allow you to risk your lovely neck.'

'Then I wish I had not told you what I was doing tonight!'

'Then I would have threatened to tell Sophia where you were.'

She gasped. 'That is blackmail.'

He gave her one of his most sardonic looks. 'Precisely so. And believe me, I won't hesitate to use it again if I deem it necessary.' The footman opened the doors. Nicholas stepped out and then held out his hand. With some hesitation, she took it and allowed him to help her out. He walked up the steps with her.

He looked down at her face. 'We will talk tomorrow. You can drive with me in Hyde Park.'

'I do not wish to drive in Hyde Park.'

'Yes, you do.' He smiled gently. 'Otherwise I might

mention to Sophia how delighted I was to escort you home from Thérèse's.'

She looked as if she wanted to hit him. At least it was an improvement over the dispirited woman in his carriage. Without saying a word, she turned and stalked into the house.

Brunton watched Thayne's carriage rumble away from Lady Simons's house. He had been sent to follow Thayne and, as last time, Thayne left with Lady Carrington. Except this time they left in Thayne's carriage and without the added interest of ropes. A pity. Although his preference would have been to have the lady bound.

He moved his horse forward out of the shadows. No matter. The guv'nor should pay him well for this information.

'Will you need anything else, my lord?' Samuels asked.

'No. Not tonight.' Nicholas waited until his valet departed and then walked over to the wing chair near his bed. He threw himself into it, stretching his legs before him. He doubted sleep would come any time soon. A frown creased his brow as he mulled over the night's events. Did Phillip indeed have something to hide? But Carrington had been his godson and Nicholas had sensed Phillip was sincerely grieved over Carrington's death.

But perhaps Phillip merely wanted to protect Julia, keep her from doing exactly what she had done: come to the conclusion that Carrington's death was connected to his investigation for the Home Office when it was nothing but a coincidence.

His frown deepened. He meant what he had told Julia. He would not allow her to pursue this on her own. She'd been desperate enough for information to kidnap him. He hated to think what else she might do if she thought it was necessary. He'd keep her from doing something else rash if he had to abduct her in return.

How the devil had he managed to get this involved in her affairs in the first place? It was the last thing he wanted. When he first returned to London, he vowed he would stay away from her. But when he saw her at the Bathurst ball, looking rather lost and trying to pretend she did not see him, his resolution went to hell. Kingsley's sly machinations had little to do with his decision, except to make certain he obtained a proper introduction before asking her to stand up with him. He had thought only to tease her, perhaps flirt with her a little and then he would put her out of his mind.

But as he had looked down into her upturned face with her expressive hazel eyes and inviting mouth, his hand resting lightly on the slender curve of her back, he realised he still desired her. He wanted to possess her in a way he had felt with no other woman but Mary.

He was not in love with her. Nor would he ever be. In her own way, she was as unobtainable as Mary had been. Only an idiot would fail to see Julia still loved her husband.

And he still loved Mary.

So, what to do? As much as he might like, he could not avoid Julia. The ring he wore was a reminder of that. He had avoided wearing it for two years because it had reminded him of his failure to protect Mary.

He would not let the ring symbolise his failure to protect Julia as well.

Chapter Ten

Julia stood in Sophia's drawing room, looking down into the square. Nicholas was due to arrive any minute. Disgusted that she was peering through the curtains as if she was actually anxious for his arrival, she turned away, only to find Sophia watching her with a little smile.

'Do not worry, I know he will be here soon enough,' Sophia said.

'I am hardly worried about that. If anything, I rather wish he would change his mind.'

Sophia laughed. 'Men do not cry off. And why, if you are so reluctant to go with him, did you agree?'

'He coerced me.' That at least was the truth. Arriving home last night before Sophia had not done much to relieve her guilt. Sophia's kindly questions about her dinner and her elderly friend had not helped either.

'Did he? Splendid! Otherwise, you would have neatly fobbed him off.'

'I doubt anyone could do that,' Julia said crossly.

Sophia laughed again. 'Poor Julia. At least think of it as a chance to show off your new bonnet and spencer. You look lovely.'

The stylish bonnet trimmed with purple ribbon to match the braid-trimmed spencer had arrived today. Sophia had insisted that she wear them. Julia had to admit having new clothes was pleasurable—she rarely bothered because there seemed little point in purchasing fashionable clothing when she had few occasions to wear them. Particularly when she must worry about the cost as well.

She turned when she heard footsteps in the hall and then Nicholas was shown into the room. Sophia rose to greet him. 'How nice to see you, Nicholas.'

'And you.' He bowed over her hand and then looked up. His gaze fell on Julia. 'Lady Carrington.'

'Good day, Lord Thayne,' she said coolly, trying to ignore the fact his dashing appearance in a perfectly fitting drab coat and light-coloured breeches made her pulse leap a notch.

His expression was quizzical, but he said nothing. After he exchanged a few more pleasantries with Sophia, he turned to Julia. 'Are you ready?'

'I have been ready for the last three-quarters of an hour,' Julia said stiffly. She had no intention of letting him think she was coming with him willingly.

'I am flattered,' he drawled, giving her a sharp look.

'I hope you will enjoy yourselves,' Sophia said. She glanced from Julia to Nicholas with a rather worried face.

Which made Julia feel ashamed. None of this was Sophia's doing, or for that matter, his, and she knew Sophia was fond of Nicholas. She managed a smile. 'I am sure I will.'

She went with him down the stairs and out of the house. His curricle, pulled by a handsome pair of matching bays, waited in the street. He helped her in and then gracefully took his place next to her. After he dismissed the groom, he set the horses to.

He said nothing until they were out of the square. He glanced down at her. 'Are you comfortable?'

'Yes. It is very nice.' She had not ridden in anything so dashing for an age. The sensation was pleasing. She gave him a tentative smile.

He looked taken aback. 'Good.' He manoeuvred around a cart and then turned back to her. 'I take it Sophia did not discover last night's activities.'

For a moment she had nearly forgotten why she was here. 'No. She did not suspect anything.'

'You do not sound particularly pleased.'

'I dislike deceiving her. But she would be even more distressed if she knew what I was doing.'

He frowned. 'What made you decide to meet with Haslett last night?'

'Thomas was killed after he left Thérèse's. Thérèse gave me a list of all the patrons who had been there that night as well as written narratives of her observations and those of her employees. Robert's name was on the list. He had been a good friend of Thomas's and I thought he might know something. He did.'

They were approaching the entrance to Hyde Park. The increasing number of carriages and riders forced him to slow down the horses. 'What did you hope to do next?' he asked without taking his eyes off the horses.

'I have the list. I recognise some of the names and I thought I could contact some of the others.'

His mouth tightened. 'No.'

'No, my lord?'

'No. It is too dangerous. Give me the list. I will make any of the necessary contacts.'

'I do not think—'

He cut her off. 'It makes sense. For one thing, I may know some of the men on the list. And, my dear, I have one other factor in my favour.' He slanted her a glance. 'I am a man. I have access to places you do not and with much less trouble. Unless, of course, you look forward to spending the rest of your time in London deceiving Sophia.'

'Of course I do not. I should hate it!' And he was right, of course. No one would question why he visited a gaming saloon. He undoubtedly belonged to White's or Brook's and could easily meet with any of the members, whereas she had wondered how in the world she would manage to approach most of the men on the list. But she hated to be beholden to him any more than she already was. More troubling, she had no idea why he seemed determined to help her.

'So is it settled? You will give me the list?' he asked.

'I am not certain,' she began, only to be interrupted by a voice.

'How very interesting. First a waltz and now a tête-à-tête drive in the park. Does this mean there is to be an interesting announcement?'

Startled, she saw George had ridden up beside them on a handsome chestnut. Engrossed in their conversation, she had nearly forgotten where they were.

'Good day, Kingsley,' Nicholas said, ignoring his comment.

'And good day to you, Thayne. And, of course, my dear Julia.' He lifted his quizzing glass to his eye and surveyed her. 'Can I believe my eyes? A new bonnet?

Most flattering, my dear. Very *au courant*. You look ravishingly lovely, do you not think, Thayne?'

'George!' Julia said, wanting to disappear. 'Do be quiet!'

'I was merely soliciting Lord Thayne's opinion on your appearance. I assume he has one.'

'He is not obligated to state it, if he does.'

'But why not? I thought the purpose for wearing new clothing was to elicit a response from one's companions, particularly eligible gentlemen.'

She didn't want to disappear, she wanted to commit murder. 'You are mistaken in my case,' she said between clenched teeth. 'I really do not care if Lord Thayne has an opinion or not.'

Nicholas turned to look at her. The corners of his lips twitched. 'Actually, Kingsley is right, I do have an opinion. The bonnet is very becoming on you. And you do look lovely.'

'You were not obliged to say that,' she said stiffly.

'Are you accusing me of insincerity?'

'Of course I am not.' Now she was flustered. 'Please, can we discuss something else? I cannot see that it matters what I wear.'

'Actually it does, my dear,' George said. 'However, I will not belabour the point. Ah, I see the charming Lady Jessica has sighted you and undoubtedly wishes for a chit-chat. So I will be off.' He made a slight bow and, with a flourish, turned his mount around.

They were approaching a trio of young ladies on horses. One of the young ladies broke away from the group and trotted towards them at their approach. 'Nicholas!' Lady Jessica exclaimed.

Nicholas stopped the curricle and she reined in her

mount, a dainty grey. She beamed at them. 'Good day, Lady Carrington. How nice to see you again!'

Julia returned her smile, finding the girl's sincere warmth hard to resist. 'I am glad to see you again as well. What a lovely horse you ride.'

'She was my first gift from Adam after we were married. Her name is Sultana.' Jessica patted the mare's neck. 'Is she not the sweetest thing?' She turned her gaze to Nicholas and gave him a teasing smile. 'I see I now have something else to write Sarah. I believe this is the first time I have caught you driving in the park during the fashionable hour. She will be quite astonished when I tell her.'

'I had no idea driving through the park was such an accomplishment,' Nicholas said drily.

'Oh, but it is. At least for some people,' she added. She smiled back at Julia. 'I had hoped I might see you soon. I know it is rather late notice, but I wish very much to invite you and Lady Simons to a small picnic we are giving in a few days. It will be at our house in Richmond so it is not a great way from here. I will, of course, send you and Lady Simons an invitation, but I had wanted to extend the invitation in person as well.'

'A picnic sounds lovely,' Julia said, rather taken aback by Lady Jessica's warmth towards her, a person she had briefly met just once before.

'I hope you can come. Nicholas will be there as well.'

His brow shot up. 'Will I?' he asked. 'I am beginning to feel slighted at the lack of an invitation extended in person.'

She grinned at him. 'You have one now.'

She turned her mount to catch up with her two companions. Nicholas urged the horses forward again. By now the park was crowded with fashionable carriages of every sort, as well as riders and a number of persons on foot. Their carriage was travelling at a mere snail's pace.

'Your cousin's wife is very kind,' Julia said.

He glanced down at her. 'Yes, she has been very kind. More than kind under the circumstances.' There was a harshness in his voice she did not understand.

'Sarah is your sister?' she asked, hoping that would be a neutral topic.

His face relaxed a notch. 'Yes. She lives in Kent. Her husband is Jessica's brother.'

'I see.' That would explain several things, although not why he had looked so grim. 'Lady Jessica seems very fond of your sister.'

'She is.' He was forced to stop the carriage while they waited for the occupants of a barouche and another curricle to finish their conversation. 'They consider themselves sisters.'

'How lovely,' Julia said a bit wistfully. She had always longed for a sibling, but Thomas had been an only child as well and so there had been no siblings by marriage either. 'I always wanted a sister or a brother. They are very fortunate. So are you.'

The barouche finally moved on and Nicholas urged the horses forward. He looked down at her. 'I am. Did you not have any cousins or such growing up?'

'No. My cousins were all much older than me. My stepfather did not encourage friendships outside of the family. It was not until I went away to school that I finally had a good friend. And then after I married Thomas, there was Sophia.' She smiled. 'She has always been as a sister to me. And Thomas as well. He was my best friend.'

'You were fortunate,' he said softly.

'Yes, I was.'

He looked at her for a moment, his expression unreadable. 'I'd best take you back to Berkeley Square,' he said curtly.

He said nothing more until they reached Sophia's townhouse. The groom dashed forward to hold the team. Nicholas jumped down and then held out his hand to Julia. She stepped down and he released her hand. 'Can you send me the papers today?'

'Yes.' She looked up at his face. 'Why are you doing this? After what I did to you, I would think you would run as far away as possible.'

'Because I would never forgive myself if anything happened to you,' he said shortly.

Under different circumstances and with a different man she might be tempted to take his words as a declaration of love. But she had the sense he was not talking about her at all, but some other woman entirely.

The note was waiting for her in her bedchamber. After Nicholas had left, she had gone directly upstairs to change for dinner. She and Sophia were to dine early with Phillip and then would proceed to a ball at Lord and Lady Middleton's home.

She pulled off her kid gloves and went to place them on her dressing table when she saw the note. She picked it up. The handwriting was unfamiliar. Puzzled, she opened the sheet.

The message was short, the handwriting crude. *You were at Thérèse's. Do not interfere.*

She stared at it for a moment, and then dread slowly washed over her.

Someone had recognised her, despite her mask. Someone knew she had gone there for a purpose other than gambling.

But who? Thérèse, Robert and Nicholas, of course. And André and Hayes. But Hayes had been there only a year and had never met Thomas. André had been with Thérèse for as long as she could remember and had always been nothing but discreet.

She could not imagine that Thérèse or Robert would mention her visit. Or Nicholas, despite his threats to reveal her whereabouts to Sophia.

Or that any one of them knew something about Thomas's death they did not want her to learn.

She sank down on her bed, her legs trembling. The note was clearly an effort to frighten her or warn her, or both. Someone did not want her asking questions.

And it was unlikely the sender of the note would be any more pleased if Nicholas started asking questions. She had already been assaulted, and there had been the highwaymen. What if the note writer decided to progress beyond threats on paper?

Which meant she must explain to Nicholas as soon as possible why she could not accept his help.

Without removing her bonnet or spencer, she sat down at the small writing desk and pulled out a sheet of paper.

The ball was in full swing by the time Nicholas stalked into the Middletons' ballroom. He'd had no intention of attending this particular ball held in honour of the second Middleton daughter, but Julia's polite little note had quickly changed his mind.

He paused just inside the door. A quick perusal revealed no sign of Julia. The dancers were engaged in a lively country dance and the sides of the ballroom were crowded with chaperons and their charges who were not fortunate enough to be engaged with a partner.

A frown crossed his brow and then he spotted Sophia. So, at least she was here, which presumably meant Julia was as well unless she had decided to elude Sophia for another meeting. His frown changed to a scowl. He'd have her head if that was the case.

He started across the room towards Sophia when he suddenly saw Julia standing near the French doors on the other side of the room. She stood with Kingsley, her back to Nicholas. As if sensing Nicholas's interest, Kingsley looked over and saw him. He turned back to Julia and said something to her and then, taking her arm, led her through the French doors to the outside terrace.

Nicholas muttered a curse. What the devil was Kingsley up to now? The music stopped and the dancers began to drift towards the sides of the ballroom. He was forced to step aside as he waited for the crowd to disperse.

'Lord Thayne,' Lady Middleton said. She bustled up to him, beaming. He nearly groaned. Not only was she a notorious gossip, she routinely pounced on eligible bachelors as partners for her daughters. 'How honoured we are to have you! But your poor arm! I do trust it is better! How shocked we were to learn what had happened!'

He stared at her. 'I beg your pardon.'

'The highwayman. How fortunate that you were able to make it to shelter where you were cared for.'

She wagged a finger at him. 'Now, if only we can learn the identity of the mysterious lady who bound your wounds!'

He nearly reeled. Where the devil had she heard this? Not from his grandfather or Phillip. Or Julia. Which left Kingsley. He looked forward to killing him.

He realised Lady Middleton was regarding him with an odd expression. 'There is no mysterious lady, I fear,' he said.

'No?' She arched a brow and then smiled in a disbelieving manner. 'Of course not. I quite understand. But come, let me find you a partner. My Lydia would be honoured to stand up with you.'

He glanced towards the doors, only half-attending. Julia still had not appeared, nor had Kingsley. 'I fear I am obligated for this dance.'

'The next one, then?'

'Yes, the next one,' he said automatically.

'Splendid!' She beamed again.

He finally managed to extricate himself and to escape through the French doors onto the terrace. Lamps at intervals provided light. A few couples stood on the terrace and, at one end, a group of men were engaged in a heated discussion.

Julia and Kingsley had to be in the garden. He quickly ran down the steps. A couple stood in one corner, but the lady was too stout to be Julia. He frowned. And then from his right, he heard Kingsley's unmistakable drawl. 'My dear Julia, did I tell you how lovely I find you? A veritable rose in the moonlight.'

'I think you have finally gone mad!' Julia's voice was filled with exasperation.

Nicholas rounded the corner of the terrace. They sat

on a bench behind a large potted tree. Julia was attempting to rise but Kingsley's grip on her hand prevented her.

'Well?' Nicholas said between gritted teeth.

Julia froze. She sank back down on the bench, her expression a mixture of mortification and apprehension. Kingsley merely smirked. He released Julia's hand. 'Ah, your protector has arrived. And just in time to save you from my ungentlemanly advances.'

Nicholas fixed him with a hard stare. 'Is that what you were attempting?'

'Yes. I fear the moonlight, coupled with the presence of—'

'He was doing no such thing!' Julia declared. She jumped up, her eyes flashing with fury. 'He has spent the entire time telling me the most idiotic gossip and would not let me go in, and suddenly at the last moment decided to possess himself of my hand and pay me an idiotic compliment.'

'I see.' It was all too apparent Kingsley was amusing himself, but Nicholas had no idea why. Just as he had no idea why Kingsley had decided to spread the tale about his encounter with the highwayman. He was beginning to suspect they were related.

He kept his eyes on Kingsley. 'I believe, Kingsley, it is time you and I meet,' he said dispassionately.

'No!' Julia said. 'Please do not!' She looked almost sick. 'George looks very frivolous but he…he is deadly with swords and your arm cannot be completely well!'

Nicholas swung around to stare at her. 'What the devil are you talking about?' Then it dawned on him. 'Don't concern yourself, I am not planning to call him out. Yet.'

George rose in a leisurely movement. 'This little comedy has been extremely amusing. Despite the ungracious remark about my frivolous appearance.' He turned his gaze on Nicholas. 'Just let me know when you wish to meet me, my dear fellow. I will be completely at your service.' He sauntered off.

'I…I should go in as well,' she said, not quite meeting Nicholas' eyes.

He stepped in front of her. 'Not yet. We are going to talk first.'

She frowned at him. 'Are we? I do not think we have anything to talk about.'

'You are quite wrong. We have a number of things to talk about. Such as your note dismissing me from further involvement in your affairs.'

'I decided I did not need your help after all.'

'Indeed. And what caused you to change your mind?'

'After some reflection I…I decided that Phillip was right and there is nothing more to discover about Thomas's death.'

He merely looked at her until she began to fidget. 'Now tell me the real reason,' he said.

'I just told you.'

'What happened in the scant hour since I left you and before your note arrived at my house?' He smiled coolly. 'I can still tell Sophia about your little adventure the other night.'

'No.' She took a deep breath. 'Very well, I will tell you. I received a note as well. I found it on my dressing table after I left you. The note was unsigned. It said not to…to interfere.'

'What else?'

'And that the sender knew I was at Thérèse's.'

He drew in a breath. 'Do you have the note?'

'Yes.'

'Then give it to me. Along with the other papers.'

'No! I cannot! I do not want you involved.' She glanced away and then looked back at him. 'I cannot allow you to be hurt.'

He stared at her. 'You are worried about me?'

'Of course. You have already been injured because of me. I do not want anything more to happen to you on my account.'

'And you were worried Kingsley was going to run me through?'

'Well, yes. That would have been due to me as well.' Her eyes, fixed on him, were large in the pale moonlight. 'I do not think I am a safe person for you to associate with.'

'Probably not.' He stepped towards her, causing her to step back. 'But, as I told you before, I am too tangled in your affairs to extricate myself.'

'You needn't be.' Her voice was breathless. 'You could walk away right now.'

'I do not think I can.' His gaze strayed to her lips, soft and inviting. 'Because then you might be hurt if I do.'

Her eyes widened. 'I...'

He bent his head towards her. He was undoubtedly mad, but he was going to kiss her. 'Julia.'

'Lord Thayne!'

Lady Middleton's shocked tones jerked him back to reality. He spun around to find her behind him. She stared at him and then her gaze narrowed speculatively as it fell on Julia. 'Good evening, Lady Carrington.'

'Good evening, Lady Middleton. We...we were just

about to return to the ballroom,' Julia said in a hollow voice.

Lady Middleton continued to watch her. 'Lord George said I might find Lord Thayne out here. Lord Thayne is obligated for the next dance.' Her tone implied Julia had deliberately kept Nicholas out in the garden in order to thwart her plans.

Nicholas started and then vaguely recalled agreeing to such a thing. Good God. The last thing he wanted to do was stand up with the flirtatious Lady Lydia.

Julia glanced at him. 'Yes. He…he was just saying that, which is why we were about to return to the ballroom.'

'Very good.' Lady Middleton sounded mollified. 'Then you will not object if I whisk him away from you.'

'No, of course not,' Julia said. 'I will go in as well.'

Nicholas had no choice but to leave. He cast one more look at Julia who wore a fixed smile, then he turned and mounted the terrace steps with Lady Middleton. He should be relieved he had been saved from an act of pure folly. Instead, he wanted to roundly curse Lady Middleton for her damnable timing.

Chapter Eleven

Any hopes Julia entertained that Nicholas would forget about the papers were dashed when he came to call the next morning. Julia and Sophia were having breakfast in the small library which overlooked the back garden.

He was shown in, impeccably dressed in a dark blue morning coat and buff pantaloons, his Hessians polished to perfection. Her heart thudded at the sight of his elegant maleness and she had no idea whether it was from nervousness or something else entirely. Sophia smiled. 'Good morning, Nicholas. Will you not join us?'

He returned her smile and shook his head. 'Thank you, but I am not here on a social call. Lady Carrington has an item she is to give me.'

Sophia glanced over at Julia, her expression bemused. 'Indeed. Did you wish it fetched for you?'

'Oh, no. I can do it.' Julia glanced quickly at Nicholas, who merely raised his brow. Why must he ask her in front of Sophia? She rose from the table and frowned at him. 'Could I speak to you for a moment, Lord Thayne?'

'Of course.' He did not move.

'In the hallway, if you please.'

He smiled coolly. 'After you bring me the item.'

He apparently had no intention of budging. Aware of Sophia's curious look, Julia turned and left the room. Really, why ever had she thought he would listen to her? He was as stubborn as Thomas had ever been. Perhaps worse.

The papers were in the bottom of a wardrobe where she had left them. She pulled them out. She had already gone over the list and marked the patrons she knew had had some connection to Thomas. She took this list and returned the other papers to their place.

She clasped the list to her chest and stood, hesitant to go downstairs and turn it over to Nicholas. What choice did she have? If she did not turn it over, he would undoubtedly hound her for it. She could say it was lost, but he was not likely to believe that.

She reluctantly returned to the library. He was alone and stood in front of the tall window looking out at the garden. He turned when he heard her. 'Well?'

'I do not want you involved.'

'You made that clear last night.' He moved towards her and she was suddenly reminded of last night in the garden. Her gaze flew to his mouth and her heart began to thud. Had he really been about to kiss her? Why was she thinking of that now? She forced her mind on to the topic at hand. He stopped in front of her. 'Let me have the paper.'

She stared at his hand. The ring glinted up from his fourth finger. It fitted his strong, lean finger well, as if it had always belonged there. She swallowed, a peculiar lump rising to her throat. Without looking at him, she placed the paper in his hand.

He took it and frowned. 'Is this it?'

She forced herself to speak. 'I have the narratives Thérèse wrote. I did not think there was anything very remarkable. But this is the list of patrons that night. I marked those who knew Thomas.'

'I see.' He looked at her closely for a moment and then turned to the list.

She covertly watched his face, the strong planes of his cheekbones, the long lashes of his eyes. His golden-brown hair, thick and silky, curled just slightly at his neck and she suddenly remembered how soft and silky it had felt under her hands the night she had abducted him.

He glanced up. 'I will start with those you have identified.'

'Yes,' she said distractedly.

'Is something wrong?'

'I beg your pardon?'

'You are staring at me.'

'Oh!' Her cheeks heated. She hurriedly came up with an excuse. 'I...I was wondering how your arm is. Has it healed properly?'

'My arm? I was talking about the paper.'

'Yes, but I was wondering about your arm.'

His gaze travelled over her face and a slight smile touched his mouth. 'What is it? Are you still worried about my welfare? My dear, if you continue in this vein I may start to believe you care about me.' His voice was lightly mocking.

A stab of hurt shot through her. 'There is no need to be horrid about it!' And then could have bitten her tongue. Why could she have not said something light and mocking in return?

An odd expression flitted across his face. 'I did not

mean to be,' he said softly. His hand holding the paper dropped to his side. 'So, are you saying you care about me?'

Mortified, she backed away. 'Of…of course I am concerned about you. I shouldn't want anything more to happen to you because of me.'

'I see. You do not want my death on your conscience?'

'Well, no. That is, I would not want your death anyway. Or anyone else's for that matter.' She had no idea what she was saying.

His expression shuttered. 'It is gratifying to know I at least occupy the same level of esteem as most of humanity in your eyes,' he said shortly. 'I assume that means you don't abhor me.'

'Why would you think I abhor you?' she asked astonished. 'If anything, I would expect the reverse, that you abhor me!'

His brow snapped down. 'Why the devil would I abhor you?'

'Because I abducted you.'

Now, he appeared astonished. 'What the devil does that have to do with anything?' He fixed her with a scowl. 'I don't dislike you at all.'

'Well, I do not dislike you either!'

He stared at her and then suddenly laughed. 'Are we now clear enough on that point? I am glad to discover you do not dislike me.'

'I never have.' She smiled back at him, feeling unexpectedly shy.

'Good,' he said softly. He looked down into her face and his expression slowly changed, the laughter fading from his eyes. She caught her breath, her heart pounding as she met his gaze. Her lips parted, almost as if anticipating his kiss.

He slowly pulled his eyes away. 'I should leave you,' he said abruptly. His voice was husky.

'Yes.' She looked away as well, her cheeks flaming. She prayed he had not noticed her wanton reaction to him.

After he departed, she sank down on a chair, her hands at her still-heated cheeks. She must be going mad. What else could explain her growing preoccupation with him? No, it was not just a preoccupation—it was an attraction. Almost as if she were developing a *tendre* for him.

Which would be completely horrible. She could not allow such a thing. Undoubtedly it was some sort of aberration due to their forced togetherness under such unusual circumstances.

Which undoubtedly accounted for any attraction he might feel for her as well.

The best thing would be to avoid his company as much as possible except as absolutely necessary. She would be civil, of course, but only as befitting the merest acquaintance. And certainly she would endeavour to never find herself alone with him. She feared she might be tempted to do something exceedingly rash.

A night later, Nicholas sat in Thérèse's and watched the Honourable Edward Palmerston, seated across the table from him, polish off his fourth glass of brandy. Nicholas doubted he'd gain much more information from the man now. Not that he'd been particularly helpful—his recollection of the night Carrington had been killed was hazy—undoubtedly he'd been in the same inebriated state he was in now.

Which presented a problem. Not only was he interviewing witnesses about an event that took place three years ago, most of the witnesses who had last seen Carrington had probably been foxed as well. His inquiries so far had yielded nothing of importance.

Nicholas rose. Palmerston set his glass down. 'Leaving so soon, Thayne?' His words were slurred.

'I've another appointment at White's.' He was to meet Adam there shortly.

A gleam of awareness actually crossed Palmerston's face. 'Look at the betting book. Might interest you.' He slumped back down in his chair.

Nicholas shrugged. In his more youthful, albeit wilder days, White's betting book held some curiosity for him. He rarely glanced at it now.

He left Palmerston starting on his fifth glass and quit the private room. Thérèse left the table where she had been presiding, and stopped him on his way out. 'How is Julia?' she asked in a low voice.

'She is well.'

'Good.' Thérèse put a hand on his arm. 'I am glad you are helping her. I do not want her pursuing this matter on her own.'

He stared at her. 'You know what I am doing?'

'But of course.' She arched a delicate brow at his expression and dropped her hand from his arm. 'It is not a secret you have been asking questions about Thomas's death. The question, of course, is why. The general conclusion is that you wish to fix your interest with Julia.'

'Hell.' He scowled.

She looked amused. 'I see you have been too busy

to listen to gossip. Which is rather remarkable since much of it concerns you.'

He stifled a groan. 'What else?'

'There is the tale of your heroic wound by a highwayman and the mysterious woman who nursed you.'

'I've heard that. Kingsley, no doubt.'

'Probably.' She sobered. 'There is the betting book at White's. I have not heard the precise nature of the wager. I fear, however, most of it concerns Julia as well.'

'Blast.' He felt like uttering something much stronger. The gossips would soon suspect Julia was the mysterious woman—if they did not already. 'She will hardly be pleased.' Which was an understatement.

'I fear she will not.' She caught his arm again and looked directly at him. 'I do not want her hurt, Nicholas. She has a kind heart.'

'I've no intention of hurting her,' he said. 'Or of allowing anyone or anything else to do so either.'

The entry in the book at White's hardly improved his temper. *Wager: Lord G. Kingsley wagers the Hon. W. Buntford a certain sum Lord Thayne will wed Lady C. within two months.*

Adam peered over his shoulder. 'Good God! What the devil possessed Kingsley to make such a bet?'

'A death wish. He knows I will have his blood.'

Adam put a restraining hand on his arm. 'I wouldn't if I were you. Unless you want a scandal. And a rift between your family and his.'

The words he'd left out hung unspoken over Nicholas's head. *Unless you want another scandal. And to cause another rift between two families.*

'Of course, you are right,' he said bitterly. 'I can do nothing.'

Adam dropped his hand. 'Except keep your temper. As much as Kingsley probably deserves your wrath, Lady Carrington does not need the additional gossip.'

'No.' It would distress her no end. Particularly if knowledge of this blasted wager got about. She would undoubtedly find some way to blame herself.

He realized Adam was regarding him curiously. 'Well?' Nicholas demanded.

'I was merely wondering what led Kingsley to think you would not be adverse to, er…accompanying Lady Carrington to the altar?'

'I've not the least idea!' Nicholas snapped and then scowled. 'Just the knowledge I was under her roof for five days, I suppose.' He wasn't about to tell Adam about the scene on the sofa. Which meant nothing.

'Is that all? You are rather frequently in her company.'

'That hardly signifies.'

'No? Apparently to Kingsley it does.' Adam regarded him thoughtfully. 'So, what is your next course of action? You had best hope Kingsley does nothing to advance his cause.'

Nicholas smiled rather grimly. 'He will not have the opportunity. I intend to avoid Lady Carrington's company as much as possible.'

'Indeed,' Adam said. 'Does that mean, then, you are not coming to Richmond tomorrow? Lady Simons and Lady Carrington have both accepted Jessica's invitation. I warn you, however, Jessica will be most put out if you do not decide to come. She will undoubtedly write to Sarah as well,' he added with a grin.

Nicholas stifled a groan. How the devil had everything become so damnably tangled? He'd forgotten about the picnic, but he could hardly cry off now. It would distress Jessica and she had been far too kind to him to disappoint her.

Except as politeness dictated, he would stay as far away from Julia as possible.

Julia and Sophia arrived in Richmond shortly before noon. Adam Henslowe's Richmond estate was small but beautifully situated in a large green park. The house, of red brick, had been built a half century ago and stood at the end of a long curving drive.

Since Phillip had gone to his estate near St Albans for a day, George had escorted the ladies. The weather was perfect for a picnic, warm with the sky a nearly cloudless blue. The footman showed them to the large lawn at the back of the house where a number of guests, mostly female, were already present. Long tables had been set up and a number of servants were bringing out trays of food.

Lady Jessica broke away from a small group of ladies when she saw them. She came forward, lovely in a white-sprigged muslin gown tied with a dark green sash and a bonnet trimmed with matching green ribbon. She greeted them, a smile of pleasure on her face.

'I am so glad you could come. How pretty you both look!'

'And so do you,' Sophia said with an answering smile.

Lady Jessica turned to Julia. 'Nicholas has already arrived. I fear, however, the men have already abandoned us to look at the trout stream.' She made a little face.

'Men have a habit of doing such things,' Julia said lightly, trying to ignore the reference to Nicholas. She planned to stay as far away from him as possible.

'Julia?'

She turned and found Robert Haslett standing at her elbow. 'Robert, how nice to see you,' she said, surprised.

He smiled, his eyes crinkling at the corners. 'And how nice to see you as well.'

Jessica looked from one to the other. 'I did not know you knew each other.'

'We are old friends,' he said. His gaze fell on Sophia. 'I do not believe we have met,' he said slowly.

Sophia smiled at him in her friendly way. 'No, we have not.'

Julia quickly performed the introductions. Sophia held out her hand and Robert bowed over it. 'I did not realise Stanton had such a lovely sister,' he said, releasing her hand.

Colour rose to her cheeks. 'I did not realise you knew my brother.'

Several new guests arrived and Jessica excused herself to greet them. 'Shall we find a place to sit?' Robert asked. 'There are some chairs under the trees or we can sit on a spread if you would prefer.'

'Oh, I would like to sit on the spread,' Sophia said. 'I think when one is on a picnic one should be on the grass. Or at least as close to it as possible.'

Robert smiled down at her. 'I agree.'

They found a spot under a spreading oak and seated themselves. Sophia and Robert were soon chattering away with an easy familiarity as if they had known each other a very long time. Watching his rather sober face light up with a smile at something Sophia said, Julia thought he was decidedly smitten.

She could hardly blame him. The light blue of Sophia's gown brought out the lovely blue of her eyes and her porcelain cheeks glowed with soft colour. A pang of envy shot through her.

Not because she wanted Robert for herself. She had always liked him very much, but her feelings were those of a sister. And she could think of no two people who were more deserving of happiness than Sophia and Robert.

So, why did she have such a feeling of longing? She certainly had no desire to fall in love again, to lose herself in another person so completely as she had Thomas. When he died, she felt as if she had died with him.

'Julia? Are you well? You have been so quiet.' Sophia was watching her with concern.

'I was merely thinking. I am fine.' She smiled and attempted to shake off the melancholy that had gripped her for a moment.

Sophia's face relaxed and she smiled back at Julia, a hint of mischief in her eyes. 'Nicholas has returned, I see.'

'Has he?' Julia said with as much disinterest as she could muster. Why did everyone think she was interested in his whereabouts? First Jessica, and now Sophia.

'He is over near the tables.'

'How nice.' She kept her gaze fixed on the stream.

Sophia gave her a peculiar look. Just then Adam appeared near the tables and announced it was time to eat. Robert promptly rose and offered to fetch a plate for each of the ladies.

Sophia looked after him for a moment and then turned to Julia. 'Have you quarrelled with Nicholas?'

Having expected Sophia to comment on Robert, Julia was startled. 'Of course not. Why would you think that?'

'Because he has been casting the most dark glances this way.'

'I have no idea why. We hardly know each other well enough to quarrel.'

Sophia stood. 'Then you won't object if I invite him to sit with us.'

'Sophia!' But Sophia had already walked off towards the tables.

She could get up and leave herself. But that would be too obvious. Besides, whom else would she sit with? Except for Lady Jessica and her husband, and George, she hardly knew anyone else. She was not about to sit near George.

Perhaps Nicholas would refuse. There were undoubtedly a dozen other guests he knew. She stole a glance towards the tables and then nearly blanched. Nicholas was heading in her direction, two full plates of food in his hands. She scooted over onto the other side of the tree. And then felt ridiculous. He might not even be coming in her direction.

Her hopes were dashed when two well-muscled legs clad in buckskin breeches appeared in front of her. She stared at his boots and froze.

'Good day, Lady Carrington.'

Her eyes flew to his face. 'Lord Thayne.' He had a stiff cool look on his face that did not bode well.

'Sophia asked me to bring you a plate of food.'

'How kind,' she said faintly.

'She also invited me to join you.'

'Please sit down.' What else could she say?

He did in a remarkably graceful fashion for a man with two full plates in his hand. She probably would have spilled both of them. He held out one to her. 'This is for you.'

'Thank you,' she said, taking it and then staring down at it. The plate was piled high with lobster patties, and chicken and salad. Even if she had an appetite, she could hardly eat that much food.

'You do not care for lobster patties?' he asked.

She looked up. 'I do. It is only—how much food do you think I can eat in one sitting?'

He made a wry face. 'I beg your pardon. I fear I am out of the habit of procuring plates of food for ladies. I did not want you to go hungry.'

'That seems unlikely.'

He settled back against the tree trunk and balanced the plate of food across his legs. 'So, Haslett is here as well. I imagine you were pleased to see him again,' he said casually.

'Yes, of course.'

'Have you seem him often since your husband's death?'

'No.' She was puzzled by his question, but even more by the fact he was not looking at her. 'The other night was the first time since shortly after Thomas's death.'

'But you know him well.'

'Yes.' She glanced at him. 'Why are you asking? Do you think he has something to do with...with Thomas?'

'No,' he said shortly.

'Then why the questions?'

He shrugged. 'I merely wondered why you were

holding his hand at Thérèse's.' He forked a piece of chicken and brought it to his mouth.

She nearly dropped her plate. He had seen that? And why ever was he bringing it up now? 'If you must know, he had just told me he lost his wife. I was offering him sympathy,' she said icily.

'I am sorry.' He was silent a moment and then he looked at her. 'Do you always hold men's hands when you offer sympathy?'

'No. Not that it is any of your concern.'

'Would you hold mine if I needed sympathy?'

Her mouth fell open. 'I beg your pardon?'

'I was merely inquiring as to how far your sympathy would extend. So, would you?'

Heat stole into her cheeks. 'This is a…a most ridiculous conversation! Have you had too much wine?' She had no idea how to read his mood. And where were Sophia and Robert?

'Not yet.' He put his fork down. 'I've made a few inquiries,' he said abruptly.

'Inquiries?' Her mind was blank for a moment. 'Oh! Have you discovered anything?' she asked.

He started to speak and then looked over her shoulder. 'Sophia and Haslett are returning.'

No further opportunities for conversation presented themselves. Robert seated himself beside her and Sophia sat next to Nicholas. They were soon joined by several other guests. Robert looked at Julia's plate. 'You have not eaten much.'

She smiled. 'It would be hard to tell with so much food.'

His mouth curved in an answering smile. 'Very true.' He sobered. 'Have you learned anything more about Thomas's death?' he asked in a low voice.

'Not very much.' She debated whether to tell him that Nicholas was helping her and decided against it. She feared it would make things more complicated.

'I will be glad to help you any way I can,' Robert said.

She flashed him a grateful smile. 'Thank you.'

'I do not like the idea of you making the sort of inquiries you did at Thérèse's.'

He was starting to sound like Nicholas. And every other male in her life. She glanced at Nicholas and found he was watching her with a cool, impenetrable stare, as if he'd caught her in some wrongdoing. Had he overheard? She hastily turned her gaze back to Robert. 'I am doing nothing dangerous. You must tell me how long you have been in England and how you find it after living away for such a time.'

He complied and they spent the rest of the meal in an easy discussion which Sophia soon joined. Julia had a difficult time keeping her mind on the conversation. She was all too aware of Nicholas, who seemed to be engaged in a flirtation with Lady Serena Lyndon, the dashing daughter of the Earl of Mooreland. She was a young woman with a sultry voice and equally sultry dark eyes. Too sultry, in Julia's opinion, for someone who could not be much past twenty. Despite her intention to ignore him, she found herself glancing their way, only to be met by the maddening sight of Nicholas actually smiling at something Lady Serena said. She felt like throwing her plate at him. How dare he smile at Lady Serena when he did nothing but glare at her?

But why should he do anything else? She had done nothing but bring him trouble and had managed to embroil him in her affairs. He had made it clear, perhaps not in so many words, that he was only doing so out of some sense of guilt over the lady he had loved.

She took a few more bites and set her plate down. Sophia and Robert had fallen into conversation again. Julia stood and Sophia looked up. 'I thought I might take a short walk,' Julia said.

'Do you wish us to go with you?' Robert asked.

She shook her head and smiled. 'And disturb you when you are so comfortable? I will not go far.'

She walked across the lawn towards the stream. She saw George watching her and hoped he would not decide to accompany her. She was not in the mood for his odd remarks. However, one of his cronies said something to him and he turned away.

A narrow dirt path ran along one side of the stream. She started along the walk, the sun warm and pleasant on her arms. The stream bank was shaded by trees and a tangle of shrubs. After a while, she stopped to watch the water as it tumbled over the rocks into a deeper pool before continuing on its way. The gurgle of the stream and the chirping of the birds were the only sounds she heard and she realised she had gone farther than she had intended.

She stood for a few moments and reluctantly turned around. And then gasped. Nicholas stood behind her, his arms folded across his chest. 'What the devil are you doing?' he demanded.

She lifted her chin. 'I am taking a walk, which should be quite obvious.'

'What is quite obvious is you are by yourself.'

'Not quite. You are here.' She gave him a defiant little smile.

He took a step towards her. 'Now I am.' He sounded as if he was about to lose all patience. 'Before

I was not, which means you were alone. Which means, my dear, if someone decided to cause you harm, you would have no recourse.'

She had not thought of that, but she wasn't about to let him know. 'At a private picnic? How ridiculous, Lord Thayne.'

His brow snapped further down. 'You do not know that.'

'No?' she said sweetly. 'And you do not know that someone will. At any rate, my welfare is none of your concern.' She had no idea what she hoped to accomplish by goading him in such a way, but ever since she had watched him with Lady Serena she had been possessed with the strongest urge to annoy him.

'Isn't it, my dear?' He came towards her, his expression black. Despite her resolution to remain still she found herself backing towards the stream.

His face changed. 'Julia! Stop!'

But it was too late. Her foot caught in an exposed root; the next thing she knew, she was tumbling backwards down the sloping bank. She hit the water with a splash and went under for a moment before she came up, gasping. Her feet slipped on the rocks, but she managed to grab a branch before she fell again. Suddenly Nicholas was in the water beside her.

He grabbed her arms and pulled her up. She landed against his chest and he staggered as he pulled her up onto the gently sloped bank. He fell back on the bank with her and suddenly she was on top of him and staring down into his face.

'Are you all right?' he asked. 'My God! You could have drowned!'

'I can swim.' Her mouth barely formed the words. She was wet and stunned and all she could think of

was the fact his brown eyes were flecked with gold
and his lashes were thick and long. And his mouth
was a mere breath away from her own.

His eyes darkened and suddenly she could not
breathe. 'Good,' he whispered. His hand tangled in her
hair and, just before he pulled her to him, she realised
her bonnet was gone.

She closed her eyes. His lips were warm and firm
as they moved over hers in a gentle caress. The
warmth from his body seeped through the dampness
of her clothes. His arm now draped across her back
moulded her to his hard male curves.

Her lips parted under the insistent pressure of his
mouth and his tongue slipped inside her mouth. He
tasted male and intriguing. A slow heat began to form
in her stomach. Through her thin damp gown she
could feel the evidence of an answering desire.

Evidence that suddenly brought her to her senses.
Whatever was she doing? Her eyes flew open. He
abruptly removed his mouth from hers and stared at
her for a moment, his expression dazed.

'Perhaps I should get up,' she whispered.

He released her. Embarrassed, she rolled off of him
and sat up. Reality returned as quickly as the loss of
his warmth. She was in a dirty, wet gown with her
hair hanging down her back. She undoubtedly looked
like a half-drowned puppy.

Nicholas had sat up beside her. She stole a quick
glance and saw his breeches were wet and his coat
spotted with water. 'I am sorry,' she said, averting her
gaze.

'Why?'

'Because of me you are now wet. I have probably
ruined your clothes.'

'The kiss more than made up for any damage you might have done to my attire.'

She started. 'The…the kiss?'

Although she still stared at the stream, she could almost see his brow rise. 'Yes, the kiss. Perhaps you recall? The exercise where our lips met and…'

This time she did look at him. His expression was quizzical. 'I know perfectly well what we did!' she snapped. 'Please, I would rather not discuss it!' It was bad enough she had allowed such a thing to happen. Worse had been her response. And her desire for much more.

He stared at her for a moment. 'Very well,' he said shortly. He stood up in one smooth movement and then held out his hand to her. 'I need to get you back to the house.'

She put her hand in his and he helped her to her feet. She started to pull her hand out of his warm grasp, but his grip only tightened. 'Wait,' he said.

She looked up at him, puzzled by his tone.

'Did you really think I meant to hurt you?' he asked.

'I beg your pardon?'

'Before you fell. You were backing away from me.' He gave a short laugh. 'As if you thought I was going to hurt you.'

For an odd moment, she glimpsed the vulnerability beneath his cool façade. 'Oh, no!' she said. 'That was not it at all. For a moment, you looked rather fierce, but I was not really afraid of you. I just stepped away and then I tripped.' Impulsively, she laid a hand on his arm. 'I do not think you would ever hurt me.'

He stood very still and looked down at her hand. 'No. I would not hurt you.'

'So you need not blame yourself. It was an accident.'

He lifted his head. 'Was the kiss an accident as well?'

'Yes. I think so.'

A slight smile touched his lips. 'You are not certain? Should we find out?'

Her pulse quickened. 'I think that is a very dangerous idea.'

'Undoubtedly. But everything about you is dangerous.' He cupped the back of her neck with a gentle hand and her eyes fluttered shut as he bent his head. His lips touched hers and then he suddenly jerked his head up. 'Damn.'

Her eyes flew open. Nicholas dropped his hands, his gaze going to something over her shoulders. With a feeling of dread, she slowly turned. George and Lady Serena stood in the clearing at the top of the slight rise from the stream. Behind them was Adam Henslowe.

George smiled. 'Well, perhaps this means there is to be an interesting announcement after all.'

Nicholas moved so he half-shielded her from the others. 'She fell into the stream,' he said coolly.

'Which, of course, explains why you were embracing her,' George said, his voice bland.

Nicholas started towards him, the look on his face murderous. Julia stood rooted, unable to move. Lady Serena gasped.

Adam caught his arm. 'Nick,' he said in a low voice. 'Lady Carrington is cold. Perhaps we should take her back to the house.'

Nicholas stopped. He stared at George in such a

way, that for once, the smirk vanished from George's face.

'Was it really necessary to spoilsport, Mr Henslowe?' Lady Serena inquired archly.

'Yes,' Adam said curtly. He walked down the bank to Julia's side. He asked no questions and merely removed his coat. 'Put this over your shoulders. Jessica can loan you some dry clothes.'

'Thank you.' She found she was shivering, but it was not only from the cold.

They made it back to the others without bloodshed. Adam stayed at her side as if he intended to protect her. She dared not glance at Nicholas, who walked on Adam's other side. George and Lady Serena trailed behind them in silence. When they finally reached the lawn behind the house, Sophia ran to her side, her eyes wide with worry. 'Julia? What happened?'

'I fell into the stream. Lord Thayne pulled me out.' Julia avoided looking at him.

'Nicholas?' Sophia turned to him. 'Thank goodness you were there. But how did such a thing come to happen?'

Julia touched her arm. 'It…it was such a stupid thing. I tripped.' Despite the coat she was starting to shake again.

By now the other guests had gathered around with murmurs of sympathy and shock. Jessica appeared at her side and took her arm. 'Come, we will go in the house.'

An hour later, Julia sat in Jessica's dressing room on a chaise-longue, a quilt over her knees and a cup of hot tea on the small table next to her. Jessica had been everything that was kind, sending the maid to help Julia out of her wet clothes, and to clean the mud from her skin and hair. After that she had provided her with a change of dry clothing.

And then Jessica had left Julia in her dressing room and told her she must rest before joining the others. But now, in the quiet of the room, Julia's mind refused to co-operate. How could she have been so stupid? Not only to fall into a stream, but to allow Nicholas to kiss her? Not that it was entirely his fault. She had kissed him back, which somehow made it even worse.

And then to be discovered in such a way! She wanted to shudder every time she thought of it. Adam had said nothing but George had had a most odd gleam in his eye. And what of Lady Serena? Could she be discreet enough to keep what she saw to herself? It was only a kiss after all. And a very discreet one. Not like the first one. If the others had arrived a few minutes earlier…this time she did shudder.

Besides, neither she nor Nicholas were married, and she was a widow, not a innocent young debutante, so perhaps nothing would be made of the incident.

She could only pray so.

Adam entered the dressing room just as Nicholas finished tucking the loaned shirt into a pair of Adam's black breeches. His shoulders were broader than his cousin's and his legs longer so the items were tight, but at least they were dry.

'You look a bit more civilized,' Adam remarked, leaning against the doorway.

Nicholas grimaced. 'I feel more civilized. I will own, the swim was unexpected.'

'I doubt Lady Carrington expected it either.'

Nicholas cast a swift glance at his cousin. 'How is

she?' he asked cautiously. He'd hardly blame her if she refused to speak to him again after today. His behaviour had been despicable in every regard. He'd allowed the wholly unexpected and possessive jealousy he had felt over Haslett's attentions to her override his judgment. So, when she had ended up in his arms, her soft curves pressing against him, her lovely face hovering over him, he had not been able to resist.

Of course, if that wasn't enough, he had kissed her again and then tried to mow Kingsley down.

'Jessica has loaned her dry clothing. She is in Jess's private drawing room.' Adam eyed Nicholas curiously. 'I must commend her, she seems to be quite composed considering she not only fell into a stream but was caught with you in a rather compromising position.'

To his chagrin, Nicholas felt heat creep up his neck. He gave a short laugh. 'Don't be fooled, she probably hopes she'll never lay eyes on me again.'

'I somehow doubt that,' Adam said. 'You played rather nicely into George's hands, you know. I will say nothing, but I cannot vouch for Lady Serena, although I hope she realises it would not be in her best interest to spread rumours. But Kingsley is another matter. Have you thought what you'll do if he decides to use this to further his cause?'

Nicholas turned around and stared at him. 'What will I do? As much as I am loath to give Kingsley the satisfaction, he will win his wager.' He smiled grimly. 'I will marry her.'

Chapter Twelve

Sophia set down her coffee cup and looked at Julia, who was seated across from her at breakfast. 'I do not wish to pry, but did something happen between you and Nicholas? Beside your falling in the stream?'

Julia glanced quickly up from her nearly untouched plate of toast. 'Why do you ask?'

'You have been so subdued since yesterday. Nicholas was not much better. In fact, after you both changed your clothes and returned to the company, you appeared to be avoiding one another.' She made a little face. 'I fear I was not the only one who thought so. Did you quarrel?'

'No, we did not quarrel.' If only that had been all that had happened.

'Are you certain?' Sophia asked. 'He wore such a black look when he saw you had gone to walk along the stream and then when he followed you, I feared he meant to say something dreadful to you! And if he did, I will make him extremely sorry!'

Julia stared at her, astounded by the vehemence in her friend's voice. Sophia looked so militant, Julia feared she really would say something to Nicholas if she did not learn the truth. 'He kissed me.'

'Good heavens!' Sophia exclaimed. Her eyes widened for a moment, and then her mouth curved in a smile. 'I wondered when he would get around to doing so.'

'Sophia!'

'It is quite obvious he has wanted to for an age.' Her blue eyes sparkled with teasing laughter. 'Good heavens! I am not certain you both needed to be so glum about it, however.'

Julia sighed. 'That is not the whole of it.' She might as well confess everything. She feared it would soon reach Sophia's ears any way. 'George, Lady Serena and Mr Henslowe saw us.'

'Oh, dear.' The teasing look left Sophia's face. 'That was rather unfortunate.' She paused and then asked delicately, 'Was it a very…that is, a very complicated kiss?'

'A complicated kiss?' Julia stared for a moment and then Sophia's meaning dawned upon her. 'No, that particular kiss was not.' And then felt her face heat. She hadn't meant to disclose there had been more than one.

'Well, that isn't so bad,' Sophia said doubtfully.

'But that isn't the worst.' Julia took a deep breath. 'George made some stupid remark about whether there was to be an announcement and Nich—Lord Thayne started towards him. If Mr Henslowe had not stopped him, I think he would have knocked George down. Lady Serena accused Mr Henslowe of spoiling sport.'

'Oh, dear,' Sophia said again. 'Shall I speak to Phillip? He can handle George, although I do not know what to do about Lady Serena.'

'Please do not say anything to Phillip.' He took the promise he made to Thomas to watch over her too seriously. The rift between him and George was too great already and she did not want to widen it further. Most certainly she did not want to cause any tension between him and Nicholas.

'But…' Sophia began.

'Please, I am certain everything will be fine.' She gave Sophia a reassuring smile. 'I do not want Phillip to worry about this as well.'

'If you are certain.' Sophia pushed her coffee cup away and then eyed Julia. 'So there was another more complicated kiss?'

Julia's face heated. 'I am certain it was merely an aberration.'

'Perhaps, but did you like it?'

'Sophia!'

'Well, you must have if there was a second one. And for some reason, I expect he does it very well.' Sophia arched a delicate brow. 'Well, does he?'

'Sophia. Yes. I…I suppose so. I haven't had much experience. Just Thomas.' Which was something else that had completely bewildered her. She had never thought that after Thomas she would desire another man's kisses.

'So you did like it.'

Why lie? Sophia had always said she was too transparent to tell a believable falsehood. 'Yes, but I wish I had not.'

'It has been three years since Thomas,' Sophia said gently. 'I do not think it is wrong for you to like another man's kisses.'

'I do not wish to like his.' Julia gave Sophia a shaky smile. 'My association with him seems to be nothing but disastrous. I have made up my mind about one thing, however. I intend to avoid him until I leave London.'

'Well, I don't wish to overset you, but I fear that will be rather difficult.' She gave Julia an apologetic little smile. 'Lord Monteville has sent us an invitation to join him in his box tonight at the opera. Nicholas will be there as well.'

After breakfast, Sophia sat down at the small desk in one corner of the library to answer her correspondence. Julia paced to the window and looked out at the street. The grey sky drizzled rain. Except for the green grass in the centre of the square, she could see nothing but the buildings. A wave of homesickness for Foxwood washed over her. Barbara and Eduardo would take good care of the farm and its four-legged residents, but she missed them very much.

She turned away from the window. How much longer could she stay in London? Her search for Thomas's killer seemed to be fraught with difficulties and had become inextricably entwined with Nicholas. Perhaps Phillip was right—there was nothing more to his death than a mere robbery.

Was there a way of ever knowing?

Which was perhaps the question she had to answer before she considered leaving London. And she did not know how else to do so without involving Nicholas.

The one man she should, if she had an ounce of sense, avoid. Particularly after yesterday.

This was ridiculous. She could not afford to waste time thinking about a kiss. It had meant nothing. Not to her. Or to Nicholas. It was obvious he still cared deeply for the woman he had loved and lost, just as she still cared for Thomas. As she had told Sophia, yesterday had been an aberration for both of them.

Nicholas had just entered White's when Phillip appeared at his side. 'I need to speak to you,' he said without preamble.

'Of course. I had no idea you were back in town.'

'I arrived late last night.' From the grim look on Phillip's face, Nicholas suspected the interview was not for pleasure. Had he already got wind of yesterday's débâcle?

He followed Phillip to a table in the morning room. The older man waited until they were seated and the waiter had taken their order before speaking. 'There are rumours you have been inquiring after Thomas's death. Is this true?'

'I have made a few inquiries.'

Phillip frowned. 'Why?'

'Because the alternative is to have Lady Carrington do so.'

'She has told you her suspicions?'

'She has told me she is determined to discover who killed her husband. However, I do not think it safe for her to go about asking questions on her own.'

'And so you offered to do it for her. I see.' Phillip leaned back. 'Very wise of you, but unnecessary. I assume you have discovered nothing useful.'

'No.' Unless he counted the information Julia learned from Haslett. Information Phillip already knew.

'I thought not. Certainly not after so much time has passed.'

'But you have not been able to convince Lady Carrington of that,' Nicholas said.

'No.' Phillip's brows drew together. 'It is in a sense unfortunate she saw the ring again for it has given her hope that is most likely false. But perhaps if you continue to ask a few questions, it will satisfy her enough so she will cease asking questions on her own. I hope that in time she will let the matter rest.'

'Perhaps.' For some reason, the conversation made Nicholas uneasy but he could not quite pinpoint why.

Phillip adroitly changed the topic, but it did not concern Julia. Apparently, he had not yet heard any of the rumours. Or George had yet to spread them.

Phillip left White's an hour later. The sense of uneasiness Nicholas had felt with Phillip returned in full force. He had planned to visit Tattersall's to view the contents of a stable up for auction, but he changed his mind. Instead he headed for Grosvenor Square.

Monteville's secretary was seated at a table in the small room off the library. Colton looked up as Nicholas entered and stood. He was a serious young man with sandy hair and a pair of intelligent grey eyes.

'Good day, Lord Thayne.' He removed his spectacles. 'What may I do for you?'

Nicholas came to stand in front of the table. 'My grandfather has said you are at my disposal if needed.'

Colton nodded. 'Yes, he has said so on several occasions.'

'Then I have a task for you.' He doubted if his grandfather had quite intended that he should send his secretary out of London for a few days, but he would deal with that detail later.

Chapter Thirteen

Phillip came to escort Sophia and Julia to the King's Theatre. Julia's apprehension that he had heard some sort of rumours about yesterday's affair appeared to be unfounded for he said nothing. She began to relax. Perhaps George and Lady Serena would not mention it after all. But as they travelled through the dark London streets, nervousness began to set in for another reason.

She dreaded meeting Nicholas.

She would pretend nothing had happened.

The street in front of the King's Theatre was filled with carriages. They were forced to wait until their carriage could stop near the entrance and then Phillip helped them down.

Julia had not been in the King's Theatre before. She was taken aback by the crowded lobby and the expensive, glittering clothing of the patrons. Sophia had told her no one was admitted unless in full dress.

She paused for a moment to let an elderly lady and two younger women pass, all dressed in magnificent silks and jewels, and then realised she had lost Sophia and Phillip in the crowd. Panic gripped her for a moment and then she calmed herself. Surely they would realize she was missing and wait for her. If not, she could ask someone to direct her to Lord Monteville's box.

And then someone touched her arm. She gasped and spun around.

Nicholas stood behind her. 'You seem to have lost your party already.'

'Oh!' Her hand went to her throat. Relief mixed with a dozen other emotions coursed through her. In pure black, relieved only by the white ruffles at his wrists and his white waistcoat and gloves, he looked incredibly handsome. Her mouth went dry, but she managed to say, 'What are you doing here?'

His brow rose quizzically. 'I am planning to watch an opera. And you?'

'The same, of course. That is, if I can determine where the rest of my party is.' She found herself smiling at him, so great was her relief.

He stared at her for a moment and then held out his arm. 'You are fortunate tonight, for I happen to be one of your party.'

'Yes.' She took his arm. 'Thank you. You do not know how worried I was. I know it is very silly of me but for a moment—' She realized she was babbling and stopped.

'For a moment you what?' He looked down at her, a slight smile on his face and for an instant, despite the crowd, she felt as if they were the only two people in the world. She was hardly aware of the voices and laughter swirling around them.

The awareness in his eyes mirrored her own. Her world suddenly seemed to shift and she caught her breath. 'I...I felt as if I was lost.'

He smiled. 'Here? But you are not. You are quite safe.'

'Yes.' She was now and she returned his smile.

'Ah. Determined to provide more fuel for the gossip mill, I see.' George appeared as if on cue beside them.

'Good evening, Kingsley,' Nicholas said coolly. He glanced down at Julia. 'Perhaps we should continue on to the box.'

Gone was the warmth that had sprang up between them. She felt bereft, as if the sun had suddenly disappeared behind a dark cloud. 'Of course.'

They proceeded across the lobby and up the staircase. George walked on Julia's other side. Apparently oblivious to the fact his presence was unwelcome, he filled Julia's ears with a steady stream of arch comments on the dress of everyone they passed. His monologue, combined with Nicholas's tense silence, threatened to set her nerves on edge.

Despite her trepidation at spending an evening in Lord Monteville's box, Julia was nearly weak with relief when they reached it. Her relief increased when she saw that Sophia and Phillip were already there with the Earl.

Nicholas released her arm. Sophia greeted them with a pleased smile and then turned to Julia. 'I do hope you are not too angry with us, but by the time I noticed you were not with us I saw that Nicholas had found you and I knew he would see you here.'

'And I found them and made certain they actually reached the box. Otherwise, I fear they intended to spend the evening in the lobby, staring at one another,' George said.

Julia's cheeks heated while Phillip gave him a cold

look. 'I trust you will keep such speculations to yourself.'

George shrugged. 'I can, of course, but I fear I cannot control what others might think. I merely wished to protect Julia from gossip.'

'Since there is nothing to cause gossip, she has no need of your protection,' Nicholas drawled. His face held supreme indifference, but his stance was that of a tiger about to spring.

'Isn't there, Thayne?' George drawled.

Nicholas took a step forward. 'What the devil do you mean by that?' he asked in a low voice.

Julia froze, the blood pounding in her ears. The scene had all the horrible familiar aspect of a recurring nightmare. They would not possibly start a brawl in front of their families and most of the *ton*?

'I fear you are both forgetting your manners,' Monteville said. His gaze rested on Julia. 'Lady Carrington would undoubtedly like to take her seat and, since you are blocking the entrance to the box, you are rendering that impossible. Lady Carrington, perhaps you would do me the honour of sitting next to me?'

His calm words broke the standstill. 'I beg your pardon,' Nicholas said stiffly. He moved aside and, without looking at him, Julia took her place next to the Earl. To her dismay, she found her hands were trembling.

George executed an elaborate bow. 'A most interesting encounter as usual. Good evening to all.'

Julia didn't dare look at anyone. Her throat was dry and her stomach was knotted and she wanted nothing more than to disappear.

'My dear, there is nothing to distress yourself about,' Monteville said gently.

She looked swiftly up at him. 'I am very sorry.'

He raised a brow. 'I cannot imagine why. Unless of course, you deliberately provoked the regrettable behaviour of both my grandson and Lord George.'

'No, I did not, my lord, but—'

'Then you've nothing to reproach yourself for. I suggest you enjoy the performance and put the rest of this from your mind.' He spoke kindly but firmly.

She managed a smile. 'I will try.'

'Good. Have you been to the King's Theatre before?' he asked.

'I have not.' She tried to follow his lead, keeping her voice polite and conversational as if nothing untoward had happened.

She found any sort of concentration impossible once the performance began. She scarcely noticed when the curtain came down and the interval arrived. Their box was suddenly filled with visitors and she found herself smiling and nodding and attempting to respond to the remarks addressed to her. The effort was tiring. Lady Middleton entered the box with her eldest daughter and soon cornered Nicholas. She only relaxed when Robert appeared and engaged her and Sophia in conversation. She glanced at Nicholas once and found him regarding her with a dark expression. She looked quickly away. What was wrong with him now?

She was taken aback, however, when they finally took their seats for the second half, to find him taking the place next to her. She cast him a startled glance. His brow shot up. 'I am merely sitting by you, not planning a ravishment.'

'I hardly thought that!'

'Good. I wouldn't want Kingsley's remarks to worry you.'

'I assure you they did not. I have scarcely given them a thought.'

'No?' He looked completely disbelieving.

'No!' She frowned at him. 'Perhaps we should watch the performance.' She turned away. They were speaking in low tones, but she feared they would be overheard.

'If you wish. Although I wasn't aware you paid much heed to the first half.'

She looked back and levelled her most cool look at him. 'And how would you know?'

'Because I was watching you.' He gave her a satisfied smile.

'You should have been watching the stage.'

'You are more interesting.'

She flushed in spite of herself. 'I assure you I am not!' She turned away again, determined not to respond to anything else he might say. To her immense relief, he said no more.

Flustered, she stared at the stage. Had he been flirting with her? No, that was completely impossible.

Nicholas stole a glance at Julia's delicate profile. From all appearances, she was so engrossed in the performance his presence was completely forgotten. The only thing that gave her away was that if he so much as shifted, her hand tensed around her fan.

Or if he stared at her as he was doing now. He slowly pulled his gaze away and back to the stage where the soprano was singing an impassioned aria. Why the devil did he persist in teasing her?

He scowled. He knew perfectly well why. Teasing her was a mask for his real desire. A desire to pull her into his arms and make love to her until she lost all resistance.

And then what? She was not the sort of woman he wanted as a mistress. His few liaisons since Mary's death had been with upper-class women who expected nothing more from him than his body and a few expensive jewels. He had quickly curtailed the one relationship that might have promised more.

But even if he were to make such a foolish proposition, she would never accept. He'd seen the awareness in her eye, but she would fight him every step of the way. Three years ago, before Mary, before his world had shattered, he might have considered Julia a challenge and set out to seduce her with very little conscience. But that was before he learned that the emotions of others were not something that could be so carelessly dismissed in the pursuit of pleasure.

Nor were his.

With a start, he realised the audience was applauding. Had the interminable performance ended at last? Apparently so, for the music had ceased and the singers were on stage taking their final bows.

The party made their way out of the box and to one of the downstairs rooms where they waited for the carriages to be brought around. The room was crowded and conversation difficult. Although he had determined he would avoid Julia as much as possible, he was hardly gratified to find she apparently had the same thought in mind.

When they finally made their way to where the long line of carriages waited, she kept to Sophia's side.

Which was why, when she stumbled, he had no hope of catching her.

She fell directly into the street between two carriages. Sophia screamed. The startled horses shied back and heedless of the prancing animals, Nicholas shot forward, terrified she would be crushed.

She had fallen face first. He barely registered that Haslett had sprung forward to calm the horses. Nicholas reached down and lifted her into his arms and carried her out of danger. Her face was pale and her eyes fluttered open to look at him. 'Oh, dear,' she said weakly.

'Don't try to talk.' He levelled a frown at her. 'Do you hurt anywhere?'

She gave him a faint smile. 'How can I answer that if I can't talk? Please, my lord, put me down.'

'No.'

The horrified crowd had gathered around. Sophia, her face white, had just pushed past a large gentleman when someone touched Nicholas's shoulder. He turned and saw Robert Haslett at his side. His face mirrored Nicholas's own shock. 'Perhaps it would be best if you brought Julia to my carriage,' Haslett said. 'I regret to say, it is the one she nearly fell in front of.'

Hell. Haslett was one of the last persons he wanted to entrust Julia with. He was about to refuse when Sophia spoke up. 'That would be very kind. Do you not think, Nicholas?'

Julia made a movement in his arms. 'Please, I'd rather walk.'

'Not now.' He hesitated. He had no intention of putting her down. But making his way through the crowd to Stanton's or his grandfather's carriage seemed impossible.

'This is not the time to let your personal feelings

overcome common sense,' Haslett said with more than a touch of irony.

Nicholas looked at him for a moment. 'You are right.'

He carried her to the carriage and set her gently on the seat. She looked as pale and fragile as she had the night she'd been hurt at Foxwood. A fierce desire to protect her surged through him. 'How do you feel?' His voice was more abrupt than he intended.

'I am fine. Just horribly mortified. To fall on my face in front of half of London.' Her voice trembled as if she was about to cry.

He resisted the urge to gently touch her cheek. 'There is no need to concern yourself over that. In the future, however, you'd best step into a carriage rather than the street.'

His feeble attempt at humour brought a faint smile to her face. Then her brow creased. 'I really had not meant to take a step at all.'

Before he could ask what she meant, he heard Phillip's voice behind him. 'How is she?'

He turned. 'Well enough under the circumstances.'

'Thank God.' Phillip's face wore a peculiar expression.

Nicholas frowned. In the commotion he realised he'd paid scant heed to the whereabouts of either Phillip or his grandfather. And the fact they had not been at Julia's side was decidedly odd. 'What is it?'

Phillip hesitated and then spoke in a low voice. 'Several witnesses claim she was pushed.'

Nicholas felt as if he'd been punched. His mind searched for any other rational explanation. 'How can they be certain? There is enough of a crowd that it would be impossible to tell. Perhaps she was merely jostled.' Even to his own ears his words sounded feeble.

'I would have said the same except for the identity of one of the witnesses. His impression I cannot question.' Phillip looked straight at him. 'You see, Monteville saw the entire incident.'

Chapter Fourteen

Nicholas had just left his bank the following morning when he once again saw Ernest Grayson. Grayson was descending the steps of Fisk and Fisk, a business on the opposite side of the street, with the furtive air often seen in those visiting a moneylender.

Grayson was as soberly and inconspicuously dressed as he had been when he had first approached Nicholas. The older man looked down the street both ways and then started off.

Nicholas dashed across the road, heedless of the disgruntled traffic. Grayson was just about to cross the next street when Nicholas came up behind him.

He turned and his face paled. Nicholas smiled coolly. 'I have been hoping to find you again.'

Grayson eyed him with disfavour. He was a thin, neatly dressed man in his mid-thirties with the air of a harried clerk. 'Indeed, my lord. I had the most distinct impression that you had no desire to pursue the matter any further.'

'I've changed my mind. I wish to talk to you.'

Grayson gave him a hassled look. 'I do not know if the offer is still open. I would need to consult with my client first. If you will pardon me, I have another appointment.' He started across the street.

Nicholas fell into step beside him. 'Precisely who is your client? I am beginning to think I should deal with him directly.'

Grayson looked straight ahead. 'I cannot tell you.'

'You cannot or will not?'

He hesitated a fraction. 'Both.'

'I am willing to pay you handsomely for the information.'

Again hesitation. 'I think not, my lord.'

'Fisk is not known for his patience in waiting for repayment of his loans. I am certain he would not object if I offered to pay your debts. Of course, you would then be indebted to me.'

Grayson swallowed. 'I…' He cast a furtive look around as if he expected Fisk to pounce out of the shadows. 'I cannot discuss this here. Perhaps, my lord, we could meet elsewhere.'

'Your lodgings?'

'No!' He appeared almost terrified. 'I do not want you calling there. I fear that I may be followed. To-night. At Vauxhall. I will be there with a small party. Four gentlemen and three ladies. We will arrive by boat and proceed to a private box where—'

'At the end of the Grand Walk. At eleven.' He feared the man was about to describe their supper plans next. 'And if you fail to meet me, I've no doubt I can discover your whereabouts easily enough.'

'Of course.' With a distracted expression, he dashed off.

Nicholas watched him go. He'd run Grayson to ground if the man failed to show up. After last night, he wanted more than anything to find out who was behind the attacks on Julia. He intended to make sure the man would rue his existence.

He walked to his carriage. Guilt mixed with anger had assailed him ever since last night. She had been injured under his nose. He had failed to protect her.

He could not fail again.

'Good day, Lord George!'

George urged his horse alongside the phaeton in which Lady Serena Lyndon sat with her widowed cousin, Mrs Harriet Winslet. He bowed and smiled. He knew Lady Serena's habit of driving daily in the park and had been lying in wait for her stylish phaeton.

After last night, it was time to play his hand.

Lady Serena was a notorious rumour-monger. The only thing that kept her from being ostracised was her huge fortune and the fact that most of the tales she spread had more than a hint of truth. He bestowed one of his most charming smiles upon them. 'Ah, two of England's most lovely flowers. Good day, Lady Serena, Mrs Winslet. I am delighted to see you both.'

Mrs Winslet smiled a trifle nervously. She was a timid woman who undoubtedly allowed her companion to ride roughshod over her. Lady Serena acknowledged the compliment with an insincere nod. 'And I am very delighted to see you, Lord George,' she said with a meaningful look.

'Indeed.'

'Yes.' She leaned forward a little. 'I was so concerned, as all of us were, about Lady Carrington. And since she is a guest of your aunt…I do hope she is quite well after such a terrible accident. Imagine! Being shoved in front of a carriage!'

'She is quite uninjured due to Lord Thayne's quick action in plucking her from harm's way.'

The mention of Thayne had the desired effect. Her eyes widened. 'Yes, it was fortuitous he was there. As he was near the stream. But then, he always seems to be at her side, does he not?'

'Indeed, he does seem to be underfoot a considerable amount of time. But perhaps under the circumstances it is understandable.'

'Really.' Her dark eyes opened even wider. 'But what circumstances are those?'

George smiled and shrugged apologetically. 'I fear I have said too much already. But suffice to say he has cause to be grateful to her. The highway robbery, you understand. And sometimes gratitude may lead to other…developments. As of yet, there is no announcement.' He paused and then looked uncomfortable. 'I pray you will say nothing.'

'Oh, most certainly not. I am the soul of discretion!' She settled back against the cushions with an excited air. He had no doubt she was already turning over the possibilities. He quite looked forward to the end result of her musings.

Satisfied he had fulfilled his goal of setting the cat among the pigeons, he engaged the ladies in a few more comments and insincere compliments before continuing on his way. The resulting gossip as well as a few other cats he planned to let loose should be quite effective in thrusting Julia and Thayne to the altar. And thrusting a considerable sum his way.

Nicholas took a pace around. He'd been standing in the appointed meeting place for the last ten minutes and there was no sign of Grayson. He scowled. He should have called on the man in his lodgings instead of trusting he would keep his word.

He would give him another quarter of an hour and then he'd hunt the man down. Discovering the man's lodgings had been easy enough. With a little entice-ment, Fisk had been more than willing to provide the information and Nicholas had already sent a servant around to verify Grayson indeed lodged there.

Nicholas had had the man followed. His servant had informed him Grayson had arrived with the party as he'd said. A half-hour before ten Grayson had slipped away and then Nicholas's man had lost him.

The path was now quiet. He could hear the sounds of the fireworks and assumed most of the crowd had gone to watch. And Grayson was not coming. He decided he would take a different path back in the chance Grayson had come another way.

He had not gone more than a few steps when he heard a rustle behind him. The hair on the back of his neck prickled. He started to turn, his hand on his pistol, But the blow came from the other direction.

He went down without a sound.

The abigail had just left the room after helping Julia dress when Sophia entered the bedchamber. Her nor-mally calm face was filled with distress.

'Sophia?' She looked so dreadful Julia's heart slammed into her throat. 'What has happened? Are you ill?'

'No. 'Tis not me.' Sophia took a breath. 'Phillip was just here. He told me…oh, dear. It is Nicholas. He has been hurt.'

'Nicholas is hurt?' Julia stared at her, uncompre-hendingly.

'He…he was attacked last night. At Vauxhall.'

The blood pounded in her head. 'Is…is he very hurt?' she whispered.

In a rush of concern, Sophia put her arm around Julia's waist. 'Oh, my dear, you must sit. Come.'

'No.' She looked into Sophia's face. 'I am fine. Please, just tell me about Nicholas. Is he conscious?'

'Oh, dear. I fear I am making a botch of this. He is conscious but with a rather nasty bump. The physician says he will be fine so you need not worry.'

'Thank God.' She sat down on the bed. 'But why was he at Vauxhall?'

'He was to meet a man there. A Mr Grayson.'

'Mr Grayson?' Julia turned to stare at Sophia. 'But that was the man who wanted to buy the ring.'

'Yes. He did not show up.' Sophia paused for a moment—still looking troubled. She sat down next to Julia and put her arm around Julia's waist. 'I fear that is not all. When Nicholas was attacked, the ring was stolen.'

'The ring?' For a moment she could hardly think what Sophia referred to and then she felt ill all over again. 'Oh, dear heaven.'

'I am so sorry. I know it meant so much to you and now it is gone again.'

'Oh, Sophia. The ring hardly matters.' She rose from the bed. 'In fact, I am beginning to think it is cursed.' She turned to look at Sophia. 'I must see Nicholas. Will you come with me?'

'Of course.' Sophia caught her hand and pressed her fingers against Julia's. 'We can leave as soon as you wish.'

Chapter Fifteen

Nicholas scowled at his grandfather. 'I see no reason to spend my day lying about like a damnable invalid. I've a bump on my head, not an amputated limb.'

'None the less, you are to remain in bed a day.' Monteville looked down at him. 'Next time I hope you will inform us of any plans to accost suspects on your own. Particularly in secluded areas.'

'There wasn't time.' His gaze fell to his left hand and his mouth twisted bitterly. The pale line where the ring should be was a painful reminder of how much he had failed. 'I should have demanded the information from Grayson even if it meant abducting him.'

'He still may not have told you. You were fortunate you were not injured more seriously. If Grayson is to be found, I've no doubt Phillip will do so.'

Nicholas fell back against the pillows on the sofa and then winced. At least he had persuaded his grandfather to allow him downstairs in the library. He'd have felt even more like a foolish schoolboy if he had been forced to remain in his room.

The footman appeared in the doorway. 'Lady Carrington and Lady Simons, my lord.'

He sat back up and cursed. What the devil were they doing here? Julia was the last person he wanted to see. Certainly not in this condition. And not after losing the ring. 'I am obviously not receiving today.'

'I think it would be best if you were,' Monteville said. He turned to the footman. 'You may show them in.'

Nicholas forced himself to rise, and then folded his arms and stared at a point near the mantelpiece while the two ladies were shown in. His grandfather stepped forward to greet them.

'We came as soon as possible,' Sophia said. 'We were so worried about Nicholas. How…how is he?'

'You may ask me directly.' Nicholas said, taking a step. He ignored the sharp pain that shot through his head. 'I am quite well.'

'Should you not be in bed?' Sophia asked. Her wide blue eyes were filled with concern. 'You cannot be feeling at all the thing.'

'I assure you I am.'

'But you look quite pale,' she insisted. 'I think you should at least lay on the sofa.'

Julia spoke. 'I must agree with Sophia. You should not be up after such a blow.'

He turned his gaze upon her, trying not to notice how pretty her face looked beneath the wide rim of her bonnet. 'If I recall, you objected to my laying on your sofa.'

Her eyes met his. 'But this is your house and you may do as you please.'

He stared back at her. '*Touché*, my dear. And my pleasure is to remain standing. At least as long as you are.'

'Under the circumstances standing on such formality is ridiculous.'

His brow shot up. 'A pun, my dear?'

She looked as if she wanted to hit him, a circumstance he considered most pleasing. He gave her a superior grin and leaned against the arm of the sofa.

Monteville regarded them with faint amusement. 'Perhaps you would not object to entertaining my grandson for a moment, Lady Carrington. I have recently purchased a pianoforte I intend to give to my granddaughter. I thought perhaps you would try it, Lady Simons, and give me your opinion.'

Sophia smiled. 'Of course. I would be delighted.' She ignored Julia's dismayed look.

Monteville glanced at Julia. 'I trust you will persuade my grandson to return to the sofa.'

Julia started and gave him a strained smile. 'I will try.'

Nicholas frowned after his grandfather. What the devil did he mean by leaving him alone with Julia? He stared at the panelled door as a staggering possibility hit him. Could it be his grandfather actually desired a match between himself and Julia?

The thought nearly made him reel.

'I really think you had best sit down.'

He jumped and stared at her. 'Sit down?'

'Yes.' She gave him an odd look. 'Perhaps you have heard of it, my lord? It is where one—'

'I know what it is.' He scowled at her. 'You first, my dear.'

Her face wore an odd expression and she sat on the nearest piece of furniture, an uncomfortable Queen Anne chair.

He took a seat on the sofa, remembering not to lean

his head against the back. His head was beginning to hurt, but it hardly kept him from staring at her. The thought that Monteville might approve of her for his wife made his throat go dry. Not that she'd ever accept him willingly. Which would hardly stop his grandfather if he thought they were well suited. His sister's marriage was a case in point.

'Is there something wrong?' Her face now held concern. 'You look very strange.'

'Nothing is wrong.'

'Are you certain? You are pale.' The worry on her face was unnerving.

'I am fine,' he snapped. 'Did you call for a purpose?'

'Yes, if you must know,' she snapped back. 'I had wished to assure myself you were not seriously harmed, but if your rude manners are any indication you were not.'

'I beg your pardon,' he said stiffly. He rose again and went to stand near the mantelpiece. 'And I must beg your pardon for another matter as well. I fear I was robbed of your husband's ring.' He avoided her gaze.

'Sophia told me,' she said quietly.

'You are welcome to ring a peal over my head if you wish for my carelessness.'

He glanced back at her and was completely taken aback when she jumped up, fury written all over her face. 'If you must know, I do not care about the ring. What I do not understand, my lord, is why you were so idiotic to arrange such a dangerous meeting on your own in dark woods! You could have been killed!'

He stared at her as she came towards him. She stopped in front of him and glared. 'And do you know how I would have felt? Knowing you were murdered because of the stupid ring! In fact, I am glad the ring is gone! Perhaps whoever wants it is now satisfied and will stop hitting people over the head and shoving people in streets!' He blinked. She pointed a finger at his chest and he took a step back. 'And why? Why are you so horribly stubborn that you are not sitting down? Why are men so…so idiotic about these things?'

He had no idea if she was about to cry or strangle him. 'I…er…have no idea.' He caught her shoulders. 'My dear, there is no need to be so overset.'

She stared into his face. 'Yes…yes, there is.' Her voice trembled and her fine eyes filled with tears.

'Damn it,' he murmured. He pulled her into his arms and awkwardly patted her shoulder. Her body felt light and delicate against him and he leaned his head on her soft silky hair.

'Don't cry,' he murmured.

She sniffed and turned her head, but didn't pull away. His arms tightened around her and he pulled her more firmly against him. Which was a mistake. His desire to comfort her was rapidly becoming entwined with a desire to do much more. Such as complete the kiss he had started by the stream.

The sound of footsteps in the hall yanked him back to reality. He would play neatly into his grandfather's hand if he gave in to the impulse. And Kingsley's. He released her abruptly. His head did seem to be spinning. 'Perhaps you are right, I'd best sit down,' he said, his voice husky. He didn't move.

'Yes.' She looked as dazed as he felt. Her lips were slightly parted and he nearly groaned with the desire to taste them.

'Julia,' he murmured.

She swallowed. 'Should you not sit down?'

'I suppose I should.' His gaze remained fastened on her lips.

'I know Sarah will be delighted,' Sophia said from the doorway.

Nicholas jerked around and found Monteville and Sophia had both entered the room. His grandfather's look was curious, and to his embarrassment, he felt heat rise to his cheeks.

Julia backed away, her own cheeks flushed. 'I...I was just trying to persuade Lord Thayne to sit down.'

'Of course,' Monteville said blandly.

Nicholas moved to the sofa and sat. Julia took a seat as far away from him as possible. He wanted to curse. What the hell was wrong with him? He hadn't behaved in such a callow way since he was a youth in the throes of calf-love. Not even with Mary.

The thought was disturbing. And he had no idea why.

Julia forced a smile on her face as Sophia presented her to Lady Catherine Reynolds, a formidable dowager with a double chin, an intimidating bosom and a pair of sharp grey eyes. Julia and Sophia had just reached the door leading from Mrs Hawkesbury's crowded drawing room when Lady Catherine had intercepted them.

She fixed Julia with a piercing stare. 'So, you are the young woman who is causing such a stir.'

Julia was perplexed, as she had been all evening, by such mysterious remarks. She was also rather tired of them. This was the first time she and Sophia had been out in company since the opera three evenings ago. Were they referring to her being pushed in front of a carriage? She managed a polite little smile. 'Indeed. Surely such a mishap shouldn't cause that much of a stir, Lady Catherine.'

Lady Catherine cackled. 'A mishap? It was a bit more than a mere mishap, I should think. And a most fortunate one for you. As for it causing a stir, why should it not? One of the *coups* of the season.'

Julia met Sophia's eyes. She looked as confused as Julia. Sophia turned to Lady Catherine. 'I fear we do not know what you are referring to. Lady Carrington's accident was most unfortunate and we are only thankful she was not seriously injured.'

'Which you owe to Lord Thayne, do you not?' She cackled again. 'That only served as confirmation. But I can see you intend to keep it under wraps, although it is a bit too late, I fear. Best make an announcement and get it over.'

After a few polite remarks they managed to extricate themselves from Lady Catherine and slipped into the hallway. It was only a trifle less crowded than the drawing room, but at least the staircase and front door were nearer at hand.

Sophia turned an exhausted look on Julia. 'This has been the most tiresome affair. I never thought we would escape.'

'Nor did I.' Julia pushed a strand of hair from her heated face. 'I will own I have never been so confused in my life. After Lady Catherine, I am beginning to think that they were talking about something entirely different from my fall at the Opera House.'

'I am certain they are not,' Sophia said brightly, but her face looked worried. 'We will hope that, in another day or so, it will all be forgotten. I need to find Phillip and tell him we wish to leave. Will you be all right if I leave you here?'

'Of course.' She would be glad to escape the crowded rout for a few minutes.

She waited until Sophia disappeared back into the drawing room and then moved to stand next to a table beneath a portrait of a stern man in a wig and an old-fashioned frock coat. A marble bust stood on the table under the painting.

At least, partially hidden next to the table, she could rest for a moment. The evening had been disturbing. No, not just the evening, but the entire day. She could not recall the visit to Monteville House without a blush. Whatever had possessed her to throw herself into Nicholas's arms in that fashion?

She was supposed to be avoiding him, not using every opportunity to accost him. It was just she had been so worried and he had made her so angry.

Which was no excuse at all.

'Lady Carrington.'

She glanced up and found Lady Serena standing in front of her. Her heart sank. She was not someone Julia looked forward to meeting. 'Good evening, Lady Serena.'

'I had so wanted to speak to you.'

'Indeed.' Julia said in her most discouraging tone. Not that she was hopeful it would have an effect on Lady Serena.

'Yes. To congratulate you. I dare say I should not say a thing, but there will be an announcement soon, will there not?' She managed to look guileless and shrewd at the same time.

'An announcement? I fear I have no idea what you are talking about.'

Lady Serena opened her cornflower-blue eyes very wide. 'Why, your betrothal to Lord Thayne, of course.'

Chapter Sixteen

Colton returned to London two days after Nicholas was attacked at Vauxhall. He reported to Nicholas the morning after his return. Sitting in his grandfather's study, Nicholas listened, his uneasiness growing with every word. When Colton finished, Nicholas frowned. 'You are telling me that Halford, the elder Halford, who is reputedly senile, is not so doddering after all. And he remembers such a ring?'

Colton nodded. 'Yes, my lord.'

'You were certain he was lucid?'

'Quite. He rather puts me in mind of my own grandfather who, although he is laid up with gout, is extremely shrewd. I thought perhaps, if the information regarding Mr Halford was incorrect, that the information pertaining to the ledger was as well.'

'And was it?'

'Unfortunately not. Several of the older ledgers were burned in a fire nearly six months ago.'

That had been too much to hope for. 'Did he remember the man who sold him the ring?'

'He recalled a gentleman who spun a tale about the ring's mysterious origins which is why he clearly remembered the ring. As well as the ring's unusual appearance.'

'Anything else? What did the man look like?' Nicholas asked.

'He could not tell me.' Colton cleared his throat. 'Unfortunately, his daughter-in-law returned just then. She appeared most displeased that he had been conversing with me and rather forcibly suggested that I leave.'

Nicholas was not able to elicit much more from Colton. After Colton departed, Nicholas stood in front of the study window. There were too many pieces he did not like. Such as why Phillip had said Halford was senile. Had Phillip actually visited the elder Mr. Halford or merely accepted the word of the younger Halford?

He could bring the information before Phillip. But for some reason he was reluctant to do so, as if he was questioning Phillip's competence in the matter— or did not trust him.

He paced away from the window and picked up a paperweight from the desk. The second attack on Julia had filled him with fury. The attack on him and the robbery of the ring had turned his fury to a cold determination. He was going to find Carrington's murderer and put a stop to this.

He set the paperweight down. Grayson's disappearance only added to his resolve. He had briefly considered Grayson as suspect and dismissed it almost as fast. His manner had been too furtive and nervous for someone who committed such well-planned attacks.

No, he was looking for someone much more devious, much more cool-headed and clever.

He was beginning to think it was time he paid a visit to Sheffield as well.

He looked up as his grandfather entered the room. In his hand was a newspaper. 'I take it you have not seen this morning's *Post*?'

'No, sir.' The odd expression in Monteville's eyes alerted him. 'What is it?'

'I believe there is something that might interest you.' He handed Nicholas the paper. 'The third notice in the first column.'

Puzzled, Nicholas quickly perused the paragraph. 'Lady M. is to pay an extensive visit to relations in Lancashire, I see.' He glanced up at Monteville. 'Fascinating to be sure, but I fail to see how it concerns me.'

'That one may not, but the next one might.'

Nicholas turned his attention back to the paper. He froze for a moment and then slowly looked up. 'Damn him,' he said softly. 'I should call him out.'

'Which would only start a new round of rumours. I suggest you consider other alternatives,' Monteville said.

'What?' Nicholas's mouth twisted. 'According to this, her angelic ministrations during my recovery have resulted in a passion of finer feelings with an interesting announcement to be expected any day.' He slammed the paper down on the desk. 'My only alternative is to marry her.'

Monteville eyed him thoughtfully. 'Do you find the prospect that alarming?'

He glanced at his grandfather and gave a short laugh. 'You are remarkably calm. If it were not for the fact that I know you are above such machinations,

I might suspect you of placing such an announcement merely to force my hand.'

'I am pleased to discover you apparently hold me above such measures,' Monteville said drily.

'I beg your pardon, sir. I did not mean to imply...' He coloured. 'I had some idea you thought Ju—Lady Carrington might be suitable for the next—' He broke off under Monteville's quizzical gaze. Now he was stammering like a schoolboy.

'The next Countess? You are correct, I have considered it, but only because I suspect neither one of you would be completely averse to the idea.'

'You are wrong on that account.' Nicholas took a wild pace around the room. 'She would rather go to the gallows than wed me. Nor do I wish to wed her.'

'You will eventually need to consider marriage.'

'I would prefer not to wed at all.'

'Because of Lady Mary?' Monteville watched him for a moment. 'I think it is time for you to let her go,' he said gently.

'I cannot.' Nicholas moved to the window and looked out at the street below.

'You will need to. If you wish your marriage to Lady Carrington to succeed.'

He looked back at his grandfather, a ghost of a smile on his lips. 'So I am to marry her?'

'I think so. She doesn't need more scandal. Nor do you.'

'I doubt she'll have me.'

'Then you will need to persuade her. Preferably as soon as possible. Once she gets wind of this, I doubt very much if she intends to remain in London much longer. I do not think Phillip will be able to keep her here.'

He stared at his grandfather, beginning to feel like a fox trapped by a pack of hounds. And when the footman entered and announced Lord Stanton was below, he knew how the fox felt when it realised its doom was imminent.

Julia found Sophia in the small drawing room off her bedchamber. She was seated at her writing desk, a pile of letters in front of her. She looked up when Julia entered and made a face. 'I fear I have been a dreadful correspondent of late.' She put her pen down and looked more closely at Julia. 'Should you be up? I doubt very much you slept much last night.'

Julia seated herself on the chair near Sophia's desk. 'As much as I was tempted, I do not think hiding away in bed past noon will solve a thing.'

Sophia considered. 'Sometimes it does. Occasionally the problem will resolve itself if one leaves it alone.'

Julia sighed. 'I do not think this one will. Which is why I have made up my mind what I must do.'

Sophia looked at her with a little frown. 'And what is that?'

'I am leaving London.'

'But, Julia, whatever for?' Sophia said, her face filled with distress.

'Oh, Sophia!' Julia said, touching her hand. 'You have been so kind and I shall miss you terribly, but I cannot stay here any longer. Not after last night.'

'Lady Serena is a dreadful gossip!'

'Sophia, surely you must see she is only saying what everyone else was thinking? That Lord Thayne and I are…are…' Julia bit her lip.

'Betrothed.'

'Yes.' Julia's face heated at the mention of the word. 'It is ridiculous! How did anyone come up with such a notion? How can I ever face him? What if he thinks I did something to encourage such fustian?'

Sophia had propped her chin on her hand and was regarding Julia with an interested look. 'I doubt if Nicholas will think such a thing.'

'But there is Lord Monteville as well. He has been more than tolerant, more than kind, and how do I repay his kindness? By attempting to trap his grandson into marriage!'

'Is that what you are doing?'

'Most certainly not! Sophia! I do not think you are taking this at all seriously!'

Sophia sighed. 'I am, but only because it is upsetting you. But I do not think everything is so dreadful that you must run from London.'

'I do. It is the only possible way to circumvent these ridiculous rumours. If I am gone then no one will see us together.'

'I am not certain that will stop the talk. They will undoubtedly invent a new tale to explain your absence. A lover's quarrel or perhaps a desire to leave so rumours of your engagement will be proved wrong until you decide it is time to make the announcement.'

'Sophia!'

'I am only teasing you. But, Julia, you cannot leave London, it may not be safe.'

'I have considered that as well. But now that the ring is stolen, I am certain nothing more will happen. I am certain the ring is the only thing this…this person wanted.' She spoke more confidently than she felt; there were still several things that puzzled her greatly. Such as why it had been necessary to push her into the street. She was beginning to think that had been a mere coincidence after all.

'Perhaps.' Sophia appeared doubtful. 'I think, dear, before you do anything we must talk with Phillip.'

'I have quite made up my mind.' No matter what Phillip had to say. She suspected he would try to talk her out of it, but this time Julia had no intention of listening.

The footman appeared in the doorway. 'Madame Blanchot is below. She wishes a word with Lady Carrington.'

'Thérèse?' Julia asked, stunned. Thérèse, always mindful of her position as the proprietor of a gaming house, rarely set foot in more respectable establishments. She feared something was very wrong. She stood. 'I shall go down directly.'

'No, you may show her in here,' Sophia said firmly. She glanced at Julia after the footman left. 'It will be more comfortable for a visit here. And besides, I have wanted to meet Madame Blanchot for an age.'

Thérèse entered the room a few moments later. There was no mistaking the fact something had shattered her natural poise. 'Lady Simons, I must apologise for calling on you in this way. But I felt I must speak to Julia without delay.'

'Of course,' Sophia said with concern. 'Are you unwell? Perhaps you should sit down.'

'You are more than kind, but, no, I am not unwell. What I have to say concerns Julia.'

'Thérèse, what is it?' Julia asked quickly. A feeling of dread was slowing creeping over her.

'Have you seen the *Morning Post* today?'

'No.' Julia realised Thérèse carried a folded newspaper. She glanced at Sophia, who appeared equally lost.

'I worried you had not.' Thérèse unfolded the paper with an agitated hand and pointed to a paragraph. 'There is something you must see.'

Sophia and Julia both peered over her shoulder. Sophia gave a little gasp. Julia stared at it and her heart took a sickening dive. 'Oh, dear heavens.' She looked at Sophia, whose face reflected her own sick dismay. 'I really think I must leave London as quickly as possible.'

The footman appeared in the doorway again. 'Lord Stanton is below. He wishes to speak to Lady Carrington.'

Julia stood as Phillip was ushered into Sophia's drawing room, and wished her knees would not tremble so. She also wished Sophia and Thérèse were still present, but Phillip had insisted on speaking to her alone.

She forced a smile to her lips although her heart sank when she saw the newspaper in his hand. 'Good day, Phillip.'

He did not return her smile. 'Good day, Julia. Please sit. I have something of grave importance to impart to you.'

She sat back down on the chair. 'I suppose it is about the piece in the *Morning Post*.' She clasped her hands together. 'I have already decided what I am to do. I will leave London as quickly as possible.'

'You cannot do that, I am afraid.' He spoke in his usual firm manner, and she knew he expected her to acquiesce as she usually did.

'But I am.' She forced herself meet his eyes. 'I have

made up my mind on this. I cannot stay. It is bad enough that Lord Thayne has had to endure two injuries on my account. I refuse to have him endure such outrageous nonsense as well.'

'Leaving London will not help him. Or you.'

'I am leaving tomorrow.'

'You are not.' He came to stand over her, a flinty expression in his eyes she had only seen a few times, but never before directed at her. It took all her willpower to keep from shrinking. 'Nicholas is waiting to speak to you. You will hear what he has to say. And you will accept his offer.'

'His *what*?' A nightmarish sensation washed over her.

'His offer.' He strode to the door and looked back at her. 'If you really wish to protect him from scandal, you will accept.'

She rose, her legs trembling, hardly knowing what she was about. She had never crossed swords with Phillip before, never been the recipient of his anger. The encounter left her shaking.

But even worse was the thought of facing Nicholas. Whatever was she to say to him? He couldn't possibly be planning to make her an offer.

She whirled at the footsteps behind her and clutched the back of the nearest chair for support. Her heart slammed into her ribs as she took in his expression. Nicholas looked as if he was reporting for his execution.

'I would like to speak to you,' he said grimly.

She swallowed. 'Would you? I...I cannot imagine why.'

'Can't you?' He shut the door behind him, his eyes never leaving her face, and advanced across the room.

She forced herself to stay still despite a cowardly urge to run. 'You really do not have to say a thing, my lord. In fact, I think it would be better if you did not.'

He stopped a few feet from her. 'Would you prefer my offer in writing then?'

'Actually I would prefer no offer at all.'

'That is unfortunate because I am making you one. And you are going to accept it.'

She gasped. 'I am not! I have no intention of marrying you.'

'Yes, you will.' He folded his arms and stared at her.

'And how do you know that? Are you omniscient?'

'No, but you're marrying me none the less.'

'Well, really!' She had no idea whether she wanted to hit him or burst into tears. 'I have never heard anything so...so high-handed. This whole thing is so ridiculous! You cannot possibly feel you must marry me because of that stupid thing in the paper.'

'I do.' He was beginning to look exasperated. 'Damn it, Julia, if we do not marry neither one of us will have a shred of reputation left. We've no choice.'

'If you must know, I do not give a fig for my reputation. And I would never marry a man who makes me an offer in such an arrogant, and...and callous manner. Even if he feels compelled to!' To her chagrin, her voice trembled. She gulped and looked away. She would rather die than cry in front of him.

'I beg your pardon. I seem to always be making you cry.'

She turned and glared at him. 'You did not make me cry.'

'You looked as if you were about to.'

'Well, I was not.'

He scowled at her. 'I know I'm making a botch of this. I've not had a lot of practice in making offers. In fact, last time the lady was no more pleased than you are,' he added bitterly.

She stared at him and realized he felt as confused as she did. 'I am sorry.'

'Don't be.' He frowned. 'Is there someone else? Haslett?'

'Robert?' she said in amazement.

His brow snapped down. 'You have been remarkably friendly with him.'

'He is an old friend, that is all. Besides, I think he is developing a *tendre* for Sophia.'

'Is he?' Was it possible he actually looked relieved? Before she could consider what that might mean, he spoke again. 'We do not have a choice in this matter.'

His words made her feel more trapped than his arrogance ever had. 'I don't want to marry again.'

'I know that. It won't be so bad, I promise you.'

'But Lord Monteville...he cannot possibly want this.'

To her surprise, he looked almost amused. 'Actually, on that point you are quite wrong. Consider the advantages. You will have my fortune at your disposal. If you wish to repair your farm you may.'

The generous offer only made her more wretched. 'I do not want your fortune,' she whispered.

He shrugged. 'Probably not. But my fortune and my name is what I have to offer you. But the formidable Mrs Mobley, not to mention Betty the goat, might appreciate a leak-free roof.'

She stared at him, stunned. His eyes met hers and something in his expression made her breathless. He took a step forward and reached out his hand. For an eternity they stared at each other and then he abruptly dropped his hand. He backed away. 'I will call on you tomorrow.'

'I...' But he had already turned and was out of the door before she had a chance to find her voice.

She stared at the closed door and then sank down on the sofa. She could not marry him—it was impossible. Perhaps she hadn't meant to but it had happened—she had trapped him into marriage. A loveless match. She closed her eyes. *But my fortune and my name is what I have to offer you.*

'No.' She opened her eyes. She could not do that to him. Or to herself. She would leave London even if it meant sneaking out in the dead of night.

Chapter Seventeen

George rapped neatly on the door of Sophia's town-house. He had come directly from a musical soirée where Sophia, who fixed him with a cold stare, had informed him that Julia was home with a headache. Her brusque manner indicated he was fully to blame. His congratulations on the upcoming nuptials had no softening effect at all.

In fact, no one seemed pleased with the results of his machinations. Julia least of all, if her absence was any indication.

Which was why the news of her supposed headache aroused his suspicions. He would not put it past her to bolt.

And thus, he decided a visit to the reluctant bride-to-be was in order.

Sophia's prune-faced butler admitted him. George's request to speak with Lady Carrington was met with a frown of disapproval. 'Lady Carrington is not receiving.'

George had come prepared. He pulled a folded paper from his pocket. 'Perhaps you will give this to her and then let her decide if she is receiving or not.'

Williams took the paper between his fingers and held it as if it were a hot coal. George watched him go and moved to idly observe one of the dull portraits the late Lord Simons seemed to favour.

After a few more minutes, Williams appeared. 'Lady Carrington will see you, Lord George. In the drawing room.'

She was standing near the mantelpiece, her whole body rigid with tension. He paused for a moment, taking in her slender figure and the soft brown of her hair. And the sensible travelling dress. He had no doubt Thayne would be most displeased if his intended bride should run off so quickly.

She looked up. 'Good evening, George.' Her voice held as much enthusiasm as William's had.

'Good evening, my dear Julia.'

A flicker of annoyance crossed her face. 'You had a message from Sophia?'

He walked towards her. 'She was concerned that you were indisposed and wished me to be certain you were not in need of a physician. Am I to assume, that since you are up and dressed, you have recovered?'

'Yes. Is that all? I do not wish to be rude, but I really cannot engage in idle conversation at this moment.'

George ran his eyes over her gown and then smiled. 'I see you are about to embark on a trip. I would like to offer my congratulations before you leave town. Most certainly the match of the season.'

'We are not going to be married,' she said flatly.

His brow arched. 'Perhaps I misunderstood. My father informed me only today of the happy event. Or perhaps the unhappy event, in this case. So you are not to be married. Have you yet informed Thayne of this?'

Her face crumpled and filled with misery. 'Please do not tease me.'

'I beg your pardon.' He watched her for a moment. 'I take it Thayne has not been informed. What are you going to do, my dear? Do you wish me to help?'

She took a deep breath. 'I must leave here. If you could take me to Thérèse's, I could then go from there to Foxwood.'

'Thérèse's? My dear, I can do better than that. I can take you to Foxwood.'

She frowned a little. 'But I wish to leave now.'

'Of course. My carriage awaits.'

'I do not wish to go to Foxwood now,' she said impatiently. 'Only to Thérèse's.'

'Very well. We will only go to Thérèse's. I suppose you have a bandbox or two.'

'Only one.' She hesitated. 'I do not want anyone to know I am leaving. At least not right away. I rather thought I would go up to bed and then leave through the servants' entrance and go through the back garden to the mews.'

'Very clandestine of you,' he remarked. 'When can you be ready? An hour?' That should give him time to track down Thayne's location. Or he could deliver her to Thérèse's and send Thayne there to retrieve his runaway fiancée.

'Yes.' She did not look very happy.

'Very well, my dear.' He smiled. 'In an hour. I will have a servant waiting for you outside the gate.'

Julia fastened the strap on the bandbox with shaky fingers. Whatever was she thinking of? Running off

with George? Except she was not really running off
with him, merely asking him to escort her to Thérèse's. She tried to shove aside her uneasiness. George
was not the most trustworthy of men, but he had been
kind to her in his own peculiar way since Thomas's
death.

She would go to Thérèse's. Surely Thérèse would
conceal her whereabouts until she could send for Eduardo.

She had left a note for Sophia, a very brief note for
the purpose of assuring her she would be safe. Her
pen had hesitated over the second note and, in the end,
she had left it next to the one for Sophia. He would
undoubtedly be furious with her, but relieved as well.

She picked up the bandbox and slipped out of her
room. The house was quiet and she saw no one as she
made her way to the back staircase. There was no one
near the door that led to the garden and she made her
way out unseen.

The garden was dark and shadowed. Despite her
soft boots her footsteps seemed unnaturally loud on
the gravel walk. She tried to stay close to the bushes
and prayed no one would see her.

She reached the back wall and hesitated at the gate.
Her heart was thudding loudly, but she forced herself
to undo the latch and pass through.

She gasped when a man appeared out of the shadows.

'Lady Carrington?' he said softly.

'Yes.' She peered at him but could see only that he
looked rather elderly and harmless.

'Come with me.'

She nodded and prayed he was George's servant.

But who else would be lurking behind Sophia's house waiting for her?

The carriage stood in the side street. Her escort paused. 'Do you wish to carry your bandbox with you?' he asked courteously.

'Yes.' She clutched it to her and waited as he opened the door.

The interior was in shadow and she could not see George's face although she could see the coach was occupied. Her heart had began to thud again and her hands were clammy.

'George?' she said softly.

'Go on in, my lady,' her escort said behind her.

She climbed in and took her seat. The door closed firmly behind her and she glanced in the corner. With mounting panic she realized everything was all wrong—the man was wearing a black coat and breeches, not George's pantaloons and buff coat. And his shoulders were much too broad.

The coach began to move. 'Oh, no,' she whispered.

'Good evening, Lady Carrington,' Nicholas said.

Julia gasped. 'Wh…what are you doing here?'

Nicholas leaned back and folded his arms. 'Abducting you.'

Even in the dull light he could see the stunned look on her face. 'You cannot be.'

'Why not? It rather evens the score, does it not?'

'I don't understand. Where is George?'

He shrugged. 'Probably in his carriage somewhere near Bond Street. Not that I particularly care. Although I question your wisdom in running off with him.'

'I was not running off with him! I merely wanted him to—'

'To what? Help you escape London? Escape me?'

'No!' she snapped.

'So why were you stealing away from Sophia's house in the middle of the night, then?'

'I might ask why you were skulking around Sophia's back garden and spying on me!' she retorted.

He smiled grimly. 'Because, my dear, I suspected you might try something of this sort. When I learned you were not with Sophia, I decided I would call on you. And whom do I see but Kingsley leaving the house. Questionable under any circumstances, but when I found his carriage parked in a side street and Kingsley hovering around the garden, I decided to have a word with him.'

She stared at him aghast. 'Did you hurt him?'

He raised a brow. 'I fear he put up a bit of resistance when I informed him I intended to take his place. Along with some nonsense about how he intended to inform me of your plans.'

'But why? I still do not understand why you are doing this.'

'Because I've no intention of letting you run off. Not only because of the damnable piece in the paper, but because your life may still be in danger. And I don't trust Kingsley past my nose.'

'I see.' She looked away. 'I suppose you will take me back to Sophia's now,' she said calmly.

'No.'

'No?' Her head jerked up. 'Then where are you taking me?'

He regarded her under half-closed lids. 'I've no intention of telling you. At least for now.'

'But you cannot do this! You cannot hold me against my will!' A note of panic had crept into her voice. 'My lord! Please, take me back to Sophia's or to Thérèse's.'

'I am not planning a rape, if that is what worries you,' he said coldly. 'You will be quite safe. Trust me on this.'

'How can I? I have no idea where you are taking me.' She looked at him for a moment and then turned her head away. She sniffed.

'I don't suppose you brought a handkerchief with you. Here.' He handed her one. She looked as if she was about to refuse and then plucked it from his hand. 'Thank you,' she said in a small voice.

He stifled a groan. The anger he'd barely contained when he discovered she planned to run off with Kingsley was rapidly giving way to conscience. No doubt he had frightened her, but he had no intention of allowing her to run away, not even if she found the idea of marrying him so repulsive she would prefer to trust Kingsley over him.

Julia slowly awoke. Her arm felt cramped and her neck was cushioned by something rough. For a moment she had no idea why her bed was swaying. Then she remembered. She was in Nicholas's coach. He had kidnapped her. And she had no idea where he was taking her.

She opened her eyes and realized the rough cloth under her cheek was a masculine coat. And that she had been covered with a throw. She moved her head a little and realized with vague surprise that the early light of dawn was creeping through the windows of the coach.

She shifted. Nicholas was in the opposite corner of the coach, his eyes closed. His long legs, the muscles visible through his tight breeches, were stretched out in front of him. He wore only his waistcoat and shirt and she realised he had tucked his coat under her neck.

When had she fallen asleep? She remembered her eyes closing in spite of her resolution to remain awake. There had been a stop, she thought, but even that seemed like a dream.

Her eyes drifted over him. Sleeping, he looked oddly vulnerable. A lock of hair had fallen over his forehead, giving him a boyish air.

But there was nothing boyish about the strong masculine line of his jaw or the growth of beard around his firm mouth. Or the rest of his hard, lean body. She flushed and pulled her gaze away, feeling as if she was violating his privacy by staring at him while he slept.

The coach suddenly seemed too small and intimate. Just as hers had the night she had kidnapped him. Except this time he was not safely bound and gagged. And now she knew what it was like to have his arms around her, feel his mouth cover hers.

She must be going mad. She should not be thinking of a man who had just abducted her in such terms. Instead, she should be making plans to escape, not falling asleep as if she were at home in her own bed.

'You are awake.'

She gasped and looked over at him. He was still stretched out in the corner and looked as if he hadn't moved except to open his eyes.

'Yes.'

His gaze drifted over her. His eyes had a heavy sensuous look that reminded her of Thomas and how he had looked at her when he awoke and wanted to make love to her.

Heat rose to her cheeks. She must truly be depraved. She jerked her gaze to the window. Outside, she saw neat hedgerows and fields. 'I do not suppose you wish to tell me where we are?'

'Near Newmarket.'

'Why are we near Newmarket?' She frowned at him. Something tugged at the back of her mind.

'Monteville House is not far from here.'

'Monteville House?' A sense of panic was starting to rise in her throat. 'But why are we near Monteville House?'

'Because you are going to stay there while I go to Sheffield.'

Her hands went to her heated cheeks. 'You cannot possibly bring me to Monteville House. Are you mad? What will everyone think?'

He shrugged. 'They will think what they like. I've no doubt my grandfather will spin a plausible tale about how we decided a visit to the family would now be in order.'

'He knows about this?'

A smile tugged at his mouth. 'He does now. I left a note.'

'A note?' She undoubtedly sounded completely idiotic.

'Yes. I would be willing to wager you left a note somewhere as well.'

Her mouth nearly fell open. How dare he sit there and look so pleased with himself? He was planning to bring her to his family home? The possibilities had turned in her mind before she drifted off to sleep, but this had not been one of them. 'You cannot do this! I have brought nothing with me!'

'What is in that bandbox?'

'It is a toothbrush and a nightrail—' She broke off. 'This is ridiculous. I have no clothing.'

'Next time you decide to go off with someone you'll know to pack more,' he said kindly.

'I was not going off with someone! I had expected to go to Foxwood and I would have what I needed there. I cannot possibly arrive at your home like this!'

'No? Would you prefer to continue on to the border? Although I would prefer a change of clothing before we go on.'

'No!' She was about to fly into the boughs and then realised from the gleam in his eye that he was teasing her. In fact, he looked remarkably relaxed for a man who had just abducted a person and was planning to show up at the family home with his victim.

None of it made any sense. And she was hardly reassured when they rounded a bend and she caught a glimpse of a large manor house in the distance.

'Monteville House,' Nicholas said.

Her stomach lurched. She was beginning to wonder if it might have been preferable if Nicholas had had improper designs on her person after all.

If the housekeeper, Mrs Burton, was shocked by the arrival of Nicholas with a strange woman in tow shortly after dawn, she hid it well. Her manner remained quite calm when Nicholas said they had travelled most of the night and Lady Carrington was in need of a bed.

She had not shown even the merest flicker of surprise that Julia had brought only a bandbox with her as she took the young woman upstairs then opened the door to a bedchamber.

'I trust you will be quite comfortable here.' She held open the door and waited for Julia to step past her.

Julia looked around at the room, taken aback by its size and the elegance of the furnishings. She had somehow expected a chamber less grand. She realised Mrs Burton was waiting for her to speak. 'It is lovely. Thank you.'

'Is there anything else you require?' Mrs Burton asked.

'No, not at all.'

The housekeeper moved to the door. 'I shall send Fanny in to help you undress, my lady.' She left the room.

Julia stood for a moment, feeling rather lost, and finally moved towards the bed. She removed her pelisse and laid it across a chair. A looking glass hung nearby and she caught a glimpse of herself. With a great deal of dismay, she saw her hair had come almost completely out of its pins and her travelling dress was a mass of wrinkles.

Mortified, she turned away. She looked much worse than she had ever imagined. Rather like a waif someone had picked up off the streets.

She sat down on the bed. Whatever was she to do now? And, even more pressing, what did Nicholas intend to do with her?

Chapter Eighteen

When Julia awoke again, daylight was streaming across the bed. For a moment, she thought she was in Sophia's townhouse and then her mind cleared.

She was in Monteville House. She sat up, still disoriented from her heavy slumber. From the angle of the light, she thought the hour must be well past noon.

She glanced around the room. It was a pretty, feminine room, done in colours of blue and cream. A watercolour of a garden hung on one wall. A small writing desk stood in a corner near the window and on the other side of the carved fireplace was a small wardrobe.

It was the sort of room she had dreamed of as a child, warm and inviting and with a sense of permanence, unlike the room she had occupied in her stepfather's house with its bare furnishings and drab walls. Or with Thomas, who considered rooms merely a place to rest one's head.

Which was why Foxwood had seemed so wonderful to her despite its shabbiness. A real home. A place where Thomas had finally seemed content to settle.

She threw back the bedcovers and climbed out of

bed. She padded to the window and drew back the filmy muslin curtains. The day was overcast, but it failed to detract from the magnificence of the view. Below her were spread formal gardens and in the distance she saw a small lake. To the left, beyond the tree tops, she could see the rooftop of another house.

How lovely it would be to live somewhere so stately and settled. And to wake up in this cheerful, peaceful room and be able to look out of the window at gardens that were neat and civilised rather than a straggly mess. For a moment, she could almost imagine herself hiding away up here, suspended in time.

Mrs Burton's entry into the room brought her back to the present and her situation abruptly. Several muslin gowns were draped over her arm. She surveyed Julia with her placid air. 'So you are awake, my lady. I dare say you are hungry by now. A tray in your room perhaps, and then you can come downstairs for dinner. And I have brought you some gowns. They are old ones of Miss Sarah's, but since you appear to be of similar proportions they should do until your trunks have arrived.'

'Thank you,' Julia said, completely taken aback. Her trunks? Whatever had Nicholas told her?

She watched in some bewilderment as Mrs Burton bustled around opening the curtains and then the maid, Fanny, came in with a tray of food which she set on the small desk.

'After you eat and are dressed, Lord Thayne will see you,' Mrs Burton said. She hovered for a moment. 'Perhaps you should eat first, my lady.'

Julia obediently sat down and looked at the food set before her. There was cold slices of roast beef, bread and fresh strawberries. She looked up and saw Mrs

Burton still watching her. She took a bite of the beef. Mrs Burton, apparently satisfied she meant to eat, finally left the room.

An hour later, she had finished eating and Fanny had helped her dress. The cream-coloured gown was a little short but otherwise fitted her adequately.

The apprehension she had managed to keep at bay returned as soon as she left the sanctuary of the bedchamber. She followed Mrs Burton down the hallway and to the wide circular staircase. She descended the staircase past portraits of stern ancestors and finally across a lower hallway to a door. 'Lord Thayne is waiting for you in the library,' Mrs Burton said.

Julia thanked her and stepped past her into the room. It was large and panelled with dark wood and lined with bookshelves.

Nicholas stood near the window. She could see that it faced the lawn she had seen from her bedchamber. He had his hands clasped behind his back. He turned when she entered, then moved forward. 'I hope you rested well,' he said politely.

'Very much so.' She looked at him, uncertain of what to say next.

He had shaved and changed into buckskin breeches and boots and a dark brown coat. The informal attire only emphasised his lean masculinity. He looked at home and, despite the civilised surroundings, for the first time since last night she felt completely in his power.

'Good. Please sit.' He indicated a small settee.

She sat on the edge. He remained standing, which seemed to her an unfair advantage. 'Are you not going to sit?' she asked.

'Should I?'

'Yes, otherwise I feel as if you have called me in for a scolding.'

His mouth twitched. 'Indeed.' But instead of taking a proper seat, he perched on the edge of the desk.

She frowned at him. 'That is not a chair.'

'Would you prefer I sat next to you? That is my only alternative.'

Must he be so exasperating? 'You could pull the chair from behind the desk.'

'It is not very stable and tends to tip.'

'Really!' At least his customary stubbornness had the effect of banishing the peculiar feeling of being at his mercy. 'I would think you would have a few hundred chairs at your disposal here.'

'Yes, but I have a fondness for that particular chair.'

She sighed. 'I refuse to ask why you do not sit in it.'

'Good.' He actually smiled. 'Are you comfortable?'

'Oh, yes. My bedchamber is lovely and has such a pretty view.'

'It belonged to my sister.'

'Did it?' She was taken aback. 'I do not think I should be there. That is, I am hardly a guest and it seems rather presumptuous of me…' Her voice trailed off at his raised brow.

'My sister would be delighted to know you are in her bedchamber. And you are a guest. Is there anything else you wish to say to me?'

'I need to know why I am here,' she said quietly.

'Because I decided this would be the best place to keep you safe.'

'Safe from what? I fear I do not understand. The ring has been taken—surely that is what the thief was after. And I do not understand why I was in danger after the incident at Foxwood anyway. You were the one with the ring! It is you who should have been worried.'

He was silent for a moment. 'There are several things about the affair which do not make sense. Which is why I've no intention of allowing you out of my sight.'

'This is ridiculous! You cannot possibly consider yourself responsible for me!'

He folded his arms and stared at her. 'But I do. After all, we are going to be married.'

'We are not!' Her heart began to pound.

'I hate to contradict you, but we are. After I return from Sheffield.'

She rose. 'You are going to Sheffield? But why? Phillip said there was nothing to discover.'

'I have reason to believe, however, that the jeweller knows more than he is willing to tell.'

'Do you?' She felt a stab of fear. 'I don't want you to go.'

He looked at her, a frown on his brow. 'Why not? It may lead to the man who killed your husband.'

'Yes.' She clasped her hands tightly together and said slowly, 'I have wanted more than anything to discover the person who did this and see he was punished. I thought that I would do anything, including murder, if I had to. When I abducted you, I did not think of the consequences, that I might put someone else in danger. And I have put you in danger. You have been hurt twice because of me. And I cannot let you be hurt any more. Even if it means I never find his killer.'

He faced her. 'There is a man out there who has

killed at least once. He has assaulted you twice. What if he decides assaults are not enough? That to prevent discovery he must kill again? We still do not know why you were shoved in the street or why you received a threatening note. And I've no desire to find you dead because I failed to do everything in my power to find the man.'

She stared at him, taken aback by the vehemence in his voice.

'And so you will remain here while I go to Sheffield.'

'At least let me go with you.'

'No.'

'But I wish to,' she said.

He scowled at her. 'No, and I'll place you under guard if I must.' He rose from the desk. 'I have sent for my cousin, Lady Marleigh, to chaperon you. She lives four miles from here and will arrive before dinner.'

'I see.' The thought of meeting an unknown relation of his was daunting. 'When are you leaving?'

'Tomorrow if possible.'

It was all she could do to beg him not to go. Instead, she nodded.

'You may do as you please, except I do not want you going about the grounds unattended.' When she said nothing, he frowned. 'What is it? Are you worried for your safety? You should be in no danger here. I've given instructions to the servants to admit no one unknown to them. You will be guarded when you step out the door and I trust you will do nothing foolhardy such as try to go about without a chaperon.'

'I am not worried about my safety,' she snapped.

He continued to frown. 'Then what is it?'

'It is nothing!' She could hardly admit to him that the fact he was going to leave her made her want to throw herself into his arms and beg him not to go. That she would worry about him every minute he was gone.

'Then why are you looking like that?'

'I am not looking like anything! I am merely out of sorts. Being forced into a coach and then travelling throughout the night does that to one.'

'Does it? You will have a few days to rest, then.'

She glared at him. 'I doubt that. I will most likely be wondering when I will hear of your demise!' And wanted to bite her tongue as his expression changed.

He took a step towards her. 'I see. You are worried about me.' His eye held a peculiar gleam.

She took a step backwards. 'Of course I am. I would worry about anyone.'

'Indeed.' He took another step and she found herself backed into the settee. 'I am flattered none the less. Does that mean you will miss me when I am gone? That you will be here eagerly awaiting my return?'

She flushed but forced herself to meet his gaze. 'Only because I will then be free to leave.'

His smile was rather wicked. 'Why do you think that? Perhaps I never intend to let you go. We are betrothed, you know.'

She caught her breath. 'Please don't tease me!'

Something flickered in his eye. He stepped back. 'Very well.' His voice cooled. 'The house is at your disposal. I must meet with my grandfather's agent, but you may make any requests you might have to Mrs Burton.' His voice was dismissive.

'Thank you.' She kept her voice as polite as his and

walked with as much dignity as she could from the room.

And then it was all she could do to keep from bursting into ridiculous, childish tears.

His cousin, Amelia, Lady Marleigh, arrived shortly before dinner. She was shown into the study where Nicholas was seated behind the desk, staring at a pile of documents that awaited his signature.

'Good heavens, Nicholas. Whatever are you up to now?' she asked, coming into the room. She still wore her pelisse and bonnet, a confection of straw and blue that tilted fashionably on her blonde curls. She walked to his desk, stripping off her gloves. 'You have the most atrocious hand and I could scarcely make out what you wanted, except that you are in need of a chaperon. I feared I must be mistaken, for what would you be need of a chaperon for?'

He stood and came around the desk. 'You are not mistaken at all. I have a lady staying here.'

'A *lady*?'

'A person of the female persuasion such as yourself.'

She made a face and took the chair by his desk. 'Must you be difficult? Perhaps you had best tell me who this lady is and why she is here. And why ever are you at Monteville House? Should you not be in London, creating more scandal? There have been the most delicious rumours circulating about you that involve highway robbers, and a mysterious lady who nurses you back to health that you have fallen in love with—' She broke off and stared at him. 'Do not tell me you have brought her here!'

'I have. Her name is Lady Carrington.'

'Lady Carrington?' She wrinkled her brow. 'I do not know her. But you are in love with her and have brought her to Monteville House and wish me to chaperon you until you…you what?'

He fixed her with a scowl. 'I am not in love with her.'

'How disappointing.' She smiled at him. 'So, why is Lady Carrington here?'

'I abducted her.'

Her mouth fell open and then she gave a shaky laugh. 'Really, Nicholas, that is beyond the pale, even for you. I think you had best explain precisely why it was necessary to do something so deplorable.'

'I feared her life was in danger. And she was trying to leave London to escape me.' He took a pace towards the window and then turned. 'I could not think what else to do. And after I brought her here, I realised I could hardly keep her here without a chaperon. There is already enough scandal between us. You were the only person who came to mind who would not be completely shocked.'

'I am not certain whether I should be complimented or not,' Amelia said.

'There is one other thing. We are betrothed.'

She appeared momentarily stunned. 'Does Grandfather know of this?'

'It was his idea. He also knows I abducted her.'

'Heavens,' she said and then laughed. 'Of course. It all makes sense. I think you had best start at the beginning if you want me to help you.'

Julia started at the knock on the door of her bedchamber. She sat in a chair near the window and had been staring out at the garden and trying very hard to think about nothing.

She stood. 'Come in.' She was taken aback to have a tall, fashionably dressed young woman with golden hair and vivid blue eyes enter the room.

'Lady Carrington?' the young woman said. 'I am Nicholas's cousin, Lady Marleigh.'

'How do you do?' Julia felt very awkward. She had somehow thought Lady Marleigh would be much older, not someone so sophisticated and composed.

'May I come in?' Lady Marleigh asked. 'I thought I should speak to you before dinner.'

'Yes, of course. Would you care to sit down?'

'I think so. And you may take the other chair and tell me how you are. I fear Nicholas could not really say.' She took a wing chair arranged near the mantelpiece and Julia obediently sat on the other.

'I am fine,' Julia said cautiously. She had no idea what Nicholas had said to his cousin.

Lady Marleigh must have guessed her thoughts. She looked at Julia with her frank gaze. 'Nicholas told me about last night. I know you are not here willingly.' She hesitated a moment. 'I hope he did not harm you.'

'Harm me? I do not understand.' Julia stared at her and then her meaning was clear. Heat rushed to her face. 'Oh, no. He was nothing but a gentlemen.' She remembered his coat under her cheek. 'He was actually quite kind.'

Lady Marleigh smiled. 'Was he? I am glad. I did not think he would ever touch a woman without her consent, but I wanted to reassure myself. So, how did you find being abducted? I will own I always thought it might be rather romantic.'

'It wasn't really. He was angry because he thought

I was running away, so we quarrelled. After that I resolved not to speak to him and then I fell asleep.'

A gurgle of laughter escaped Lady Marleigh. 'I will own that sounds quite dull. And, of course, you would quarrel with Nicholas. He has a dreadful temper. Did he scowl at you the entire time?'

Julia found herself wanting to giggle. 'Yes, but then he always does.'

'And it does not intimidate you. Splendid, he should not marry someone whom he can ride roughshod over.'

The smile left Julia's face. 'We are not going to be married,' she said quietly.

'No?' Lady Marleigh arched a brow. 'But why not?'

'Because neither of us wishes to be married. It is only because of some ridiculous gossip that is circulating in London. He feels obligated to offer me marriage, but I will not let him because it is entirely my fault we are in this stupid fix.'

'And why is that? I cannot think you could be faulted for nursing him after he was injured.'

'No, but he was injured because of me.' Julia took a deep breath. 'You see, I abducted him first because he wore my husband's ring. I wanted it back. And on the way to Foxwood, which is my farm, we were held up by highwaymen. One of the highwaymen tried to shoot me because I would not give him my pistol and Nicholas took the ball instead. So, none of this is his doing at all.'

Lady Marleigh looked stunned. 'Nicholas did not mention this.' And then she leaned forward, her eyes sparkling with laughter. 'My goodness! I am beginning to think you are quite well suited after all.'

Chapter Nineteen

Julia paused outside the drawing room, feeling rather self-conscious. Lady Marleigh had insisted on loaning her a dress for dinner, a dark salmon silk. It was a deceptively simple gown, but the V-neckline of the bodice plunged lower than she liked. Although Lady Marleigh was several inches taller than Julia, Fanny had proved amazingly adept with the needle and had managed to put up the hem in no time. A few tucks here and there had been all that was needed to fit the bodice to Julia's more slender curves.

Lady Marleigh had supervised the dressing of Julia's hair as well and when she stood in front of the looking glass she had hardly recognised herself. She had not worn such a bold colour for an age, nor had she had her hair dressed in curls tumbling over her head.

'You look beautiful,' Lady Marleigh said. She walked around Julia. 'But your locket is not quite right. I will loan you my ruby.'

'You have done far too much already,' Julia protested.

Lady Marleigh smiled. 'Oh, not at all.'

Somehow, she had found the locket removed from her neck and a ruby and diamond necklace taking its place. And when she had glanced back at the looking glass again, her stomach had fluttered. She looked like a woman who was set on seduction.

There was not much she could do about it now. She forced herself to enter the drawing room. To her dismay, Nicholas was the only occupant. He stood near the mantelpiece dressed in a dark coat and breeches. He looked up when she entered. The arrested expression that leapt to his eyes made her pulse leap.

She flushed as his gaze travelled over her, and lingered for a moment on the ruby above her breasts. Then he moved forward. 'Good evening, Lady Carrington.'

'Good evening, Lord Thayne.' Her own mouth was dry. Her pulse thudded as he came to stand in front of her, his eyes still on her.

His eyes searched her face and came to rest on her mouth. 'What did Amelia do to you?' he asked. His voice was husky.

'She did nothing but loan me a gown. Is that so objectionable?'

'It probably should be.' His eyes darkened. 'You look far too desirable.'

Her breath caught. 'That was not my intention.'

'No?' His mouth curved in a cynical smile. 'I've no doubt it was Amelia's.'

'I beg your pardon,' she said stiffly. Really, must he make it sound like a crime? Not only that, but she felt foolish that he seemed to think she had set out to attract him. 'I believe I will view the garden, my lord.' She started to walk past him.

He caught her arm. 'No. Wait.'

She looked up at him. 'Perhaps you would release me.'

He dropped her arm. 'I did not mean to offend you. It is just...you look lovely,' he said flatly.

The confusion in his face dissolved any hurt she had felt. She arched her brow. 'And that is what is objectionable?'

'No.' He levelled a scowl at her. 'It is not.'

'I see.' Her lips curved in a smile at his bemused expression.

His gaze sharpened and he caught his breath. 'Julia, damn it.'

'Quarrelling again?' Amelia's voice reached them from the doorway. They turned. Her gaze went from one to the other. 'Or perhaps not.' She slanted a quizzical look at Nicholas. 'I am ready to begin my duties as chaperon. That is, if you are certain you want one.'

Julia forced her mind back to Amelia's question. 'How long have I known Sophia?' She looked at Amelia blankly for a moment. 'Oh, I first met her in Vienna. It was nearly five years ago.' She gave Amelia an apologetic look. 'I am sorry, you must think I am terribly rude for not attending. I am rather tired.' They had withdrawn to the drawing room after dinner and now sat on one of the brocade sofas.

'An affliction which my cousin seems to share. I do not think he heard a thing I said all during dinner.' She patted Julia's hand. 'Do not worry. There is a cure for this, you know. A pity Nicholas is leaving tomorrow.'

'I do not want him to go. I asked him not to, but he insisted.' Julia hesitated. 'I don't suppose you could talk to him.'

'I doubt he will change his mind. He wants to protect you.'

'He doesn't need to. I have tried to tell him he is not responsible for any of this.' She had found Amelia remarkably easy to confide in, despite knowing her for a mere five hours.

'I think,' Amelia said slowly, 'that he needs to protect you. He failed with Mary and I think it is a burden he still carries. If something happens to you, it will destroy him.'

Julia sat very still. 'I did not know. In fact, I know very little about Mary at all. Except that he still loves her.'

'He told you that?'

'No, but it is quite obvious.'

Amelia fixed her clear gaze on Julia. 'Perhaps, but she is dead. And he is falling in love with you.'

Shock coursed through Julia. 'No. He cannot be.'

'But he is. Probably in spite of himself. Is that really so dreadful?' Amelia asked.

'I do not want him to be.' Julia knotted her hands together. 'I do not want anyone to be in love with me.'

'Or perhaps you are afraid to be in love with him,' Amelia said gently.

Julia looked away. 'I still love Thomas.'

'But he is dead, as Mary is. You cannot bury yourself with your husband. As Nicholas cannot bury himself with Mary. It is wrong.' Amelia turned her direct gaze on Julia. 'But he has tried. For the past two years. I had hoped…we had all hoped, when Sarah married Lord Huntington, that Nicholas would start to put the past behind him as well. But he did not, despite Huntington and Sarah's happiness and despite the fact

Huntington does not hold Nicholas to blame.' She looked more closely at Julia. 'Do you know the story?'

'Only a little. I knew Mary was married and that she died.'

'Mary was betrothed to Lord Huntington when she met Nicholas. Lord Huntington is Jessica's brother. It is another story in itself as to how Sarah came to marry him.' Amelia smiled a little and then sobered. 'Mary and Nicholas had been lovers before her wedding. I do not suppose they meant it to happen, but they had fallen in love. But Mary would not break off her betrothal to Huntington and they married. A few weeks after her wedding, Mary ran away. She had meant to stay with an old nurse of hers, but she became very ill and was forced to stop at an inn. By the time she sent for Nicholas she was dying. He has never forgiven himself for causing her death.'

Compassion and pity washed over Julia for Mary, but most of all for Nicholas who was still alive and still lived with his burden. 'I am so sorry,' she whispered. 'I had no idea.'

Amelia touched her hand. 'He needs you.'

Julia stared at her. 'But what can I do?'

'I suspect he is in his study, attempting to drink himself into oblivion. You could start by putting a stop to that. I do not think he'll be fit to travel tomorrow if he becomes thoroughly foxed. And he'll probably be stubborn enough to go anyway.'

'Perhaps it would be better if you spoke to him.'

Amelia rose. 'It would be much better if you do. Actually, I am exceedingly tired and would like to retire.' She smiled a little. 'I am in the family way.'

'How wonderful!' Julia exclaimed. 'But…oh, dear, you should not be here at all.'

'Of course I should be. I would not have missed coming for the world. And since John is away for another few days, I was quite bored.' She took Julia's hands and bent forward and kissed her on the cheek. 'I think it is time for you to go and speak to my stubborn cousin. There is no need to be afraid of him.'

Julia watched her go, her thoughts in turmoil. Nicholas was falling in love with her? He couldn't be. Not if tonight at dinner was any indication. He had said little, answering in monosyllables, clearly distracted. Once or twice, she had found him watching her, an odd expression on his face, almost one of longing. But it had nothing to do with desire. She had felt vulnerable and a little frightened, and she had no idea why.

And then she thought of Mary. And of the bleakness she had glimpsed in his face more than once. And of him alone in his study, attempting to drink his pain away. She stood. She had felt the same bleakness, the same desire to obliterate the pain in some way. Which was why she could not possibly walk away from him now.

Nicholas scowled at the decanter of brandy before him on the mahogany desk. So far it had done little to erase the empty hole that gaped inside of him. Or the damnable longing he had thought he'd buried.

Asking Amelia had been a mistake. He should have known, with her deplorable tendency towards matchmaking, that she would not leave things alone. And that damnable dress. It had caressed Julia's slender curves like a glove, the low-cut bodice revealing the creamy white mounds of her breasts. He had wanted to take her then in the drawing room and make her completely his. All of her, body, soul, and mind.

The desire to lose himself in her and with her had shot through all the barriers he had erected. And had unstopped the painful yearning for a completion he could not have.

He picked up the glass and was about to put it to his lips when the door to the study opened. He glanced up with a frown and then nearly dropped the glass when Julia stepped into the room.

She blinked and looked around as if trying to adjust to the dim light. 'Nicholas?'

His name on her lips made his hands sweat. Perhaps he was already drunk and dreaming. He rose. 'What are you doing here?'

She moved into the room. 'I came to find you. Amelia thought you might be here.' Her voice held a trace of nervousness.

'She was correct. Is there something you wanted?' She was still wearing the dress. Hell. He scowled at her. 'Otherwise I am occupied.'

'Doing what?' She took a few more steps towards him and his mouth went dry.

'Getting thoroughly foxed, if you must know.'

A frown creased her brow. 'I do not think that is a good idea at all. Will you not feel unwell in the morning?'

'Probably.'

'Then why are you drinking?'

The concern in her eyes unnerved him. 'My dear, it is none of your business,' he drawled.

The concern was replaced by a flash of anger. 'Well, it is since you are going on my business tomorrow! If you have a headache and your stomach is unwell you will hardly be able to carry out the business properly.'

He crossed his arms and leaned against the desk. 'Is

there a purpose for your being here? Besides lecturing me on my drinking?' His behaviour was boorish, but the alternative was yanking her into his arms.

He was stunned when she glared at him. 'No! There is not! If you must know, the only reason I am here is because Amelia said you might need me, but I can see she is wrong!' She whirled around and marched towards the door, but not before he glimpsed her mortified expression.

Before he could say a word she had left the room, closing the door behind her with a bang.

He stared after her. She was here because Amelia said he needed her? She had come to tell him that? The look on her face had told him what it had cost her to come. His behaviour had been despicable.

He walked to the desk and picked up the glass of brandy. He stared at the amber liquid and then slammed the glass down with such force it shattered in his hand, spilling the contents across the desk. When he took his hand away, he saw, mixed with the brandy, the red of his blood.

Julia yanked the pins from her hair and threw them down on the dressing table. How could she have told him she was there because she thought he might need her? She had been so angered and so hurt by his cold behaviour that she had blurted out the first thing that came into her head. Then had wanted to die of humiliation.

And his expression. He had looked as if she had slapped him. It was obvious that she was the last person he wanted for any reason. The only thing she could hope for was that he would become so thoroughly drunk he would forget she had even appeared in his study.

The anger left her and she sank down at the dressing table in despair. Why ever had Amelia said he was in love with her? She must be mistaken, had to be mistaken. Just as she was wrong when she had said Julia was afraid to love him.

She rose and shivered. She had always been so certain there would be only one true love in her life, and that love had been Thomas. Now, she was not certain of anything.

She started at the knock on her door. Was it Amelia? Perhaps she had decided to see if Julia had succeeded in her mission. Her stomach knotted up. She could only tell Amelia the truth—that he did not want her.

She opened the door and then her heart leapt to her throat. Nicholas stood in the doorway. She took a step back, her hand to her chest. 'What are you doing here?'

His dark gaze was fixed on her face. 'I've cut my hand. May I come in?'

She looked down. He held a white handkerchief over one hand. A dark stain had seeped onto the snowy cloth.

'Oh, good heavens!' She took another step back. 'Come in, then. Whatever have you done?'

'I cut it on a glass.' He stared at her, looking slightly confused as if he couldn't comprehend that he had done so.

'Come over to the light and sit down.' When he did not move, she touched his arm. 'I need to look at it.'

He followed her obediently to the chair near the bed. A lamp stood on the table next to the bed. He sat down. She knelt down beside him and took his hand and gently unwrapped the handkerchief. The cut was on the side of his first finger and not very bad. It had stopped bleeding, but should undoubtedly be bandaged. She looked up into his tawny eyes. 'I think you will live, my lord. But I should call Mrs Burton and have her clean and wrap it.'

His head was bent towards her. 'You called me Nicholas earlier.'

'Did I?' She flushed a little. 'I do not recall.'

'When you came to find me in my study.'

Any hope he had forgotten the incident was dashed. 'I will call for Mrs Burton.' She started to rise, only to find his hand clamped around her wrist.

He pulled her back to him. 'Don't go, Julia.' His eyes had darkened. She could smell the brandy on his breath.

'Your hand needs to be tended to.' She tried to tug her wrist out of his grasp.

'You can do it later.' His gaze drifted over her face. 'Amelia was right, you know. I need you.'

She swallowed, not quite sure what to do with his odd mood. Was he drunk? But his eyes were clear and his words unslurred. A peculiar sensation was starting in her stomach. 'I...I am certain Mrs Burton will do an admirable job of bandaging your hand.'

'I don't want Mrs Burton.' He slowly rose and pulled her to her feet. He dropped her hands and stood looking down at her, his gaze slowly travelling from her feet up over her thighs and the curve of her hip, lingering for a moment on the swell of her breasts and then over her face. Although he stood a little apart from her, not touching her at all, her entire body felt as if it was on exquisite fire.

She did not move when he stepped towards her. 'It is the dress,' he said as if explaining something very obvious. And then he pulled her into his arms.

She had expected an assault, but instead his kiss was gentle. He moved slowly across her lips, his arms so light around her she almost wondered if he held her. His mouth drifted down her neck and briefly caressed the soft skin of the top of her breast before moving upwards to claim her mouth once again.

The light pressure nearly drove her mad. She made a small sound of protest and pressed her body hard against his. Her hands crept up and entwined themselves in the thick silkiness of his hair, pulling his mouth more firmly to her own. Her tongue touched the corner of his lips.

He groaned against her mouth and lifted his head. 'I need you. Desperately.'

'I know.'

'And you do not object?'

She took a deep breath. 'No. Not tonight.'

He gave a shaky laugh. 'I suspect I should question that qualification but I won't. Not tonight.' He drew in his breath. 'Will you come to bed with me?'

'Yes.'

The flare of passion in his eyes nearly engulfed her. He held out his hand and she put hers in it. He brought it to his lips and the chaste kiss he planted on her wrist set her on fire.

'Nicholas.' His name was almost a moan.

He looked up and saw her face. And then pulled her into his arms with such fierce desire she was nearly breathless. She struggled for a moment and he instantly loosened his hold. But it was only so she could throw her arms around his neck and pull his head more firmly to hers.

Chapter Twenty

She was not certain what brought her from the slumber she'd fallen into. But she woke and knew something was not right.

The bed was still warm from his body. She sat up, the cover falling from her bare shoulders. It took a moment for her eyes to adjust to the dark. She saw him then. He had put on his breeches and his shirt. He sat in the chair near the window, slumped forward, his head in his hands.

Without a second thought, Julia slipped from the bed. She found the quilt on the floor and picked it up and draped it around her shoulders.

She moved to his side and knelt down by the chair. 'Nicholas.'

He did not move. 'Nicholas.' She touched his hand. 'What is it?'

He lifted his head but did not look at her. 'You should be in bed.' His voice was dull.

'No.' She caught his hand. 'Let me help you.'

'You cannot. Go to bed, Julia.'

'Is it Mary?' she asked quietly. She sensed more

than felt that he stiffened. 'I know about Mary. Amelia told me.'

He looked at her then and she thought she had never seen such bleakness. 'I doubt if she told you the whole of it.'

She looked at him steadily. 'She said that you blame yourself for her death.'

'I killed her.'

'How?' Her hand tightened on his. 'I do not understand.'

'When she ran from Huntington she was with child. My child. She died because she could not bear for her husband to discover she had been unfaithful before her marriage.'

His pain was tangible and more than anyone should have to bear. 'I am so sorry.' She brought his hand to her cheek. And then stood. 'Come back to bed. I want to hold you.'

He rose. 'You do not understand.'

'I understand you lost the woman you loved and you lost a child. And you bear the burden of both their deaths. It is too much for one person.'

He did not move. 'I have used you tonight. I thought if I took you to bed I could for one night erase my damnable memories. But instead, I have added one more sin to my long list. I am sorry.' He looked at her, his mouth twisting. 'You deserve better.'

'It may not help much, but I have used you, too.' She smiled a little at his expression. 'I wanted for one night to forget my pain as well. So we are even and you can, with a clear conscious, blot that sin from your ledger.'

'You are too generous.'

'It is merely the truth.' She took his hand. 'Come and sleep.'

'I have dreams.'

'I have them, too. I dream of Thomas and he is always out of my reach. Sometimes I dream that if only I could reach him I could save him but I am always too late. And when I awaken I feel such sadness that I sometimes think I cannot bear it.'

'But you do.'

'Yes. As you do.'

He looked down at her for a moment. 'I think you are right, we should go to bed and sleep. And hope that, perhaps for the rest of the night, our demons will be held at bay.'

She led him to the bed. She waited while he removed his shirt and climbed into bed and then she slipped in beside him. He pulled her to him with one arm so her head lay on his bare chest. They lay there for a long while and gradually his breathing became heavy and even and she knew he had fallen asleep. And then she drifted away as well.

When she awoke again, she was alone. She turned to her side and clutched the pillow to her chest. His scent still faintly clung to the sheets. She felt lost.

She closed her eyes, hugging the pillow more tightly to her. Her body felt stiff, a reminder that last night had not been a dream, if the fact her body was bare beneath the sheets had not been enough of a reminder.

She had no idea whether she regretted last night or not. She supposed she should, but she had gone to him willingly...no, more than willingly. She had done everything but force him down on the bed. And she had known what she was doing—she was not an innocent virgin who knew nothing of men.

What she had told him was the truth—she had hoped that, for a night, she might banish her own emptiness. And banish some of his as well.

But she had not bargained for the sense of completeness she had found in his arms. The sense of being truly united with another soul.

Which frightened her more than any of the rest of it. For not even with Thomas had she lost herself so much in another person.

She sat up. The disorder from last night was gone. The salmon dress was neatly draped over the back of a chair and she could see her shift peeking out from underneath. Someone had already been in the room unless Nicholas had tidied up the disorder himself while she slept. The thought made her flush.

Someone knocked on the door. Amelia poked her head around. 'So, you are awake. I did not want to disturb you, but I thought you should know that Nicholas has already gone.'

'Has he? I had hoped...' She stopped and flushed. She could hardly admit that after last night she had hoped he would change his mind. And then she realised Amelia was regarding her with a peculiar look and she saw the cover had fallen away to reveal her bare shoulders. She yanked the sheet up as far as possible, embarrassed that Amelia should find her undressed.

Amelia came into the room and looked at Julia's crimson face. Her delicate brow inched up a notch. 'I can see why Nicholas appeared rather dazed this morning. Could you not have persuaded him to stay one more day?'

Pretending she did not understand Amelia's meaning would only be hypocritical. 'He left while I was asleep.' She bit her lip and forced herself to meet Amelia's face. 'I am sorry. You must think that I am ungrateful as well as immoral to engage in such behaviour while under your roof. I think it would be best if I left as soon as possible. I do not—'

Amelia's brow only inched higher. 'You cannot possibly leave. Nicholas would murder me if I let you go. And I fear my husband would be most unhappy if that happened.' She crossed the room and came to stand by the bed, her expression amused. 'Besides, it is not my roof. It is my cousin's and I doubt he found you either immoral or ungrateful.'

'But Lord Monteville…'

The laughter in Amelia's blue eyes increased. 'We are not a very proper family, I fear. My grandfather would not have been shocked although I suspect he would have insisted Nicholas remain here until you had things settled between you.'

'There is nothing to settle,' Julia said miserably. 'We both agreed it was for only a night. It will not happen again.'

'Agreements can be renegotiated.' She moved towards the door. 'I am glad you made good use of the gown.'

Her cheeks heated. 'He said it was because of it.'

Amelia laughed. 'Of course. I will send Fanny in to help you dress and then we can decide what we should do to amuse ourselves until Nicholas returns.'

Amelia kept her too busy to worry about Nicholas. She insisted on showing Julia the house. After lunch, over Julia's protest that Amelia would wear herself out, she took Julia to the lake. They sat on the bench overlooking the calm water and the swans with the summerhouse behind them, and for the first time in an age Julia felt some sense of peace.

When they returned, there was a carriage in the drive. Amelia paused and frowned. 'Nicholas did not mention a thing about visitors. And I do not recognise the coach.'

But Julia did. 'It is Sophia's carriage.'

Amelia's brow cleared. 'Sophia? Lady Simons? How delightful! Then it is all right.'

They entered the cool hallway, which already contained two trunks and several valises. With some surprise, Julia saw one of the trunks was her own. Sophia stood in one corner dressed in a stylish travelling gown, conferring with Mrs Burton. She saw them and her face lit up. She came towards Julia, hands outstretched. 'My dear, I had to come and assure myself you were all right.' She caught Julia's hands and smiled. 'Are you?'

'I am. But, Sophia, it was such a long journey for you and in the middle of the Season!'

'London already seemed dull without you.' She turned to Amelia. 'Dear Amelia, I apologise for coming so unexpectedly. But when Lord Monteville asked for Julia's trunk to be sent here I decided I would accompany it myself.'

Amelia smiled warmly. 'We are delighted to have you. Nicholas has left for a few days and so we have the house to ourselves.'

'He has left?' Sophia glanced back at Julia with a little frown. 'Perhaps that is for the best. Phillip left London yesterday morning and so George insisted on escorting me,' she said in a low voice.

'George is here?' Julia asked. She felt suddenly uneasy and then chided herself.

'I am, indeed.'

She turned and he sauntered into the hallway. Despite the journey, his coat and pantaloons were immaculate and there was not a hair out of place. She forced a smile to her face. 'Good day, George.'

'Good day, my dear Julia.' He gave her a bland look. 'There is no need to look so apprehensive. I intend to procure a room at the local inn. I do not think Lord Thayne's hospitality quite extends to myself. In fact, I had best leave before he discovers me in his hallway.'

'You need not worry. He has gone to Sheffield,' Amelia said.

George swung around to stare at her for a moment. Then he laughed. 'How very odd of him. Not a place where one wishes to find oneself, most certainly not voluntarily.'

Amelia looked as if she was about to say something else, then glanced at Julia and stopped. 'Would you care for refreshment, Lord George?' she asked instead.

'You are most hospitable, but I believe it would be in my best interest and most likely yours, as well, to decline. Now that I have my dear aunt safely delivered, I will proceed to the inn.' He turned his enigmatic gaze on Julia. 'I trust you are not too distressed that matters did not quite play out as you intended two nights ago. I fear there was some interference.'

'I quite understand,' Julia said.

He departed a few minutes later. Sophia turned to the others with an apologetic look. 'I fear I could not persuade him to stay in London. I am grateful he did not think it would be wise for him to stay under the same roof as Nicholas. I must own I was surprised he had that much sensibility.'

'So Nicholas has a quarrel with Lord George? Whatever for?' Amelia asked.

'I have no idea,' Sophia said. 'They seem to hold one another in extreme dislike. They nearly came to blows at the Opera House because they were quarrelling over Julia.'

Julia made a face. 'Sophia! That is most untrue!'

Amelia's eyes sparkled. 'But of course. I can see this is one Season I should have insisted on going to London. But John dislikes London and will not go unless he absolutely must. This year he used the excuse that it would be too taxing for me. Well, I suppose since Nicholas is not here we will not have a quarrel to look forward to.'

'Thank goodness,' Julia murmured. That was the last thing they needed. But as she followed Amelia and Sophia into the drawing room she could not quite shake off her sense of uneasiness. And she only hoped Nicholas was all right; if anything happened to him, she would never forgive herself.

A day after he left for Sheffield, Nicholas was shown into the Halfords' drawing room. Although the room was small, the furnishings were good. He had not thought a jeweller in a town such as this would live quite as well. And Mrs Halford, a thin woman with a narrow face and protruding teeth, was well dressed.

She smoothed down the skirt of her muslin dress in a nervous gesture, apparently flustered at having so distinguished a visitor in her drawing room. 'Please, be seated, my lord. Do you wish for refreshment?'

He remained standing. 'No, that will not be necessary. If you could tell Mr Halford, your father-in-law, that I would like a word with him.'

She avoided his eyes. 'My father-in-law is indisposed, my lord.'

'Indeed.' He looked at her, trying to decide on the best tactic. 'I would, of course, be willing to pay you well for your trouble and his. I suspect a household such as yours has considerable expenses.'

'You cannot imagine the half of it! My husband has no idea of the expense incurred to put a joint of beef on the table each Sunday, and the cost of candles to light six rooms, and he will insist on a fire except on the hottest days. And one would think such things as coats and gowns would not cost so much, but I am certain the prices are nearly as much as those in London. And…' She stopped. 'My husband does not like having him disturbed.'

'But he does not need to know.'

She eyed him with a calculating look. 'It cannot be more than a quarter of an hour. I will not have him worn out. Very well, I will get him for you.'

She started out of the drawing room and then screeched when a figure appeared at the door. Nicholas saw it was an older gentleman wearing a wig and dressed very properly in clothes of a few decades ago. He only hoped it didn't mean his mind was firmly entrenched in that period as well.

Mrs Halford had her hands over her heart. 'Why…what are you doing up? You gave me such a fright!'

'Sally said a lord had come to visit. I thought he might be here for me.'

'Why would you think that?' she asked indignantly.

'Haven't had too many lords here for you. The last one came to see Joshua.' He looked at Nicholas. 'So you wish to see me, do you? Best come to my room, then.'

'I will not have you bringing a lord to your room,' Mrs Halford said.

'I can't have a proper conversation sitting on those fancy chairs of yours.'

Mrs Halford glared at him. Nicholas followed Mr Halford down a narrow passageway to a small room. The older man stepped aside and gestured for Nicholas to go in. 'Sit down, my lord. The wing chair is the most comfortable.'

Nicholas found himself in a small crowded room that somehow managed to hold enough furniture for two rooms. The household extravagances obviously did not extend here. The furniture was old and worn. A desk, piled high with books and papers, stood near the window squeezed between a dresser and a book-case. All the chairs seemed to be covered with papers or books including the indicated wing chair. 'Just place the books on the bed,' Mr Halford said from behind him.

Nicholas did so and sat down. The old gentleman removed a brocade dressing gown from another chair and then seated himself. 'Well, which lord are you?' he asked eyeing Nicholas with a great deal of curiosity.

'Lord Thayne.'

'Ah. The Earl of Monteville's heir. So, what business do you have with me?'

'You had at one time in your possession an old ring.' He pulled the sketch from his pocket. 'This ring, I believe.'

Mr Halford took the sketch and looked at it. 'The old Spanish ring. I remember it. Although with the number of visitors inquiring about it recently it would have been difficult to forget it.'

'Who else has been inquiring about it?' Nicholas asked sharply.

'Nearly a week ago, a young man came who had the look of a solicitor. Said I reminded him of his grandfather. And then, a day ago, a big burly man with a Scottish accent. My daughter-in-law did not know about him,' he added with evident satisfaction.

What the devil was Mackenzie doing here? He frowned. 'Anyone else?'

'Just you, my lord.' His eyes had lost some of their blandness and had sharpened. 'So, perhaps you will tell me what your interest is in the ring.'

'The man who sold you the ring stole it from the finger of a man who was murdered. It is possible the man who sold you the ring is also the murderer.'

'That was some years ago. How did you finally come to me after this time?'

'The ring was given to me.'

'By a young lady?'

Nicholas stared at him, his gut tightening. 'Yes.'

'Very dark and pretty, but too sad for one so young. She had seen the ring in the shop window and wanted it. I was rather surprised as it was so unusual. I doubted if anyone in the village would want such a piece. I asked her where she was going but she only said north.' He looked at Nicholas. 'She bought the ring for you.'

'Yes. She is dead now.' He waited for the harsh sense of loss to grip him but it did not come.

'I am sorry.' Mr Halford looked distressed for a

moment. He glanced down at Nicholas's hand. 'You do not wear it?'

'It was stolen again. Possibly by the same person or persons who took it before.'

'I see. And you wish to recover it?'

'I wish to find the man who killed Lord Carrington. His widow's life is in danger.'

Mr Halford placed the tips of his fingers together and regarded him. 'I quite understand. Perhaps not all the connections, but enough. I will tell you what I know.'

He did not add much to what Nicholas had learned from Colton, but there were a few details that Colton had not picked up. Nicholas finally rose, something else nagging at the back of his mind. It came to him just before he left Mr Halford's room. He turned. 'One more thing. You mentioned that a lord had come to see Joshua. Your son, I presume?' At Halford's nod he continued. 'Do you recall the name of the lord?'

He smiled gently. 'There are times when I find eavesdropping rather unavoidable in such a small house. His name was Lord Stanton.'

Nicholas had one last call to pay before he left Sheffield. The younger Mr Halford was not at first willing to see him, but he had taken a second look at Nicholas's grim countenance and changed his mind.

Nicholas left Halford and Sons and stood for a moment in the street outside the establishment. Halford had confirmed Nicholas's suspicions and had also let slip Mackenzie had seen him as well. Most of the unrelated pieces surrounding Carrington's death had fallen into place with cold, shocking clarity.

Two ladies glanced at him curiously as they passed

by. He realised he could hardly stand in the road. He
moved towards his curricle. Julia should be safe in
Amelia's care and he did not want to face her until he
had confronted Stanton. He only hoped he reached
London before Mackenzie. Having Mackenzie hang
for killing a peer would hardly do Julia good.

Besides, he wanted the pleasure of putting his fist
through Phillip's face.

Chapter Twenty-One

Amelia looked up from the note she had just received. The three ladies were seated in the drawing room looking through the most recent *Ladies Gallery*. 'Nicholas is going to London. Or is he in London? Really, I cannot make out his hurried scrawls at all.'

'I wonder why he went to London?' Sophia asked.

Julia said nothing, but was conscious of a lurch of disappointment. It had only been two days since he had left. In spite of herself, she missed him terribly. All of him, even his scowls. Worse of all, she wanted to feel his arms around her, feel his strong heartbeat under her hands and smell his particular scent.

She rose and went to the window and looked out. The sky was blue with only a few clouds floating lazily overhead. Staying in his house did not help her resolve to stay detached. Not when she saw reminders of him everywhere and there was a portrait of him done several years ago in the main hallway.

Amelia came up beside her. 'He will be home soon, I expect. I do not think he would have stayed away if it was not important.'

'No.' Julia turned and tried to smile. 'I am rather worried about him.'

'He will be safe.' Amelia looked at her for a moment with a great deal of understanding in her face. 'Sophia and I thought we would walk to the lake. Do you wish to come?'

'I think I would rather stay here if you do not mind.'

'Of course not.' Amelia touched her hand.

She stood by the window for a while longer after they left, only turning when the footman announced a visitor. She was taken aback when George was shown in.

'George? I had not thought to see you here.' He had seemed quite adamant about his refusal to set foot in Monteville House.

He smiled. 'As you can see, I changed my mind.' He glanced around the room. 'So, my dear Julia, where are your ever-present guardians?'

'They went for a walk.'

'Leaving you alone?' He raised a brow. 'My dear, I doubt if Thayne would approve of such laxness. But then he is not here, is he?'

'No, but he should be back soon. Do you wish refreshment?'

'Not now.' He moved towards her. She took a step backwards and found herself backed against the window. He stopped uncomfortably close to her and she felt a sudden flash of fear, which he must have seen. 'Afraid of me, Julia? But why? We have been neighbours for an age, even before Thomas died.'

'It is merely you are standing too close to me,' she said, trying to remain calm. 'Did you wish to sit down? Or perhaps you could catch up with Sophia and Amelia. They are going to the lake.'

'I came to see you.' He didn't move. 'Actually, I came for you.'

'I beg your pardon.'

'You are coming with me.' He pulled his hand from his pocket.

In a sort of bewildered comprehension she saw he held a pistol. 'George?'

'You are leaving the drawing room with me and then you will have a cloak brought to you. After that we will go to my carriage. Do not attempt to run or scream or indicate in any way that you are not coming with me under your own free will. Or I will be forced to shoot you and anyone else in my way. I trust you understand.'

She nodded, too frightened to speak. His eyes held a cold, steely expression and she knew he would do exactly as he said. As if in a dream, she went with him out of the drawing room and across the parquet floor of the hallway. She waited while a servant fetched her cloak. In a peculiar awareness she saw there was a fresh bouquet of flowers on the table. The footman held the door open and accepted George's explanation without a blink that he was taking Lady Carrington for a short drive and would return soon.

Then she was in his carriage and he climbed in and took the seat across from her. With a sick sensation in the pit of her stomach, she felt the carriage begin to move.

She looked at him. His eyes were on her, his expression hooded. 'Why are you doing this?' she finally asked.

'I need you for insurance, my dear. My yacht is waiting in Maldon and I want to reach it and France without impediment.'

'I do not understand.' Although a sickening thought was beginning to form.

'Don't you? I am fleeing the country and plan to disappear conveniently on the continent. As long as you are with me, no one will dare interfere. I do not think Thayne will want your blood on his hands. Or my father.' He settled back.

'Why is it necessary for you to flee England?' she asked carefully. But she already knew the answer.

'Because of the ring. A pity it surfaced. I would have been safe if it had not. But when I saw it on Thayne's hand I knew it was just a matter of time before it was recognised. I had hoped, however, you and Thayne would not cross paths. It was extremely inconvenient that you did.'

She stared at him, revolted. 'You killed Thomas.'

'Yes.' He shrugged. 'It was necessary. I could not have him exposing my, er...source of income. Selling secrets to the French proved extremely profitable and amazingly simple. I fear my sire's hope that the position of a lowly clerk would install in me a sense of honour and pride failed.' He leaned back. 'My biggest mistake was taking the ring. But I needed the money.'

His callousness shocked and horrified her. And filled her with deep rage. 'You are monstrous.'

'Perhaps. But I am a survivor.'

'I will die before I allow you to escape with me.'

His disbelieving smile made her want to slap him. 'May I remind you I hold all the cards? And I doubt, when it comes down to it, you will want to die at all.'

Nicholas resisted the urge to shove Stanton's butler against the wall. 'What do you mean he has left for Maldon?'

'He left this morning, my lord. That is all I can tell you.'

Why the hell had Stanton left for Maldon? He turned and dashed down the steps of Stanton's town-house. Kingsley had not been at home either, although he had not been able to elicit much information of his whereabouts.

He was about to step into his carriage when some-one spoke behind him. 'My lord.'

He turned. Mackenzie stood behind him. 'What the devil are you doing here?' Nicholas demanded.

'The same as yourself. Wanting a word with Stan-ton.' He frowned at Nicholas. 'Where's the Countess?'

'She is at my grandfather's estate. My cousin is with her. Stanton has gone to Maldon.'

Mackenzie's brow crashed down. 'The devil he has. He has a yacht there, or rather young George does.' He stared at Nicholas. 'I think, laddie, we'd best go to Maldon. And as quickly as possible.'

Julia paced around her small cramped room in George's cottage in Maldon. They had arrived last night and George had forced her into the room and taken the key. Her meals had been brought by a surly-looking woman who refused to speak to her. Julia had no doubt George had bribed the woman to pay no heed to anything she might say.

She stopped in front of the narrow window. From it, she could see the top of a mast. The sight made her stomach churn. Thank goodness the tides had not been right for leaving last night or she had no doubt they would be well on their way to France by now.

Except she had decided she would do anything to avoid getting on the ship with him. She had no idea what he planned to do with her when he reached France, but she knew it would not be pleasant.

The key turning in the door made her heart beat with a sickening thud. George entered. 'My dear, it is time to go,' he said, drawling. He held the pistol.

When she did not move, he grabbed her arm. 'Come.' He picked up the cloak from the bed and draped it around her.

She flinched and glared at him. 'I can do it myself.'

'Quiet.' He pushed the pistol into her ribs under the cloak. 'Now move.'

There was no chance to escape as she left the cottage and climbed into his carriage. The trip to the quay did not take nearly long enough. He helped her down and, as they walked out on to the quay, kept the pistol to her. He was nervous; she could tell by the way his eyes darted around. She feared he truly would shoot her if she tried to escape.

Her knees nearly gave away when she saw the boat. Although not large, it stood out among the smaller boats docked in the harbour. 'This way.' He took her arm and started towards it. A few fisherman were on the quay, but no one gave them more than a curious glance or two. 'If you scream, I will not hesitate to shoot you or anyone else,' George said in her ear.

Her stomach lurched when they reached the graceful masted boat. If she was going to do something, it would need to be soon. She looked down at the grey cold water and shivered. George pulled her on to the gangway.

'Let her go.'

George turned, his arm around her waist. Phillip stood behind them. In his hand was a deadly-looking pistol. 'Release her, George.'

'I am loath to contradict your order, but I have no intention of doing so.'

'I will shoot you without compunction.'

'Not a very paternal sentiment. However, I doubt if you will. Think of the potential scandal to the family name. You may put it about we have fallen in love and eloped.' His grip tightened on Julia's arm.

'This has gone far enough. Let her go,' Phillip said grimly. 'I will see you get to France.'

'I need her. Come, my love.' He started to move, his arm tight around her waist.

Phillip stared at him. 'I will hunt you down.'

George laughed. 'No, you won't. You will cover for me as you have done for the past three years.'

'Phillip?' Horrified, Julia stared at him. 'You knew?'

Phillip's eyes were full of regret. 'My dear...' he began.

George laughed. 'My dear Julia, of course he knew. But he was willing to do anything to protect the family honour and Arthur from scandal. The lengths he has gone to keep you from discovering the truth have been quite amazing. The highway robbery, the thief at Foxwood, the little incident at the theatre. And Mr Grayson, of course.'

Her eyes were still on Phillip. Anger mixed with horror began to seep through her numbness. 'Phillip? You hurt Nicholas?'

'No, of course he did not,' George said. 'I did. He merely sent Grayson to purchase the ring.' His voice was impatient. 'The conversation is becoming tedious. Come.' He tugged on her arm.

'No! Leave me!' She yanked her arm out of his grasp. Her anger and betrayal rendered her nearly oblivious to George and his pistol. She stared at Phillip. 'How could you? How could you do this to Thomas?'

'Get moving!' George grabbed her arm.

Furious, she stomped on his foot. Caught by surprise, he stepped backward and tripped on the edge of the gangway. He clutched at her and fell with her into the cold water below.

He released her before he hit the water. She went under, somehow remembering to take a breath, then made her way to the surface and trod water, gasping, as she tried to get her bearing. She vaguely heard shouting and voices.

She nearly screamed when an arm caught her by the shoulders. She started to flail. 'Don't fight me, Julia,' Nicholas said in her ear. 'I am going to pull you out.'

She sat in a chair by the fire Nicholas had demanded the landlady build. The inn was small and shabby, but the innkeeper had been kind. The innkeeper's daughter had found a clean muslin gown and a shawl. Despite the fire and the dry clothes she could not stop shaking.

Eduardo fetched a physician. He had examined Julia and had pronounced her to be in a state of nervous shock from the cold water. He had left a draught and said that she must sleep.

She scarcely looked up when Nicholas appeared at her side. 'You must go up to bed now,' he said.

'I do not want to sleep.'

'Julia.' He knelt beside her. 'You are safe. Eduardo is here. I am here. No one can hurt you.'

'Yes.' But her mind refused to work. She felt as cold and numb as she had when she had fallen in the water.

She made no protest when he reached down and lifted her in his arms. He carried her to the room and laid her gently on the bed. She hardly noticed when he removed the borrowed knit stockings from her feet. She took the draught without protest and slipped, at last, into a deep dreamless sleep where she knew nothing.

'You have a visitor.' Barbara appeared in the doorway of the drawing room. 'Lord Monteville. He seems determined to see you. I do not think you will be able to fob him off as easily as you have the others.'

Julia looked up from her embroidery. In the fortnight that had passed since her abduction, she had found it impossible to sit without some sort of stitching in her hand. Not that she was able to sit much, for most of her waking hours were spent in restless movement. If she was not walking, she was in the garden; for the first time in several years, the garden was entirely free of weeds.

She had refused all visitors. Including Nicholas. She had not seen him since she left the inn near Maldon with Eduardo to return to Foxwood. She tried not to think of their parting, the helpless concern in his face replaced by bleakness when she said she did not think it wise for them to meet again. But how could he want her, when she felt so numb, so devoid of anything?

'Shall I show him in?' Barbara asked.

'I...' Julia rose, but Monteville had already stepped around Barbara and into the room.

'Lady Carrington,' he said. He moved forward and picked up her hand. 'I have come to see if you have recovered.'

'Thank you. I have,' she said automatically. She

turned to Barbara, remembering she should at least show some courtesies. 'Perhaps you would bring Lord Monteville some refreshment.'

'Will you not be seated, Lord Monteville?' Julia said after Barbara left the room. He took the chair near the sofa and she sat back down.

He surveyed her face with a not unkind expression in his cool grey eyes. 'I do not think you have recovered at all,' he said gently.

'I am fine.'

'But you have refused to see anyone who cares about you.' He waited for a moment. 'Why?'

Her hands tightened in her lap. 'Because I can feel nothing.'

'Perhaps you are not allowing yourself, then.'

'Perhaps I have nothing left to feel.'

'I suspect that the opposite is true. You are holding such strong emotion inside that you are afraid of what might happen if you allowed yourself to feel.'

She rose and went to the window and then turned. 'I want to destroy things. I have imagined throwing every dish in the house. Or that I might scream and not stop. And then I fear I am about to go quite mad.'

'It is unlikely.' He stood and moved to stand near the mantelpiece. 'I have known Phillip for the past twenty years. I considered him one of the most intelligent and honourable men of my acquaintance. I also saw, however, he had certain weaknesses. His excessive pride in his family name. His blind devotion to Arthur, whom he saw as the embodiment of all the virtues he honoured, and his prejudice towards George, who was not.'

He looked away for a moment and back at her. 'I have, for the major part of my life, considered myself an astute judge of human character. But I failed with Phillip. I did not see, or did not want to see, how deeply his pride dictated his character. Or that his desire to protect his name would lead to such crimes against your husband and yourself. I also did not suspect the extent of George's wickedness. For that I offer my apologies to you.'

She knew how proud he was and how difficult it must be for him to admit such a thing. She realized, too, how he must feel betrayed as well. 'You do not need to, my lord.'

'I have one other confession.' He looked directly at her. 'On more than one occasion in the past fortnight, I have considered running Phillip through with a sword for the pain and betrayal he has caused his family and friends.'

'Have you?' she said, startled. 'I have thought I would like to do the very same thing. And then the fact I can feel such horrible, consuming rage frightens me. Not even after Thomas died was I so angry.'

'Yes.' He understood, she could see, and somehow his understanding began to fan the faintest flicker of hope.

'I have not wanted to feel anything,' she said. 'Not only because of the anger but because it will hurt too much when I do.'

'But you cannot stay in this state. You are hurting others as well.' He looked at her. 'And you are not allowing them to heal. Sophia has lost her nephew, and, although Phillip is not dead as George is, his betrayal has been worse than his death. She thinks you must blame her and that now she has lost your friendship as well. And there is Amelia. She is certain she is responsible for your abduction because she allowed

George into the house.' He came to stand next to her. 'And my grandson. He has shut himself away again as you have. He feels he has failed you, failed to save you and so he bears the burden of that.'

Julia looked sharply at him. 'He pulled me from the water.'

'Yes, but he left you at Monteville House, and while he was gone George reached you. And he may have pulled you from the water, but he did not save you from the pain and betrayal.'

'He could not have. He has no cause to blame himself.'

'My dear, you are lost to him. And so he did fail,' he said gently.

'I am lost to him?' She looked at him, puzzled. 'How?'

'He loves you. He would help you, if he could, but you won't let him. And so, like you, he is in his own private hell.'

She stared at him, stunned. Amelia's words came rushing back. *If something happens to you, it will destroy him.* She thought of the pain he had been in that night at Monteville House. And knew she could not bear to imagine him in such pain again.

A sob rose to her throat. 'Oh, dear God.' She looked at Monteville with tears in her eyes. 'What shall I do?' she whispered.

'It is for you to decide. But you will have to go to him. I do not think he is able to come to you.' He picked up his hat and gloves. 'I will leave you, my dear. I wish you well.'

She stood for long after he left and then finally, for the first time in a fortnight, wept.

Chapter Twenty-Two

Two days later, Julia sat in the drawing room of Sophia's townhouse. She knotted her hands together in her lap. She would hardly blame Sophia if she did not want to see her. Her treatment of Sophia had hardly been kind.

In a moment she heard familiar footsteps. And then Sophia came into the room. She paused in the doorway and Julia saw what Monteville had meant. Her face was puffed, as if she had been crying for a long while, and there were dark circles under her eyes. She stared at Julia and Julia rose. 'Sophia?'

And then Sophia dashed forward with a glad cry. 'Oh, Julia, it is you! You do not know how much I have wanted to see you!' And Julia was swept up in a joyful embrace.

The next day, she discovered from Sophia that Nicholas was rarely at home to anyone. 'Amelia does not think he has been eating or sleeping properly and he is in a foul temper most of the time.'

They were sitting in Sophia's dressing room. Julia felt sick at heart. 'I need to see him. But I do not know whether he would receive me.'

'I think you must force him to see you.' Sophia looked at her thoughtfully. 'He has been frequenting Thérèse's. You did force your acquaintance on him once before.'

'Are you suggesting I abduct him again?' Julia stared at her friend. 'He would most likely want to strangle me.'

'It would be better than what he is doing. You could take him to Foxwood again and refuse to let him go until he listens.'

'Yes, I could,' Julia said slowly. 'But how can I be sure he will be there?'

'Amelia is here in London with her husband. I think between us and Thérèse we can guarantee Nicholas will be where you want him.'

'Yes.' She had no doubt they would.

'There is one more thing.' Sophia rose. 'I will return shortly.'

Julia waited and tried not to think of all the reasons she could not abduct Nicholas again. Sophia returned. She sat down next to Julia. 'I think you should give him this.' She opened her hand and the ring lay on her palm.

'Where did you get it?' She looked slowly up at Sophia.

'From Phillip. The day after…after everything happened.' Her face was anxious. 'I know that you once said you thought it was cursed. But it was given to two people with love and perhaps it should be given once again in love.' She took Julia's hand and opened her fingers. 'Please take it.'

Julia looked it. And she slowly closed her fingers around the ring.

Nicholas glanced across the table at his opponent. 'I've relieved you of enough of your pin-money. And I'd best take you home before your protective husband notices you are gone.'

His cousin's smile was quite unconcerned from beneath her mask. 'Do not worry, he will not. And if he does, he is unlikely to call you out. When you are in such a horrid temper all the time, we are all afraid of you.'

His brow shot up. 'I had not noticed you have any particular fear.' In fact, Amelia had hounded him unmercifully to take her to Thérèse's. If he did not, she declared, she would go by herself without an escort. However, once they arrived, she had spent much of the evening craning her head around as if waiting for someone. If he hadn't known she was in love with her husband, he would have thought she was waiting for a lover.

'Oh, but I do. You quite terrify me.'

'You will be quite relieved to know, then, that I leave town tomorrow.'

Something had caught her attention. She stood and stared over his shoulder for a moment and then suddenly fixed him with a brilliant smile. 'Actually, I think you are leaving town tonight. I believe I will go watch the Faro bank for a moment or two.'

'Damn it, Amelia.' But she had already left the table.

He started to rise, intending to go after her, when someone slipped into the chair she had vacated. He caught his breath. The woman wore a dark salmon gown and her hair was caught up at the back of her head. For a moment he thought he was hallucinating.

'Good evening, my lord.' Her voice was clear and unmistakable.

He sat back down. 'What the devil are you doing here?'

'I want to play a game of cards with you.'

'And I do not want to play.' He folded his arms. 'You made it very clear, my dear Lady Carrington, that you do not want my company in any form.'

She flinched. 'You are not very sporting.'

'I do not feel very sporting. If you will excuse me, I am going to escort my cousin home.'

'Please sit down, my lord.'

His brow shot up and then he stilled. She had a pistol pointed at him. 'What is this in aid of?'

'We are going to play a game.'

He laughed without amusement. 'Are we? So, if I refuse to co-operate you will shoot me?'

She considered. 'Yes.'

'I doubt that.' He stared at her, curious in spite of himself. Her manner was as cool as it had been that first night. Except now he knew the passion under her façade. His loins tightened. 'Very well, we'll play. The same game as before. And the terms?'

'The same as before.'

What the hell did she want? He watched her shuffle the cards. She wore gloves, but they did not diminish the memory of the feel of her hands on his body. She bent forward to deal and the movement clearly revealed the valley between her breasts. He caught his breath as desire, sharp and swift, shot through him.

She looked up and caught him watching her. She

bit her lip, a gesture that told him she was not as calm as she appeared.

Her gaze on his face did not waver, however. 'Shall we begin?'

'Yes.' He watched her, paying little attention to the game. It came as no surprise when she played the winning hand.

He leaned back in the chair. 'You have won. And now perhaps you'll tell me what you want. I've no ring, although perhaps you wish money instead. Perhaps for breach of contract. We did have a betrothal of sorts or have you forgotten?'

'I have not forgotten,' she said in a low voice.

'Have you perhaps changed your mind?' He knew he was goading her, but the hurt and anger of her rejection sprang to the surface. 'You wish my fortune and title after all?'

He could see she had paled under her mask. 'I want neither your fortune nor your title.'

'Then what do you want? Revenge? Although I have no idea why. Or perhaps you wish me to admit I still desire you after all.' He ran his eyes over her face and allowed his gaze to rest on her breasts. 'Very well. I desire you. I want your lovely body with your beautiful breasts, and your graceful legs, I want to feel the curve of your hip under my hands, and I want to make love to you until you cry out with pleasure. Does that satisfy you?'

'How dare you!' She jumped up, her mouth trembling. 'I am beginning to think I should shoot you after all!'

'Go ahead.' He folded his arms. 'I find I couldn't care less one way or the other. Although I trust you can aim well enough to do the job.'

She faced him. 'How dare you talk like that! As if your life means nothing!'

He looked at her. 'Another lecture? Perhaps you would be kind enough to tell me what you want and then leave me in peace to wallow in misery as I please.'

'If you must know, I want you. And if you dare make one of your stupid, sardonic remarks I will shoot you!' She glared at him. 'So, if you will kindly get up, I am going to take you to my carriage.'

'Are you?'

'Yes!' She marched over to him. She poked him in the shoulder with the pistol. 'Stand up!'

'I suggest you do as she asks, lad.'

He nearly groaned when he heard Mackenzie's voice. The man stood in the doorway and was looking at him with a stern, unyielding expression.

Nicholas slowly rose. 'Hell.'

Julia glanced over at her captive in one corner of the carriage. He had promptly closed his eyes after settling his long frame in the seat. His temper had not been improved, as they were leaving the saloon, by the sight of Lord Marleigh standing next to Amelia near the EO bank.

Julia doubted if he was asleep. He probably wanted to avoid her. Not that she blamed him. No doubt he was extremely angry at being hauled off in a carriage at gunpoint for a second time. And even if he did desire her, it did not mean that he even liked her.

She slumped against the seat, all the energy drained from her. They would be at Foxwood soon. She would offer him a bed if he wished, and then provide him with a horse so he could return to London as soon as possible.

He opened his eyes as soon as the carriage came to a halt in the drive. 'At least there were no highwaymen,' he remarked.

'No.'

Eduardo opened the door and assisted her down. She could not quite meet Nicholas's eyes when he descended. She was aware he looked at her for a moment before he walked towards the house.

She caught up with him. 'My lord.'

He halted and looked down at her. She bit her lip. 'I wanted to tell you that you may stay here overnight and then you are free to go. I will provide you a horse in the morning and you may return to London as soon as you wish.'

'This seems to be a habit as well. You abduct me, bring me to your farm and then attempt to throw me out again as soon as possible.' He started to move towards the house again. A furry figure came out of the bushes near the front door and rubbed against his leg. 'Ah, I see my friend has come to greet me.' He bent down and rubbed the cat's head.

Barbara opened the door. 'We've been wondering when you would return. No baggage again, I see.'

'Julia needs to either warn me when she plans to kidnap me or have my valet pack a bag that she can bring with her.' He stepped into the hallway.

'So, it's like that again, is it?' Barbara looked sharply at Julia. Julia flushed and followed him in. He headed towards the staircase.

Barbara frowned and called after him. 'There is no bedchamber ready for you.'

He paused with his hand on the railing. 'I assume Julia's bedchamber is suitable.'

Julia had come to the bottom of the staircase and looked up at him. 'Then where am I to sleep?'

'With me, if you wish. Or there is the sofa in the drawing room.'

His careless tone made her want to throw something. Or cry. She turned away and looked at Barbara. 'Perhaps the drawing room, then,' she said, keeping her voice as level as possible. 'If you could bring me some bedcovers and a pillow.' She started to walk towards the drawing room.

Barbara gave her a sympathetic glance. 'He's as stubborn as ever.'

Julia pulled off her gloves and laid them on the table near the sofa. 'I do not blame him. He is probably very angry with me.'

'I doubt that is the reason,' Barbara said as she left the room.

Julia sat down on the sofa. The curtains had not been drawn and moonlight spilled across the worn oriental carpet. Wellington jumped up beside her and began to purr.

She stroked his head. The room was quiet and peaceful. The ticking of the clock, combined with Wellington's loud purr, had a soothing effect. If she could stay in such a moment, she could perhaps bear living without him. She closed her eyes and then something soft and cool brushed her lips.

'Julia.'

She opened her eyes. Nicholas knelt in front of her. 'I need to know why you brought me here,' he said.

'It was foolish of me.'

'That is not an answer.' His eyes searched her face. 'You said you wanted me.'

'Yes.' She glanced away. 'I suppose that was foolish of me as well.'

He slowly stood. 'At Maldon, when you sent me away, I knew you were lost to me. In every way possible. I had failed you. I told myself I did not want to see you again. When I saw you tonight, I knew that was not true. I suppose I wanted to hurt you as much as you had hurt me.'

She rose as well and came to stand in front of him. 'I sent you away, not because you failed me, but because I felt so empty. I had nothing to give you and so I thought I would hurt you less if I refused to see you.'

'What changed your mind?'

'I started to feel again. And I love you.' She had nothing to lose by telling him.

He stared at her for a moment and then gave an odd strangled laugh. 'Will you marry me, then?'

She looked at him uncertainly. 'Yes. Do you still want me?'

He stepped forward and caught her hands. 'Yes. In every way possible. Shall I reiterate for you?'

Her cheeks were starting to flame. 'I believe you did once tonight.'

'Yes, although you objected strongly.' He smiled a little. 'You still have not told me what you hoped to accomplish by abducting me again.'

'I had wanted to talk to you. And…' she coloured a little '…seduce you.'

He gave her a wicked smile. 'You cannot accomplish that by sleeping in here. You had best come upstairs. But first I need to make certain this is what you want.' He slowly pulled her towards him.

In the morning Julia woke before he did. She pulled on her dressing gown and slippers and went downstairs. She returned just as he opened his eyes. Nicholas looked disoriented for a moment and then his gaze fell on her. 'When I did not find you beside me I feared last night had been a dream. Where did you go?'

'Only to the drawing room.' She sat down on the bed next to him and he sat up, the cover falling from his chest. Julia looked at his beloved face with its shadow of beard. 'I have something to give you.'

She opened her hand and held out the ring. He stared at it for a moment, then his eyes went to her face. 'Where did you get it?'

'Sophia gave it me. Phillip recovered it from George's possessions.'

'I would not be surprised if you wanted to bury it,' he said slowly.

She smiled a little. 'Perhaps once I did. But Sophia reminded me that I gave it to Thomas because I loved him and Mary gave it to you because she loved you. And if it were not for the ring, I would not have met you.'

'No.' He continued to look at her.

She hesitated. 'Perhaps it reminds you too much of Mary. That is, it is not right of me to give it to you because she first gave it to you. I…I can quite understand that.'

'But then I should not wear it because you first gave it to Thomas. Thomas is gone and so is Mary. But we are here. I once thought that I had died with Mary.

But I do not feel that way now.' He cupped her face for a moment, his hand gentle. 'I love you.'

'I have not died either. And I love you as well.' She took his hand. 'Will you wear it?'

'Yes.' He watched while she slipped it on his finger. And then he slowly lowered her to the bed. She saw tenderness mixed with desire as he lay over her. When he lowered his mouth to hers, she knew their ghosts had finally been freed to rest in peace.

* * * * *

Savor the
breathtaking romances
and thrilling adventures
of Harlequin Historicals®

On sale November 2003

MY LADY'S PRISONER by Ann Elizabeth Cree

To uncover the truth behind her husband's death,
a daring noblewoman kidnaps a handsome viscount!

THE VIRTUOUS KNIGHT by Margo Maguire

While fleeing a nunnery, a feisty noblewoman
becomes embroiled with a handsome knight in a
wild, romantic chase to protect an ancient relic!

On sale December 2003

THE IMPOSTOR'S KISS by Tanya Anne Crosby

On a quest to discover his past, a prince masquerades
as his twin brother and finds the life and the love
he'd always dreamed of….

THE EARL'S PRIZE by Nicola Cornick

An impoverished woman believes an earl is
an unredeemable rake—but when she wins
the lottery will she become the rake's prize?

From Regency romps
to mesmerizing Medievals,
savor these stirring tales from
Harlequin Historicals®

On sale January 2004

THE KNAVE AND THE MAIDEN by Blythe Gifford

A cynical knight's life is forever changed when he falls
in love with a naive young woman while journeying
to a holy shrine.

MARRYING THE MAJOR by Joanna Maitland

Can a war hero wounded in body and spirit find
happiness with his childhood sweetheart, now that she
has become the toast of London society?

On sale February 2004

THE CHAPERON BRIDE by Nicola Cornick

When England's most notorious rake is attracted to
a proper ladies' chaperon, could it be true love?

THE WEDDING KNIGHT by Joanne Rock

A dashing knight abducts a young woman to marry his
brother, but soon falls in love with her instead!

Visit us at www.eHarlequin.com

HARLEQUIN HISTORICALS®

Your opinion is important to us! Please take a few moments to share your thoughts with us about your experiences with Harlequin and Silhouette books. Your comments will be very useful in ensuring that we deliver books you love to read. *Please take a few minutes to complete the questionnaire, then send it to us at the address below.*

Send your completed questionnaires to:
Harlequin/Silhouette Reader Survey, P.O. Box 9046, Buffalo, NY 14269-9046

1. As you may know, there are many different lines under the Harlequin and Silhouette brands. Each of the lines is listed below. Please check the box that most represents your reading habit for each line.

Line	Currently read this line	Do not read this line	Not sure if I read this line
Harlequin American Romance	❏	❏	❏
Harlequin Duets	❏	❏	❏
Harlequin Romance	❏	❏	❏
Harlequin Historicals	❏	❏	❏
Harlequin Superromance	❏	❏	❏
Harlequin Intrigue	❏	❏	❏
Harlequin Presents	❏	❏	❏
Harlequin Temptation	❏	❏	❏
Harlequin Blaze	❏	❏	❏
Silhouette Special Edition	❏	❏	❏
Silhouette Romance	❏	❏	❏
Silhouette Intimate Moments	❏	❏	❏
Silhouette Desire	❏	❏	❏

2. Which of the following best describes why you bought *this book?* One answer only, please.

the picture on the cover	❏	the title	❏
the author	❏	the line is one I read often	❏
part of a miniseries	❏	saw an ad in another book	❏
saw an ad in a magazine/newsletter	❏	a friend told me about it	❏
I borrowed/was given this book	❏	other: _____	❏

3. Where did you buy *this book?* One answer only, please.

at Barnes & Noble	❏	at a grocery store	❏
at Waldenbooks	❏	at a drugstore	❏
at Borders	❏	on eHarlequin.com Web site	❏
at another bookstore	❏	from another Web site	❏
at Wal-Mart	❏	Harlequin/Silhouette Reader	❏
at Target	❏	Service/through the mail	
at Kmart	❏	used books from anywhere	❏
at another department store or mass merchandiser	❏	I borrowed/was given this book	❏

4. On average, how many Harlequin and Silhouette books do you buy at one time?

I buy _____ books at one time ❏
I rarely buy a book ❏

MRQ403HH-1A

5. How many times per month do you shop for any *Harlequin and/or Silhouette* books? One answer only, please.

1 or more times a week ❑	a few times per year ❑
1 to 3 times per month ❑	less often than once a year ❑
1 to 2 times every 3 months ❑	never ❑

6. When you think of your ideal heroine, which *one* statement describes her the best? One answer only, please.

She's a woman who is strong-willed ❑	She's a desirable woman ❑
She's a woman who is needed by others ❑	She's a powerful woman ❑
She's a woman who is taken care of ❑	She's a passionate woman ❑
She's an adventurous woman ❑	She's a sensitive woman ❑

7. The following statements describe types or genres of books that you may be interested in reading. Pick *up to 2 types* of books that you are most interested in.

I like to read about truly romantic relationships ❑
I like to read stories that are sexy romances ❑
I like to read romantic comedies ❑
I like to read a romantic mystery/suspense ❑
I like to read about romantic adventures ❑
I like to read romance stories that involve family ❑
I like to read about a romance in times or places that I have never seen ❑
Other: _____ ❑

The following questions help us to group your answers with those readers who are similar to you. Your answers will remain confidential.

8. Please record your year of birth below.
19 ____

9. What is your marital status?
single ❑   married ❑   common-law ❑   widowed ❑
divorced/separated ❑

10. Do you have children 18 years of age or younger currently living at home?
yes ❑   no ❑

11. Which of the following best describes your employment status?
employed full-time or part-time ❑   homemaker ❑   student ❑
retired ❑   unemployed ❑

12. Do you have access to the Internet from either home or work?
yes ❑   no ❑

13. Have you ever visited eHarlequin.com?
yes ❑   no ❑

14. What state do you live in?
_____

15. Are you a member of Harlequin/Silhouette Reader Service?
yes ❑   Account # _____   no ❑   MRQ403HH-1B

COMING NEXT MONTH FROM

HARLEQUIN HISTORICALS®

- **THE IMPOSTOR'S KISS**
  by **Tanya Anne Crosby,** Harlequin Historical debut
  On a quest to discover his past, the Prince of Merrick masqueraded
  as his highway-robber twin brother and found the life and the love
  he'd always dreamed of in Chloe Simon. But would Chloe forgive
  him when she learned his true identity?
  HH #683 ISBN# 29283-X $5.25 U.S./$6.25 CAN.

- **THE EARL'S PRIZE**
  by **Nicola Cornick,** author of THE NOTORIOUS MARRIAGE
  Ever since her father ruined them at the gaming tables,
  Amy Bainbridge has lived in genteel poverty and has vowed never to
  love a gambler. But when she meets Joss, the Earl of Tallant and an
  unredeemable rogue, she risks losing her heart and becoming the
  rake's prize!
  HH #684 ISBN# 29284-8 $5.25 U.S./$6.25 CAN.

- **THE SURGEON**
  by **Kate Bridges,** author of THE MIDWIFE'S SECRET
  When his troop played a prank on him, John Calloway, a mounted
  police surgeon, found himself stuck with an unwanted mail-order
  bride. Though he wanted nothing more than to send the stubborn
  beauty back home, he needed to know if she could help him find
  his long-buried heart....
  HH #685 ISBN# 29285-6 $5.25 U.S./$6.25 CAN.

- **OKLAHOMA BRIDE**
  by **Carol Finch,** author of BOUNTY HUNTER'S BRIDE
  Feisty Karissa Baxter wanted to secure land for her injured brother
  by illegally sneaking into Oklahoma Territory, but Commander
  Rafe Hunter stood directly between her and her crusade. Though
  she was breaking the law he had sworn to uphold, Rafe couldn't
  deny his smoldering passion!
  HH #686 ISBN# 29286-4 $5.25 U.S./$6.25 CAN.

KEEP AN EYE OUT FOR ALL FOUR
OF THESE TERRIFIC NEW TITLES